THE HALLOWED

Book Two in The Scrying Trilogy

JACI MILLER

Solitary Pen Press

The Hallowed: Book Two
The Scrying Trilogy
Copyright © 2018 by Jaci Miller
Solitary Pen Press
Cover Design by Streetlight Graphics

Print ISBN: 978-0-9988069-2-1
Ebook ISBN: 978-0-9988069-3-8
First Edition: 2018

This is a work of fiction. Names, characters, places, and incidents are either a product of the author's imagination or are used fictitiously. Any resemblance to actual persons, living or dead, business establishments, events, or locales is purely coincidental.

www.jacimiller.com
www.solitarypenpress.com

To my parents who taught me to love literature and my husband who supports my creating it.

"Multitudes who sleep in the dust of the earth will awake: some to everlasting life, others to shame and everlasting contempt."
(Daniel 12:2, New International Version)

PROLOGUE

Thanissia Universe—after the Great War.

TOWERING STONE ARCHES LOOMED AHEAD of her as she walked up the path toward the Hall of Elders. The council summons, at the request of the Guardian of Deities, surprised her. Never had she interacted with either the elders or the Guardian, for it was forbidden. Only her twin brother Gabriel, or one of the other Seraphs, Michael or Raphael, intermingled with them. As commander of the sentinels, the warring celestials who constitute most of her race, she reported only to the Seraphs. A council summons of a sentinel, even the commander, was unheard-of. With much to do before stasis, this unexpected interruption was disconcerting and amplified her already irritated state.

She had just returned from Dywen when the summons came. There was a Warlician warrior who would remain there to protect the Book of Realms, and she had been charged with ensuring his readiness for stasis. This Warlician was known to her. She had engaged him before and invariably it always ended the same way; her being provoked by his continued contempt for rules and lack of formal conduct, and him goading her into exasperation.

The sentinels under her command are professional and regimented; a fierce fighting army trained to battle with discipline. The warriors of Dywen are anything but. Emotions and passion control the witches of their realm and in her judgment, it made them undisciplined. It was a trait she found weak and dangerous in any race, but in Warlician warriors, it was most unfavorable. Due to their innate power of foresight, Warlicians are deemed invincible making them egotistical as well as emotional, and therefore, utterly chaotic.

The warrior staying on Dywen—the worst of them all. He was not merely arrogant; his insolence and bravado were also insufferable. She was glad they would never again cross paths.

What was his name? She thought as she walked toward the Hall of Elders. *Oh, yes, Rafe.* Just the notion of him left an acidic taste in her mouth and her irritation surged back when she recalled their tense encounter.

Ignoring it she focused instead on her present dilemma—the elder's sudden penchant to meet with her. She paused, her hand fidgeting with the sword at her hip. Her mind spun as she tried to determine the reason for their summons. It was illogical. The portals to the other realms were sealed, stasis had begun, and Michael was readying the remaining elders for their final journey back into the ether.

Why then were they disrupting their preparations to speak with her?

She took a deep breath as she crossed under the immense stone arches, each leading her closer to the council and the reason for their beckoning. The walk up the mountainside toward the Hall of Elders was an imposing one. Even though she occasionally made the trek in the past, the overwhelming sense of intimidation never diminished.

The white mountain, known as Elderon, was surrounded by an immense chasm. The perpetual darkness of the ether shadowed its unknown depths. It was accessible only by the long, wood and stone bridge joining the mountain to the Leylands; the moors where the sentinels lived and trained. The bridge was dominated by five massive stone arches, each represented one of the five distinct realms of the Thanissia Universe's territory. Passing under the arches, she noticed the light burning behind each of the race symbols weaken as the ancient magic of the realms faded into stasis.

The Hall of Elders was carved into the white stone of the mountainside. The soft quartz sparkled in the light as tall gaping windows scrutinized her approach. She stumbled, mindful of the hall's silent and daunting presence. Lightning flashed in the sky. The static in the air crackled as the lilac-hued atmosphere darkened. A natural response to the ancient magic becoming weaker throughout the universe. The sky was not the only thing fading; the brilliant white stone of Elderon and the surrounding foliage had also begun to dim, their magically infused luster waning.

A pang of sadness surprised her as an unfamiliar heaviness pushed on her heart. The Great War had sealed their fate, the time of the immortals was ending. Her world would be no more.

She reflected on the past as she proceeded toward her destination. Her mind drifted back, remembering the ensuing chaos that erupted not long ago. The war devastated the worlds of the Thanissia Universe and its people. The realms, once considered impregnable, were decimated easily under the wrath of an ancient evil; a dark entity that fed off magic.

3

Although the races had ultimately conquered the intruder, it came at a significant cost. The Guardian of Deities made the ultimate sacrifice to preserve the remnants of the realm's civilizations. Unfortunately, his sacrifice was not enough. The Thanissia Universe could no longer sustain life as the irreversible damage fractured the elemental magic's connection to the ether.

From the ashes of this world, a new one had been born, a non-magical world filled with static individuals known as humans.

A race, she thought, *not worthy of the majesty of Thanissia.*

Survivors of the Great War had already relocated to the new world. She and the celestials would not follow. They would exist among the stars, patiently watching the new world grow as the old one diminished.

Her shoulders shuddered as she took a ragged breath hoping to quash her jangled nerves. The last archway was behind her, and the massive wooden doors of the sacred hall stood ominously before her. The dark-hued grain embedded in the wood was a stark contrast to the white stone of the mountain. Groaning their displeasure as she thrust them open the doors heavy metal hinges grated. The sound reverberated off the interior surfaces as she entered the hallowed hall. Inside, the air was stale and saturated with a haunting silence. Clammy tendrils encircled her the moment she stepped over the threshold. The noise her boots made on the polished stone resonated through the immense space. Frustration at being pulled away from her tasks erupted again as she quickened her pace and continued to her destination.

As she entered the council room she saw her brother, Gabriel, standing to the left of the long meeting table. Michael and Raphael to his right. Not one acknowledged her as she stepped into the chamber. Their stares set straight ahead, locked on something unseen at the far side of the room. The sight of the Seraphs in their polished gray armor, black wings tucked magnificently behind them, never failed to make her feel inconsequential. They had a remarkable ability to elicit awe and fear in those who looked upon them. Their faces, exquisite masks of stoic, symmetrical beauty were unnerving. As the sentinel commander she excelled, but as the twin sister of a powerful Seraph, she often experienced an internal sense of inadequacy.

Her eyes strayed back to the front of the room where the council of elders waited. One emissary from each of the six races was present, but she recognized only one. Seri, the lone female elder and the envoy for the celestial race, was the highest-ranking Seraph within their hierarchy. Their eyes locked momentarily, and she thought she caught a flicker of empathy in Seri's irises before she cast her gaze downward.

The stifling apprehension that began as she made her way up to the Hall of Elders intensified as she stood in front of the council. The elders beckoned for her to approach. She felt a twinge as her intuition discerned something was amiss. She scanned the faces of the elders. Some looked defeated, others annoyed. The representative from the fire realm looked aghast; his whitish-gray skin paler than normal and mottled with a web of gray veins. A wariness wafted through the air. Nothing about this was typical, and it made her uncomfortable, a sensation she was not accustomed to.

Using her simmering annoyance as confidence, she pulled her shoulders back and moved forward to stand directly in front of the six council elders. Her mind whirled as she took in the daunting splendor of the council room—a place she had no business being present in. With hardened eyes, she stared at each of them hoping her annoyance at this unwelcome summons was not visible on her face.

"You summoned," she said, the tone of her voice a little too harsh, the edges tinged with the irritation she was desperate to hide. She winced.

The council elders glanced at one another. A look of concern crossed between them. Seri stood, her eyes full of compassion.

"You are chosen, my dear, blessed with a destiny that may one day bring back the time of magic. The prophetic water of the sacred pool has shown the Druid priests a time when ancient magic will be needed in the modern world. Descendants of our races will rise to once again battle the evil we could not destroy. This foretelling of a distant future, one to which you are linked, is why you have been summoned."

Seri hesitated, looking at the emissary from Dywen; a man with brilliant green eyes emanating a gentleness she was unaccustomed to seeing from a Warlician. He gazed at her, neither empathy nor hostility visible in his irises only a calm that made her relax. When he spoke his voice was husky, fractured by time yet full of wisdom and the same gentleness that penetrated from his eyes.

"Your destiny has been rewritten. Your future will no longer belong to our past nor our future. It has been foretold that you will carry our knowledge to those who do not yet exist. When the descendants of the ancients rise, you will stand with the one who carries my blood, and together you will ensure the future and the past survive."

She blinked rapidly, her blank stare a sign of her confusion. *In what world would a celestial and a Warlician warrior share an equal destiny?*

Seri placed her hand on the Warlician's shoulder igniting a

powerful essence that quietly spread across the room. In its wake, she sensed a strange and confusing emotional pulse, but before she could decipher its meaning and understand the odd connection between the two race elders, Seri spoke again.

"Go to the Ledge of Faith. The Guardian is waiting for you there. Good luck my dear, your destiny, is now our future. Remember, the past will never be truly lost."

The tension in the council room was palpable. Afraid to speak, she remained silent, her body rigid as questions flew through her mind. *What were Seri and the Warlician speaking of? What future, different from this world, could she be linked to? Why did the Guardian want to meet with her, himself?*

She fidgeted. Never had she stood in the presence of the Guardian of Deities, and she was unsure she desired to do so now. The Guardian had given up everything to end the Great War. Rumors had rippled through the sentinel camps that his powers were depleted, and his physical form altered. Claims were made that he was a mere shell of the fearsome entity he once was. Instinctively, she knew the rumors were true, but she chose to remember the powerful being as he had been. Unfortunately, that too was about to change.

The elders rose from their chairs and headed toward the exit. A sense of defeat lingered as they shuffled from the council room, eyes averted. She remained silent. Her heart pounded in her chest as she watched them go. Seri came around the table, a look of sadness welled in her eyes. "We are counting on you," she whispered. A slight smile crossed her beautiful face. As she turned a solitary feather separated from her massive wings, floating silently to the floor as she swept away to join the others.

Glancing at the Seraphs, her eyes locked with her brothers. An overwhelming sadness darkened his iridescent irises before his gaze drifted away, and he too turned to leave. She stood rooted to the floor watching, unable to utter a word as Gabriel and the other Seraphs followed the elders out. Their black, leather coats brushed the stone floor as they moved, thick black wings folded together like a pair of praying hands. Their power and grace were unequivocal as they exited the council room without a backward glance.

Alone, wrapped in the deafening silence that descended on the empty chamber, she remained rooted on the spot trying to make sense of everything. Taking a deep breath, she sighed. *Why, after all this time, had she suddenly become so important?*

A warm breeze blew in through an open window, a floral fragrance carried on its wisps. The scent released her from her self-imposed trance, and she bent, picking up the fallen feather at her feet. The tip still pulsed with Seri's magic, and she felt her own magic react, enthralled by the power of the ether.

Walking away from the loneliness encapsulating the Hall of Elders she headed to the narrow path that encircled the mountain. It ran parallel to the inside edge of the chasm and led to the Ledge of Faith where the Guardian waited. She dawdled along the path, in no hurry to meet whatever fate would befall her. As she walked, Seri's words surfaced in her mind.

What destiny could she be speaking of? What had the Druid priests seen in the mystic waters?

She had been a sentinel her entire existence; a celestial without a grand purpose. One of many protecting the realm from intruders and keeping peace among the outlying worlds. She would never be like Seri, her brother Gabriel, or the other firstborns, Michael and Raphael. Their destinies were linked directly to the Guardian—their powers unique, their status unrelenting. In the hierarchy of celestials, there were only four: The Guardian, the Seraphs, the elder council, and the sentinels. Her place had always been at the bottom, a position that suited her fine as she was unencumbered by the responsibility of those above her. She knew her place and functioned efficiently within the hierarchy because she recognized what was expected of her. Ultimately, she was left to perform her duties with little resistance from above. Although she was the commander of the sentinel army, her position did not garner the authority or prestige the title may suggest. She was one of many serving the realm.

As she approached the Ledge of Faith, static crackled above as a shadow rippled through the sky and darkened the edges further. The lilac hue continued to fade as the magic of the universe receded and with it the power of her world. Without its magic, her people could not remain in this realm. Soon they would begin their final journey back into the ether from which they were born. The time of the immortals had ended.

A golden ball of light hovered just beyond the edge of the precipice as she approached. It surged as it sensed her presence. The energy expanding and contracting as it pulsed. The Guardian's voice filled her mind. A firm whisper with a commanding tone drifted through her consciousness, a sensation that made her both fearful and comforted. As is the way of the celestials the Guardian got directly to the point.

"The Druid priests have seen the future; a prophecy that begins and ends with you and five others born from the bloodlines of the ancient races. The ancient dark has been defeated but not destroyed and it will rise again. In time its evil will infect the new world, feeding on a new kind of magic. A magic not born from the elements but sowed deep within the human soul. The new world will feel its wrath. You and the others are our only hope, the only ones who can defeat the ancient dark and save the past and future. Our fate belongs to you."

His voice changed, a conclusiveness in the tone. "You must fall, you must become mortal, and you must wait until the time comes for you to embrace your destiny. There is no other way."

Before she could utter a word in response his voice silenced, and a brilliant gold light exploded around her. Visceral pain sliced through her shoulder blades, and she could no longer feel the ledge beneath her feet. The wind whistled by as her body hurtled through time and space. The purple sky of her realm morphed into the star-filled night sky of the new world. As the light of the Guardian moved further away and her mind began to blur, memories slipping into oblivion, she heard him whisper once more.

"This is your destiny Gabriella, you must not fail. Save them all."

CHAPTER 1

THE GOLDEN MIST OCCUPYING THE room began to fade as did the haunting laughter that echoed through her mind moments before. A faint trace of burnt electricity wafted through the air; remnants of the broken light bulb, which had popped, plunging the room into an eerie darkness. Dane closed her eyes against the throbbing as it ricocheted off the inside of her skull. She knew where it came from, the chilling laughter. It reeked of death and rot and had an unmistakable stench; a heavy saturation of dirt that coated her insides with a sickening chill. *It was the ancient dark.* The encounter lasted only seconds, but its ability to get inside her mind, even for a moment, was unnerving.

Her eyes flew open as she heard Stevie gasp. The mist had dispersed, and the dark room was awash with bright strands of silver moonlight. Standing in the beams was Gabby, magnificent black wings spread wide, the tips glowing with iridescent light. Not the insecure, quiet Gabby, they'd been friends with for thirteen years, but a powerful, confident, otherworldly celestial. An immortal who had fallen from another time and place, to live among mere mortals until destiny required her to rise.

Dane's eyes locked on Gabby, waiting for her to speak. Rapture highlighted her features briefly until her gaze fell on another and a shadowed memory darkened them. "It's you," she said, disgust apparent in her tone.

Rafe's energy changed as their eyes met. The feeling of awe her transformation had elicited shifted to something resembling surprise and defiance. "Gabriella," he responded his tone as terse and uninviting as hers.

The overt tension in the air was stifling. Dane turned to question Rafe, her eyes narrowed.

"You two know each other?"

"We have met," he stated bluntly. The bland way he delivered the fact made it seem insignificant, but she sensed there was more to this relationship.

"So, you knew she was here?" Dane questioned, her confusion and frustration apparent in the frown she directed at him.

Before Rafe could address her interrogation, Gabby's voice filled the room.

"The warrior knew nothing of my destiny. His was to guard the Book of Realms not to be privy to what the Guardian of Deities had planned. He is nothing more than an undisciplined and uncouth watchdog."

Rafe's energy darkened, his ire bubbled to the surface as he brushed past Dane. The dark seed of rage that festered quietly in his depths began to grow. Dane could feel it expand as if it were inside her as well. She grasped his arm, squeezing her nails into his skin as the waves of his dark energy drenched her.

"Better an undisciplined watchdog than a rigid lapdog whose lot in life is to lead a horde of mindless sentinels under the overt shadow of your powerful brother," he spat.

Gabby's wings arched in response, her iridescent eyes flashed with rage as his words penetrated the energy swirling around them.

"Enough," Dane yelled, gasping for breath. The power in her voice surprised her, but it managed to quell the rising tension between Rafe and Gabby. She glanced at Stevie who stood dumbfounded beside her, eyes darting back and forth. Her pale face was etched with curiosity and disbelief as she turned to face Dane.

What the hell is going on? She mouthed, her hands shaking as she reached out to grip Diego's collar. Dane pushed calming energy toward her friend and gave her a reassuring smile before focusing her attention back to the immortals in the room.

"We will come back to this little walk down memory lane later," she chided. "But for now, we have other things we must take care of."

She moved cautiously toward Gabby, her foresight pulling at her mind as the ethereal energy pulsed around her.

"How are you feeling?" She asked gently.

Gabby tilted her head. Her wings lifted, stretching outward as if she were familiarizing herself with something she had not used in a very long time. Ignoring Dane, she looked down at her hands, watching as the iridescent light highlighting the tips of her fingers ebbed.

"I am beginning to fade," she announced, to no one in

particular. "I must remove myself from this realm. I need the life force of the ether or I shall cease to exist."

"That will not be necessary," Rafe said, reaching into his pocket and removing the vial. He held it toward her. "We brought the ether to you."

Gabby's eyes narrowed as she looked from the vial in his hand to his face. "You might not be as worthless as I thought."

"Gabby," Dane warned, not wanting the obvious dislike the two had for one another to escalate. She cast Rafe a stern glare to ensure he too got the message.

"It is fine," he responded as he turned to face her. His body language softened as her energy reached toward him. "I am not sure what your friend was like in mortal form, but I can only assume she was very different from her true self."

Gabby groaned, indignation dripping from the sound.

Dane gave her a look of disdain, silencing her, as Rafe continued.

"When Sebastian said, 'they were nothing like the image of angels that man had created' he was speaking the truth. Celestials are not empathetic or forgiving; they are distant, judgmental, and forthright. They speak their minds without prudence and do not care if they denigrate other races. They think of themselves as superior and are neither comforting nor inviting beings. Celestials are nothing more than a warring species. An entire race of sentinels whose mindset is to protect the agenda of the Guardian of Deities at any cost."

Rafe's eyes narrowed as he hesitated briefly to confront Gabby's penetrating stare. "The Guardian, himself, is an unyielding but equitable entity who has kept the peace within the realms since the beginning. His sentinels, unfortunately, are not as amicable."

"Our task is not to be agreeable, but effective," Gabby

countered. "Warlicians are unable to attain such discipline because of your inability to maintain any sort of emotional distance. It is the reason your race carries the dishonor of being a castigated one."

"Only in your eyes Gabriella. I had a perfectly agreeable relationship with your brother."

Dane watched Gabby wince at those words.

"Gabriel saw the worlds differently than I," she said.

"Perhaps you should have heeded Gabriel's example."

Gabby bristled. Her eyes flashed as she stretched her wings to their full length. "The Seraphs had their position in our societies hierarchy, and I and the other sentinels had ours— neither inclusive of the other. Please do not think you know my kind warrior, for our existence, is far above your inferior understanding."

Rafe chuckled, again holding out the vial toward Gabby, "I am encouraged to see after all this time, nothing has changed between us."

Nodding, she took the vial from his outstretched hand, removed the cork and drank the contents in one swallow. Almost immediately the iridescent light pulsing just below her skin brightened, spreading outward until she was once again encircled with a heavenly glow. Her wings softened as they folded over one another and dropped behind her. The glow in the feathered tips flickered as they brushed the floor.

Dane heard a low growl erupt from behind, a raw, instinctive guttural sound. Turning, she was surprised to see Diego, hackles raised, eyes glowing with malice, and teeth bared, crouched in an aggressive stance as he snarled at Gabby. In the shining light of the moon, he seemed bigger. His bulk easily hiding Tyson whose timid eyes peeked out from behind him.

"Diego, *stop*." Stevie hissed, pulling on the collar she still held in her grip. He ignored her, his eyes trained on Gabby as his growling intensified.

Dane sensed Rafe move toward Diego, surprise evident in his aura.

"Is that a Dragonwolf?" He inquired, directing his question to Stevie.

Stevie's brow furrowed in confusion. "Dragonwolf?"

"I heard there was a possibility that some had crossed through the portals from the fire realm but to see one still exists after all this time is quite remarkable."

Dane moved to where Rafe stood inquisitively inspecting Diego. Her hand stroked his back as she clarified. "He is just a dog, Rafe. Diego is Stevie's pet."

Gabby's voice filled the room behind them. "The warrior is correct, that mongrel is a Dragonwolf. I can smell his putrid scent from here."

Stevie's eyes widened, and her mouth dropped open as if she were about to say something. Instead, she looked down at Diego, her hand impulsively releasing his collar. With the pressure gone Diego began to inch toward Gabby his teeth chattering as he stalked forward.

Rafe snorted, as he turned toward Gabby. "He still has good instincts."

Gabby rolled her eyes. "Dragonwolves are as unbridled as their owners."

"An unabashed trait sentinels never appreciated."

"There is nothing to appreciate about undisciplined, erratic behavior in any species," she retorted, waving her hand at Diego, her fingers following the flow of the gentle movement. Abruptly, he stopped his approach. His body language relaxed, and he sat without incident mere feet in front of her.

Dane's head cocked, curious about his sudden behavioral change. "What did you do to Diego?"

Gabby just stared at her, cool iridescent eyes uninterested.

Rafe responded. "Celestials have an innate ability to calm and control animals. For all their feigned disgust with the unrestrained nature of certain species, their race finds animals quite intriguing. Dragonwolves, by nature, are a suspicious breed and once they bond with a master, their sense of loyalty enhances that distrust. For some reason, their breed has always had a heightened negative reaction to celestials."

He looked at Gabby, a smirk emphasizing his comment. She ignored his taunt, stretched her wings, and began to pace. Dane couldn't decide if the posturing movement was a response to boredom or a subconscious reaction to having her wings back after all this time.

"I still do not understand what a Dragonwolf is doing here," Rafe said, moving away from Dane to stand once more beside Diego. He frowned at the animal who sat completely still, his eyes following Gabby.

Stopping she stretched her wings again. "Is it not obvious," she said. Her voice dripped with indignation as she pointed at Stevie. "He has found his Dragon Gypsy."

All eyes turned toward Stevie who had retreated to the corner of the room. Her eyes widened, her pale face turned ashen. Confusion and uncertainty once again emanated from her as she squirmed under their gaze.

"Where did you get him?" Rafe inquired.

Stevie's mouth gaped but nothing came out. Her mind was frantic as she tried to understand all the strangeness unfolding in front of her.

"She didn't," Dane interjected looking at her friend with

sympathy. "Get him anywhere, I mean. He showed up on her doorstep one night."

"So, he found her," he stated.

Dane glared at him, her mouth tense. "Can you please tell me what this is all about?"

"Dragonwolves have an inherent ability to find what they are looking for, including those who possess the blood of their realm. A Dragonwolf lost on Earth would instinctively search for others like himself, those who carry the blood of the Dragon Gypsy. If he came to Stevie and has not left, it can only mean one thing."

"What?" Stevie whispered, her eyes wide, her voice hoarse.

They were interrupted by the sudden flapping of wings as Gabby's patience reached its breaking point. "Why is it that you Warlician's cannot just say what is on your mind? It is painful watching you prattle on." She redirected her annoyance and iridescent gaze at Stevie. "You carry the blood of the Dragon Gypsies, an ancient race that dwelt in the fire realm of our world." Her hand motioned toward Rafe. "As the warrior expounded, your ancestry is unique. The mongrel has identified you by your specific scent; a scent, I might add, which is less than pleasant." Crinkling her nose, she looked at Rafe. "She stinks of ash and fire. She is one of those for whom you search."

"You are sure?" Dane probed. Shock erupted inside her as she realized that her immortality may not take her further away from her friends, but closer to them.

Gabby's wings spread out again as the cool mask on her face slipped. "I do not make mistakes when it comes to recognizing the bloodlines of our realms. As you are descended from earth, she is the descendant of fire. There is no doubt."

Rafe nodded in agreement. "Celestials can identify the blood of the races. It was another reason finding her first was so important. If one who is destined is near, Gabriella will be able to detect their blood, especially now that she is connected to the ether. With her heightened senses, we may be able to find the other three without issue."

Dane glanced back at Stevie. She looked ill. Her face had lost all color and there was a film of sweat on her upper lip. Before Dane could move, Stevie's eyes rolled back in her head, and she collapsed to the floor.

CHAPTER 2

ANE'S IMMORTALITY ALLOWED HER TO move swiftly and with heightened reflexes, she had not possessed as a mortal. Sprinting toward Stevie, she caught her just before she hit the ground. Placing her gently on the floor she caressed her head and whispered her name.

Finally, Stevie's eyes fluttered open, the pupils dilating back to their normal size.

"Welcome back," Dane said.

"Sorry," she replied as she struggled to sit up.

"Easy. You fainted."

"What is going on?" She stammered, gazing over her shoulder at Rafe and Gabby. "Who is he? And what the hell happened to Gabby?"

"There is plenty we need to discuss, but first I have to know you are okay` and you won't faint on me again."

"I'm okay."

Rafe moved forward, offering Stevie his hand. She hesitated, her eyes suspicious. Cautiously, she took his hand and let him help her up.

"I am Rafe," he said smiling as he kissed the back of her hand. "The last of the Morrighann clan."

Gabby groaned outwardly. "You would think a binding would put a stop to your insolent flirting."

Dane shot her a withering glare before turning her attention back to Rafe, her eyebrow-raising in an unspoken query. He shrugged. "There is not much a celestial does not know. They are very astute and intuitive."

She shook her head, looking back at Stevie who appeared more lost and confused than before. "I will explain that later too. I promise." Dane motioned for Rafe and Gabby to leave the room. "I think Stevie needs some sleep."

Rafe moved toward the bedroom door. Gabby followed reluctantly. She released Diego from his trance as she stepped into the hall. He stretched and shook out his fur, trotting to Stevie's side as she climbed into bed.

Tyson, who had been cowering in the corner darted over to Dane. His excitement at her return, which he expressed with gusto now that the tension in the room had subsided, the only thing that mattered.

"Hey buddy," she said stroking his head as he wiggled under her touch.

"Dane, what is going on?" Stevie asked as she huddled shivering under the covers. Diego stared at Dane, a desolation reflected in his eyes as if he too realized the magnitude of what was to come.

"It's a long story and nothing for you to worry about now. Please go to sleep. I will explain everything in the morning."

"I'm not sure I can sleep. Or maybe I already am, and this is all just a bad dream." Her voice cracked as she spoke, and a shadow darkened her features. "Gabby has wings. Did you see that?" She exclaimed her eyes wide. "And she was so terse, blunt, and rude." Her eyes glazed as she thought. "She's so different."

Dane stayed silent refusing to engage further. This was not the time to try to explain the unbelievable or convince Stevie of a new reality. She would find out soon enough. Instead, she sat with her friend allowing her to talk through what had conspired in this room.

The moonlight cascaded through the bedroom window. Its beams cast a soft, sparkling ethereal glow across the floor. It filled the room with a subtle warmth as it caressed and soothed her nerves. This wasn't what she had planned when she came here this evening. Then again, she hadn't suspected two of her best friends were linked to the same ancient prophecy she was. Stevie was not the only one having a difficult time processing everything revealed here tonight.

"Where did you find Rafe?" Stevie asked, a slight twinkle in her tired eyes.

"That is an even longer story, although something tells me you might enjoy it."

She smiled at her friend, pulling the covers up tightly around her. "Goodnight, Stevie," she said as she moved from the edge of the bed to the chair and turned the light out. She sat in the darkened room listening intently to Stevie's breathing until exhaustion pulled her into sleep.

It was almost ten when Stevie and Diego emerged from the bedroom the next morning. Dane made coffee, tea and prepared a hearty breakfast for everyone. As she handed the pancakes to Gabby, Rafe grabbed the plate. "Celestials do not require nourishment," he said. "An anomaly that further increases their superiority complex."

Gabby leaned back in her chair and smirked. "The ether provides us with everything we need."

Dane shook her head. Another day of the constant bickering.

"Hi Ty," she said as she saw her dog peek around the corner. As he entered the sun-filled kitchen, tail tucked between his legs, Tyson slunk toward Diego. He was unsure about the changes he sensed in his best friend and his body language revealed his insecurity. Dane watched as the two dogs moved toward one another. Diego was much larger than before, dwarfing Tyson. There were other significant changes as well; his fur was longer and thicker, and his eyes sparkled, catching the sun's rays as they filtered through the sliding glass door.

He sniffed Tyson as he inched forward, sensing the surrounding energy. The exorbitant greetings and playful ease of their past relationship no longer present. Like Gabby, Diego had lost his *mortal* demeanor reverting to the immortal being that once inhabited a powerful magical realm. His innate suspicions guided his every action. He was cautious with Tyson but curious. Nudging his face, he circled, sniffing. Dane could sense that Diego would do him no harm so allowed the two to engage in this primal behavior.

"Why is Diego so much bigger than he was before?"

Rafe gave her a strange look, shrugging. "I can only assume the magic we reignited in Dywen is now flowing into this world and affecting any supernatural beings that reside here."

"Our realm's magic is affecting a being from another?"

"Thanissia magic is collective. The ether infuses all the realms equally. It is elemental magic that is specific."

"Oh. I guess I still have a lot to learn."

Rafe squeezed her hand. "It will come."

After scrutinizing Tyson and sniffing the air with suspicion, Diego sauntered back to lie at Stevie's feet. Tyson followed, curling up next to Diego but at a comfortable distance. Dane could see the shift in pack dynamic as Tyson accepted Diego as the alpha. A newfound respect stirred his instincts and dictated his behavior.

Stevie sat watching the three of them over the rim of her coffee mug.

"Did you sleep well?" Dane asked, putting bacon on her plate.

"Where are your wings?" She demanded, ignoring Dane's question. She had put down the mug and was pointing toward Gabby's back, where the large black wings were noticeably missing.

Gabby stared, iridescent eyes unblinking. "Celestials only show their wings when required." Her tone was flat as she stated the information like this should already be a known fact.

Stevie's eyes narrowed. Looking back at Dane, she muttered, "I'm not sure I like this version of Gabby."

Rafe chuckled to himself as he tried to suppress a smirk. "On Thanissia, the celestials are the least social and unlikable of all the races. They're aloof and superior nature often puts them at odds with the inhabitants of other realms. Even the elves, while disciplined and forthright, were less rigid than the sentinel army."

Gabby glared at Rafe before turning her back to him in silent protest.

"You will get used to her," he continued, shaking his head in jest. "Liking her is something different."

"And what about you?" She asked her suspicious eyes turning to him. "What is your story?"

Rafe grinned, looking at Dane for help. She returned his smile, raised a brow, and shrugged.

"My story is complicated, but I come from the same place as Diego and Gabriella. A world your ancestors and Danes once called home." A sadness surrounded him. "But that was long ago in a forgotten time."

"My ancestors are from Romania," she retorted, defiance hardening the edges of her tone. Taking another sip of her coffee she eyed them all.

"Your mortal ones maybe." Gabby snapped.

"That's enough Gabby," Dane said, as she took a seat beside Stevie. Clasping her friend's hand in her own she stared into her eyes.

"Stevie, I have to tell you something that even you may find unbelievable, but you have to trust what I'm telling you *is* the truth."

Stevie nodded, casting the others a wary glance.

An hour later, Dane had told her everything she knew about her family legacy, the prophecy, her journey to Dywen, the Druidstones, and Sebastian. She had intentionally left out her binding with Rafe, her immortality, and Stevie's pending birthright. Overwhelming her with inexplicable details was not going to help her adjust to a new reality or accept her destiny. Stevie would discover everything soon enough.

Stevie paled as she tried to process the information.

Dane knew it was a lot. It also didn't help that Gabby kept interrupting to infer Stevie's ancestors had possessed an infuriatingly unbridled passion.

"I hope that trait skipped several thousand generations," she said, before being quieted by Dane's withering stare.

Stevie sat for a few moments, staring down at her hands, her index finger absently playing with the ring she wore on her thumb.

"Tell me about my ancestors," she whispered looking at Rafe. "The ones that lived in your time."

Gabby began to speak.

"Not you."

Rafe smirked as Stevie managed to disarm the celestial in a way he had not seen before. With a renewed quiet in the room his mind drifted back to memories of her ancestors—the inhabitants of the fire realm.

"The Dragon Gypsies were a unique race for their powers originated from the dragons who ruled the realm before them. Thanissia was born from the ether and many magical creatures inhabited its worlds long before our kind rose to dominance."

Stevie's eyes dropped to Diego.

"Yes, Dragonwolves shared the realm during the time of the dragons."

Diego raised his head as if to acknowledge his place in their world's history.

"Unlike the other races, whose powers derive from their specific element, Dragon Gypsies enhance their inborn powers with the elemental energy. The magic of the dragon is ancient and as old as the universe itself. A magic that is both creative and destructive. It ignites passion, anger, tenacity, and an unrestrained daring. Its volatility is legendary. Dragon Gypsies were known for their unpredictability."

Gabby huffed, "That's putting it mildly."

Rafe ignored her and continued.

"Kaizi is the name of the fire realm. It is a world of molten lava rivers, charcoal black mountains, and fiery red skies. The Dragon Gypsy race was not large, in fact, before the Great War, there were only a few hundred that remained, but they were tenacious. A race that is born to exist. They were also the only race to be ruled by a royal family."

"Royalty?" Dane asked.

Gabby sighed. "It's not as grand as you may think. The Dragon Gypsies were the first of the races that emerged after the celestials—the Velkia family, the first of the Dragon Gypsy bloodline. Their family magic was powerful, more controlled than the others, so they designated themselves as royals."

Rafe nodded in agreement. "The Velkia built an empire on Kaizi, ruling it with a firm but fair doctrine. Their empire became known as the Dominion of the Dragons and was a vital part of the Thanissia trade route. Kaizi's alchemists, armorers, and blacksmiths were renowned, their wares sought after by many of the other races. The royal subjects were very skilled in their professions."

Stevie frowned, "And these are my ancestors?"

Rafe looked at her, his eyes revealed his uncertainty. "Yes, but unlike Dane, we do not know yet which of the family bloodlines you descend from. Once you accept your birthright, I suspect your ancestry will reveal itself."

Dane shot Rafe a dirty look as Stevie's curious nature took notice of the words he had just spoken. "Accept my birthright. What does that mean?"

"It's not that I was keeping anything from you, Stevie, it is just not an easy thing to tell someone," Dane said.

"What is it, Dane?"

"Your birthright is immortality," she blurted out, cringing

at how forceful her voice sounded. She had meant it to be soothing, but it had come out anything but.

Rafe glanced at her, his shoulders lifting in question.

"You have a better way of telling someone their destiny is to become immortal?" She said projecting her thoughts into his mind. He smirked and shook his head in defeat. "Please continue."

Inhaling deeply, she decided to tell Stevie the rest and deal with the consequences as they arose.

"To fulfill the prophecy our ancestors must bestow 'a birthright' on the one whose blood is pure to their race. It imbues the descendant with the ancient magic of their birth realm and knowledge of their ancestor's past. Your birthright will be received when you activate the Druidstone on Kaizi, at which time your dead ancestors come forth and transfer your birthright to you. You gain powers, ancient knowledge, and become immortal. At least that is how it happened for me."

She watched Stevie for a reaction.

Her eyes widened as the meaning of Dane's words became clear.

She gasped. "Shit, Dane, are you really immortal?"

Dane nodded.

"But you don't seem different."

She smiled, "No, I don't, but I do feel a little different."

"So, I will become immortal as well?"

"Yes. It is a sacrifice we all must make for the prophecy to be fulfilled."

"That must be what bunica meant," Stevie whispered, using the nickname that referenced her grandmother. She got up and ran out of the kitchen, Diego following close on her heels. Tyson lifted his head but stayed where he was glancing back at Dane for reassurance. She smiled, and he put his head back down, wagging his tail against the kitchen floor.

Stevie returned, a small white note card in her hand, eyes glinting with a mischievous and excited radiance.

"The Roma people have a tradition prior to the birth of a baby. The elders from the expecting mother's tribe write down fortunes for the future; specific wishes for the newborn." She waved the card in front of her. "This is the one my grandmother wrote on the day of my birth."

Her hand shook as she handed the small white card to Dane.

Taking the card, she read it aloud to the others.

"*The child shall be blessed with intelligence, tenacity, and the knowledge of our ancestors. Her path will lead to an immortal destiny and a hallowed future.*"

"Well, that is telling," Rafe acknowledged.

"There is something else I need to tell you, Stevie," she said casting a sideways glance at him. "It's about Rafe and me."

Stevie's head snapped toward him; then back to Dane. "What is going on with the two of you? You may appear the same but there *is* something different about you. I assume this one has everything to do with it," she insisted, pointing at Rafe.

Dane hesitated, which was long enough for Gabby to intervene. "They have experienced a *binding* and now share an ancient destiny. It's rare and boring. Can we move on? We need to get back to Thanissia."

Dane's eyes flashed at Gabby in frustration. She was not sure, as Rafe promised, she would ever get used to the new Gabby. Gone was her sweet, thoughtful, demure friend and in her place was this over-confident, arrogant, impetuous, and often infuriating immortal.

"What does that mean—ancient binding?" Stevie questioned, her vivacious curiosity peaking with every new revelation.

"It means that Rafe and I share not only a destiny, but we have an intense emotional connection. We can feel what the other feels."

Stevie's eyebrows raised in surprise. "So, no need for Alex then?" She asked jokingly, referring to the friend who was desperate to take Dane on a date.

"No." She smiled as Rafe's curiosity flooded through her. "I'm taken."

Stevie nodded, giving Rafe a piercing stare. "You will treat her well?"

"You have my solemn word."

There was a change in the kitchen's atmosphere as Gabby's wings reappeared, stretching out on either side and almost knocking Rafe from his stool.

"I hate to interrupt but I believe we have something more pressing waiting for us back home. If the prophecy is coming to pass, we must be ready and the power of Dywen will not be enough. The Dragon Gypsy and I need to reignite the magic of our realms, and we must find the others, so they can do the same."

"The Dragon Gypsy?" Stevie scowled. "We have been friends for thirteen years and it's always been Stevie, now it's the *Dragon Gypsy*!"

Gabby shrugged, which infuriated Stevie even more, but she refused to respond any further to her callous nature.

"Are you ready for this Stevie? Can you accept your birthright? Dane asked, disregarding the tension that pulsed around them.

Diego placed his large head on Stevie's lap his eyes eluding a calm, confident understanding. She stroked his head, a smile coming over her face. "Do I have a choice?"

Dane laughed as she remembered her conversation with Sebastian when she asked the very same thing. "Our destiny does not always give us a choice," she responded, echoing his words. "But hopefully you can find peace in it."

Stevie glanced down at Diego. The connection she had with him from the moment she found him curled up on her porch in a terrible blizzard, had always been infinite. She now understood why. Their destinies, like Dane and Rafe, were connected by a magical past. Her grandmother had predicted her fate at birth and for all her superstitions and old-world zeal, much of which Stevie found eccentric, she was correct. Stevie must honor her heritage and accept her destiny, whatever the cost.

CHAPTER 3

I T WAS ALMOST TWO IN the afternoon when they reached
the Elder Oak. The bright sun rebellious as its rays
pierced through the clearing's thick canopy. Strands of
sunlight flowed downward to thaw the frost-covered ground.
Water beads glistened on the surfaces of the fallen leaves; a
bright mosaic that littered the clearing, still untouched by the
snow that fell everywhere else. The clearing was a sacred place
where the norms of the modern world did not penetrate.
Dane's breath sent a foggy puff floating into the afternoon
chill. The clearing was quiet. Sebastian was nowhere to be
seen.

"He, no doubt, wants to make an entrance," Gabby stated,
her iridescent eyes filled with displeasure at the thought. Her
wings appeared once again, the black feathers rippling in the
breeze as it blew past her on its way to dance through the
treetops.

Dane was not sure she would ever get used to seeing
Gabby's huge wings unfold like origami as they unfolded
gracefully from fleshy slits on her shoulder blades. She had

changed into jeans, black ankle boots, and a knee-length black leather jacket, the button front open. The thin white t-shirt she wore underneath had been cut, like the leather trench, to accommodate her wings. The black streak in her hair was braided from crown to end and pulled into a ponytail with the rest of her blonde hair. She looked more like the modern celestial now.

"An entrance?" Stevie questioned.

"Like Dane and me, Sebastian is a Warlician warrior, but he was transformed by the Guardian into light stasis when our realms fell. A required sacrifice, which enabled him to endure the millennia that passed in this world before your ascension," Rafe stated. "He is a watcher and will have gained boundless knowledge from his presence on Earth. Light stasis provides the gifted with acute senses through which mass amounts of information may be gained. He will have sensed our approach and will already know the celestial and another Arcanist has been found. I suspect his delay in appearing is deliberate. It most likely relieves his boredom." He smirked at his statement.

As if on cue, the Elder Oak began to glow from within. A piercing light ebbed forward from its depths. It melded with the bark, the intensity increasing until it exploded in a sparkling, erratic shower. The shards of light crept across the forest floor toward one another, their brilliance causing the frost and water droplets on the fallen leaves to sparkle. As the shards converged at the center of the clearing they formed a shape, the edges ebbing and receding as a dark shadow emerged from the light's depth.

Dane glanced over at Stevie, who stood mesmerized by the light throbbing in front of her. Diego had placed himself in a protective position, but he too remained calm as Sebastian's normal form appeared from the radiance.

As swiftly as the light appeared, it receded back into the Elder Oak leaving Sebastian standing in all his finery in front of them. He frowned as he looked from one person to the other, his eyes pausing on Gabby. His scowl gave way to surprise.

"Gabriella. You are the fallen one?"

"Hello Sebastian, you look well considering you have been confined to a tree for all this time."

He chortled, unfazed by her condescending attitude. "Life as a mortal has not taught you humility, I see."

She sniffed, lifted her chin, and peered down her nose at him. Her wings stretched out to their full extent. The feathers caught the sun's rays igniting an iridescent sheen in the black.

The posturing was getting old.

"So, you know Gabby as well?" Dane asked.

"Of course, she was commander of the sentinel army of Etheriem, although I had no idea she had fallen."

"Etheriem?" Stevie asked.

"The realm of the celestials," Sebastian said, turning toward her. "So, you have found the one descended from the race of fire and ash." Glancing at Dane, a twinkle in his eye, he said. "This was easier than you thought, yes?"

"Yes." Dane agreed. She understood what his question referred to. "I have known both Stevie and Gabby for quite a long time."

His head bowed. "Destiny."

She and Stevie smiled at one another. "Something like that."

He turned his attention to Rafe, looking him up and down, assessing the updated version of the ancient warrior that stood before him.

He wore a dark pair of jeans, a long-sleeve white t-shirt,

and black combat boots, loosely tied, all of which belonged to Mason, Dane's ex, at one time. A green cargo jacket hung from a loop on his backpack and his sword was tied to the pack's side. He had pulled the front of his hair back and tied it with an elastic she found in her junk drawer.

Sebastian scowled. Shaking his head, he muttered something under his breath before turning his attention back to Gabby. "Gabriella, I am under the assumption you are able to release me from my light stasis. If you may, I would like to continue this journey with all of you in my regular form."

"You wish to give up the gift the Guardian so graciously afforded you?"

Sebastian did not even flinch. "Unless the coming battle will be here in this clearing, I doubt my gift will do us much good."

A ripple flowed through her wings, the feathers quivered as her muscles and tendons stretched and contracted. Sebastian clearly knew how to handle Gabby better than Rafe. "Very well." She strode forward laying her fingertips on his forehead. Closing her eyes, she began to recite an incantation. The light of the ether shimmered under her skin, its pulse matched the rhythm of the words she uttered.

"Femon, Blaedome, Areventi."

As the incantation echoed through the clearing, the light stasis streamed from Sebastian's body. Rivers of light swirled around him, their tendrils sweeping outward until they began to recede, the magical essence of the ether finding its way back into the Elder Oak. He stretched out his limbs as if the ache of a million years suddenly flowed through them. He took a deep cleansing breath, releasing it with a loud sigh.

"Many thanks."

Gabby took a step back, her head lowered as she folded

her wings in tight behind her. "There may be residual effects from the ether's magic but soon you will once again feel like your old self."

"You are able to come with us now Sebastian. You are no longer tied to the Elder Oak," Dane exclaimed.

"Yes, but regrettably I am afraid this is yet another journey you must make without me. I think my presence here is still required. The dark witch has been active, and I suspect it will continue. I will stay and watch her."

Dane hadn't thought about Lilith since she returned. It had been less than twenty-four hours and so much had happened that it hadn't crossed her mind. "What has she been doing?"

"She is creating a breach in the veil that surrounds that old mill, a kind of magical vortex. I can sense the emptiness associated with these types of anomalies. The magic she is practicing has gotten darker and there is something different about its essence. Something is lurking just behind the magical energy, but I cannot yet identify what it is."

"Maybe I should go to the mill before going to Kaizi."

Sebastian shook his head. "That is an unnecessary interruption. Until we understand her intentions, there is little any of us can do to impede her. Reactivating the Druidstones of the Five Realm's must remain our focus."

Reluctantly she agreed. Grasping his hand, she whispered, "Please be careful."

"You do not need to worry, I have been in this world long enough to understand its workings. I will not be detected by any mortal or the dark witch. I shall only observe until your return."

"I will hold you to that promise," Dane said. "Nothing

more than observing. The dark witch is unknown to us, and we are unaware of her capabilities."

He nodded. "Did you bring the portal stones for the fire and spirit realms?" He asked, changing the subject.

"Yes." She fished them from her backpack and held them out.

"May I suggest you open both now; then use the portal in Kaizi to go directly to the spirit realm?"

"That would be the most appropriate and efficient course," Gabby agreed her voice monotone.

Sebastian stepped toward the tree, coming to an abrupt halt as he sensed something that escaped him earlier. He turned, his face a mask of confusion as he stared at Diego who slept at Stevie's feet.

"Is that a Dragonwolf?" He exclaimed, disbelief and awe in his voice.

Now it was Rafe's turn to chuckle. "I had the same reaction."

"I was not aware any mystical creatures survived the Great War let alone traveled through the portal into this dimension. This is an interesting turn of events." He walked over to Diego and crouched in front of him, rousing him from his slumber. Their eyes locked as both scrutinized the other. "He is magnificent."

"He is a beast," Gabby retorted, unimpressed.

"Gabriella, you have always pretended to be indifferent to the wondrous creatures of Thanissia, but we both know different don't we."

It was a rhetorical question and Sebastian did not wait for a response. He stood, his attention redirected to Stevie. "Dragonwolves are creatures of power, grace, and stamina, revered by the royals who led your people. If this one is meant for you, your bloodline is more than just a commoner. I will be interested to see how your journey unfolds and what truths are revealed."

Before Stevie could respond he turned and walked back to the Elder Oak. His long, black cloak swished as it skimmed over the frozen leaves scattered across the clearing floor. The wind swirled, and the upper branches swayed as he placed his palm flat against the bark of the trunk. He closed his eyes and muttered an incantation, a subtle glow seeped from his palm. The trunk morphed, the rough bark disappeared revealing the panel for the portal stones. The earth stone still sat silently in its slot, the surface cold and lifeless.

Dane handed both Gabby and Stevie their corresponding portal stones. The stones sprang to life immediately as their surfaces touched skin. A low hum emanated from the spirit stone while the fire stone Stevie held, spit and crackled in her hand. Sebastian motioned toward the tree signifying that Stevie and Gabby should insert their portal stones into the corresponding spots in the panel.

Gabby placed her stone in the slot first. The humming increased as a lilac light sprang from its center, growing until a perfect door of shimmering purple light wavered before them. Stevie was next, her hand shook as she attempted to place the stone in its place. She watched in horror as it fell from her palm and clattered down the side of the tree to its base. Giving everyone a half-smile apology, she bent, picked up the stone and tried again. It sputtered and crackled as she wedged it into the slot in the panel. Sparks spit erratically as a red gel-like substance flowed from its center and down the trunk. The substance bubbled and hissed, spitting out sparks as it moved, morphing to form a circle at their feet. Flames sprang up to dance defiantly as the circle grew into a burning ring of lava and fire.

When the portal was complete, Dane took her hand.

"Are you ready?"

Stevie nodded, her wide eyes full of curiosity and dread. Dane glanced back at Rafe, ensuring he would follow. Gabby had already stepped through the portal, the red flames spit and hissed as she was engulfed in their fiery haze.

"Let's go," Dane said, taking a step forward, never releasing Stevie's hand as they moved into the red blaze of the Kaizi portal.

CHAPTER 4

WALKING THROUGH THE SWIRLING RED portal, Stevie's anxious energy erupted. Her steps faltered, and she trembled uncontrollably. Dane sensed her hesitation and squeezed her hand in reassurance as they moved through time and space toward Stevie's destiny. The moment they entered the portal the temperature skyrocketed. Dry heat from the other world scorched the portal's interior. The darkness and heat closed in around them as she pulled Stevie forward.

The portal dislodged them quickly, and they emerged into the ancient realm at the edge of a molten lava bed. Slow-moving streams of hissing orange magma slogged through crags of charred black rock. The magma flowed from a tall volcano in the distance; its throat spitting smoke and fresh lava up into the air in an angry fit of passion. The sky was tinged with a subtle red tone. A fiery moon blazed in the distance, casting an eerie flickering glow over the landscape. The black rock and the searing orange lava melded with the realm's red hues. Kaizi's entire color palate was monochromatic, a stark canvas that signified a forsaken land, void of any vibrant life. The breeze blowing across the land was hot, not humid, for there was no moisture in the air. It was heavy and dry, like the air that blows from a furnace on a cold winter night. An uncomfortable temperature that stifled the breath and caused one's skin to sweat out the heat constantly building inside. A blistering heat that leaves skin damp with an itchy, thick, sticky perspiration.

Dane had already peeled off her light sweater, thankful she had a tank underneath. Stevie also seemed uncomfortable but was too enthralled by the landscape that spread out in front of her, to care.

Rafe pointed toward the imposing volcano in the distance.

"We must head toward Saurimale Abyss. The road to the steel city of Embermire is just to its left. We will find the Druidstone underneath the royal citadel in the Temple of Fire. There is a portal located behind the royal quarters and when we are ready, we can use it to enter the ether into the spirit realm."

Beads of sweat were forming on Rafe's forehead and his already damp shirt clung to his muscular form. Dane was immediately aroused, the sight of him caused an involuntary reaction which was now heightened by her ancestral magic. A side effect of their binding she was having a difficult time controlling. He glanced over, a knowing smile appeared on his face. She shook her head and looked away, but she could still feel his penetrating stare and the seductive energy as it wrapped mercilessly around her, igniting her skin with a different type of heat.

Ignoring him as best she could, she evaluated the others. Gabby was the only one not affected by the suffocating heat of Kaizi's environment and of course Diego, whose demeanor indicated he was relieved to be back in familiar surroundings. Stevie on the other hand, her awe now under control, looked miserable.

As they trekked across the scorched earth, stepping over steaming pools and flowing rivulets of lava, an odd hollow sound whirled around them. A strange wind blew its stagnant heat across the molten land. It was difficult to breathe in this arid environment, but they trudged forward; a sense of curiosity and an understanding of the consequences of failure, spurring them on.

They wound their way through the lava pit toward the base of the volcano until they found a road. It wasn't much of a road, barely even visible, worn into the flat rock that surrounded the volcano's base. It was a path, no wider than a sidewalk and littered with small stones and dirt. The surface was covered with large flakes of gray ash that floated down from the top of the angry mountain.

They stopped to drink water, taking a moment to assess their surroundings. Stevie had been quiet for most of the trek, unaware that Dane was watching her. She took a sip from the canteen and wiped her sweaty face with the back of her hand.

"Are you OK?" she asked, as Stevie surveyed the fiery landscape.

"It's unreal," she responded, her voice taut. Her fingers absently stroked Diego's neck. "This is the home of my ancient ancestors. A race ruled by fire and dragons. Dane, we are in another time, another dimension, surrounded by immortal beings." She hesitated, a sheepish look on her face. "Sorry."

Dane shrugged. "Don't be." She understood the magnitude of the situation. It hadn't been long since she stood looking across the vast expanse of Dywen, experiencing the same conflicted emotions and awe.

They'd only been following the road for a short time before it snaked its way through a series of tall boulders. A thick, black crust scarred by deep crevices covered the rocks. As they navigated through the maze of boulders, each taller than the last, she caught a glimpse of the steel city; its metal peaks reaching upward toward the flush red sky.

Emerging from the maze they stood at the top of a precarious stone staircase. Steep steps, cracked, broken, and upheaved by time, descended into the barren valley below. The massive steel city was just to the north. A dominant iron structure surrounded by a moat of bubbling, fiery lava. From where they stood, most of the realm could be seen, a landscape of black-crusted lava rock besieged with cracks that oozed orange magma from its core. Behind them, the volcano rumbled, a palpable reminder of its visceral power. Other than the steel city there wasn't much to see on the horizon. This realm, for the most part, seemed to be a massive expanse of magma rock.

They followed Rafe as he descended the stone staircase. The sheer width and depth of the steps were intimidating. Their gratuitous size dwarfed them as they carefully moved from one to the next. When they finally reached the bottom, they were greeted by a welcome coolness as a transparent, wispy mist rolled languidly across the surface toward them. Emerging from the fog in the distance was a metal drawbridge. Its steel girders, thick cables, and iron decking were an imposing addition to the wrought iron entrance gate it was attached to. Thick walls, plated with sheets of iron and rivets, stretched for miles in either direction surrounding the metal city.

As they crossed the drawbridge, they were stifled by the heat rising from the moat far below. Bubbles burst on the surface as the thick lava oozed around boulders, its sluggish flow meandering between the thick rock walls of the moat.

Stevie stopped for a moment. Her hands gripped the iron rail so tight her knuckles turned white as she stood on her tiptoes to peer over the side. Dane could sense the awe even though the energy surrounding her was chaotic and tinged with uncertainty. Gently, she touched Stevie's shoulder motioning toward the end of the drawbridge where a large wrought iron gate, its formidable bars fused with menacing spikes, blocked their path. At its middle was a thick, metal door and their only access to the steel city within.

"Let's keep going."

As they approached, Dane could see the courtyard beyond the gate was empty. The fog rolled methodically hovering just above the ground as a hollow wind swirled back and forth. She shivered as her skin prickled. She could feel the tendrils of an invisible, eerie solitude leech from the courtyard.

Rafe moved to the gate. As he reached the door, he grasped the thick handle. The rusted iron screeched under the force, as metal grated against metal. The handle turned but the door would not budge. He tried again, this time pushing his shoulder and body weight into the door. Slowly, the door began to move. Hinges groaned in protest as it reluctantly swung inward. Gabby and Stevie followed him through the door, but Dane hesitated as a strange sensation prickled her skin and an uneasiness engulfed her. There was an unfamiliar essence floating in the warm air; a foreign energy she could not identify.

Something is not right, she thought, her eyes searching the mist as it rose up to engulf the others. Sweat trickled down her bare skin, her head throbbed from the airless heat as she continued into the courtyard. She was only feet from the door when she sensed him, but it was too late. Her foresight was sluggish, altered by the extreme temperature of the realm. A powerful arm snaked around her waist, pulling her back into the body of an unseen assailant as a sharp blade pressed firmly against her neck.

In front of her, Rafe yanked his sword from its sheath pointing the tip toward them. "Release her," he hissed, a warning she knew he would not repeat a second time. She felt the uncontrolled rage begin to rise inside him as he stared at the stranger. Fury distorted his handsome features as he realized his demand was being ignored by her captor.

The arm around her waist tightened as the blade dug deeper into her neck. She grimaced, leaning her head further back onto his shoulder. From her peripheral vision, she could see part of his face. His skin was pale, a faded pallor of whitish-gray with thin blue capillaries visible just below the surface. His eyes were a strange color, a deep red that reminded her of the color of deoxygenated blood. His hair was unlike anything she had seen before. Its length blew haphazardly in the hot breeze, each strand a different shade of gray and white.

Gabby's voice penetrated the tension as she whispered loudly. "He's a royal."

Rafe stiffened, his body leaning as he tried to get a better look at the man holding her captive. His body was flat against hers, hidden from Rafe's prying eyes.

"Has it really been so long that you no longer recognize a royal by their one categorizing feature—the white hair," Gabby hissed in disgust. "Dragon Gypsies have black hair, the entire race, except the royals. It is the singular genetic trait related to the Velkia family bloodline." She motioned dramatically at the stranger's head.

Subtle. Dane thought.

Rafe's fury diminished. His eyes scrutinized the man that peered out from behind Dane. Her captor pushed her forward but continued to use her as a human shield. He walked warily toward the others who waited unsure of what he might do.

Rafe tensed as he saw Dane grimace again. A small nick in her skin near the blade was bleeding, his eyes cold as it trickled down her neck. He did not care who he was, if he hurt her, he was going to die!

I am fine! She communicated telepathically, imploring him not to do anything rash. His eyes locked on hers, but he did not advance or make any sudden moves to lash out at the stranger. Instead, he waited, allowing her captor to dictate the interactions.

"Who are you?" The man's voice was hoarse and deep.

"I am Rafe, of the clan Morrighann, son of Gareth. These are my traveling companions, Gabriella of the spirit realm, and Stevie who carries the blood of fire and ash, a descendant of your people. The one you are currently holding against her will is a daughter of Seri and the only one to still carry the Callathian name." Dane rolled her eyes at the formal introductions, but his words must have affected the stranger because the blade's pressure decreased and his grip on her waist lessened slightly.

"Callathian." The way he said her ancestor's name was

less a question and more a recall of a memory. "Has the prophecy come to pass then?"

"It has not yet, but it is moving toward the future, which is why we have returned. We mean you no harm, we are only here to reignite the magic of the realms and prepare for the battle that is to come."

The blade dropped from her throat and the stranger released her. He sheathed the knife as he moved from behind her. His dark red eyes studied her intently before he spoke. "My apologies Callathian, we have been here alone for a very long time, it can make one distrustful."

She looked around the courtyard, its emptiness echoed back. "We?"

The stranger waved his hand toward a steel tower in the distance, a glint of light reflected in the window.

There was someone watching them.

"I am Drow," the stranger said. "The last of the Velkia bloodline."

He pointed again to the tower as someone emerged from the shadowed doorway and walked toward them. "That is Killenn, commander of the royal elite guard."

The man approaching them was dressed all in black. His pants were tucked into knee-high leather boots, and he wore a leather breastplate emblazoned with a red dragon. Long dark hair was tied into a knot on top of his head and his eyes, like Drow's, were a deep, cabernet red. A thick stubble covered his angular jaw, and he carried an impressive looking metal crossbow, which he pointed toward the ground as he reached them.

He must be Drow's sniper, she thought, recalling the glint of light she had seen in the tower window.

Killenn stood before them his eyes full of suspicion, his

jaw tense as he flexed his free hand. "Prince Drow, are you alright?"

All eyes flashed back to the *prince* as his title was unceremoniously revealed.

Drow nodded, motioning toward the strangers who appeared in his homeland. "They are friends. They come to us from the new world."

Dane could tell Killenn was unsure of how to react to the strangers he found in front of him. When he did speak, the calmness in his voice was surprising and curious.

"How did you get through the portal?"

"We have a portal stone."

He looked at Dane his brow furrowed as he considered her words. "So, the prophecy has come to pass then? The ancient dark, has risen?"

"No," Rafe interjected. "But the ancient dark has made its presence known. It is growing in strength and it will not be long before it finds its way out of its prison."

"Then we must prepare." Drow's raspy voice was somewhat unnerving and now that Dane was free from his grip, she had an unfettered view of the prince. She studied him with interest; besides the pale skin, grayish-white hair, and dark red eyes, he bore a distinct mark in the middle of his forehead—a raised scar that resembled a line with two dots on either side. She wondered if it was specific to the royal lineage, considering Killenn did not have a similar marking. He was dressed in similar pants and boots as Killenn, but he wore a knee-length coat of plush, dark, red velvet over a white silk shirt.

"Come," Drow said. "We will discuss this further in the royal citadel."

Killenn slung the crossbow over his back and followed Drow through the empty courtyard, motioning for the others to do the same. They headed toward a set of metal doors located at the back of the courtyard. Drow pushed open their bulk, stepping aside and bowing graciously as they swung open revealing the heart of the steel city.

"Welcome to Embermire."

Dane detected pride in the prince's voice when he said the name of his city, yet it was tainted by a layer of sadness. Stevie had gotten over her initial shock and was now fully immersed in the adventure. Her eyes sparkled with wonder as she looked around the expanse of Embermire.

From the top of the volcano staircase, the front half of the city was not visible. Dane was astonished at how many streets and buildings existed inside the stone and iron walls. They moved at a hurried pace through the empty streets, passing stores, trade smiths, market areas, all echoing the solitude that had infected the realm since the Great War. They moved without pause through the abandoned streets toward their destination. The red haze of the sky serving as an ominous backdrop for the black charred stone and thick metal that created this impressive city.

As they emerged from an alley, Dane could see the towering peaks of the citadel. Massive metal towers reached high above the other buildings. Banners flowed down their sides, long black silk scrolls emblazoned with the same red dragon head that Killenn wore on his breastplate. *The Dominion of the Dragons* was, without question, a powerful and proud empire that thrived in the time of the supernaturals. As they walked down the final street and headed to the entrance of the citadel, she wondered if Stevie could be a descendant of the Velkia bloodline. If Stevie could be *royalty?*

CHAPTER 5

THE ROYAL CITADEL WAS THE largest building in the city, taking up at least three city blocks. Its entirety was constructed from metal, an impressive piece of architecture that included, sloping rooflines, towering peaks, and suspension cables supporting a network of catwalks. Large stained glass windows dotted the exterior, each piece a different color of red or black. The gables between the intersecting roof pitches were covered with small metal shingles. Each gable adorned, at the peak, with a filigree metal bracket.

"Remarkable," Stevie whispered, more to herself than the others.

The citadel entrance featured a massive set of arched steel doors. Large metal rivets bordered the edges and metal dragon heads protruded from both sides. A large iron ring hung from the mouth of each, metal teeth clenched tightly together. The burnished metal reflected the translucent red light that filled the sky casting the entryway in an eerie hue. Above the doors, a gargoyle perched. Its expansive wings spread wide as it crouched menacingly. Vacant eyes stared at everything and nothing—*an ancient otherworldly protector.*

Passing through the main doors of the citadel, they emerged into a wide hallway. Numerous painted canvases housed in sculpted iron frames lined the walls, portraits of the Velkia royal family. Each likeness had the same whitish-gray hair as Drow and each bore the strange mark on their forehead.

"This way," Drow instructed, leading them to a set of doors at the far end.

The portraits dark red eyes followed them as they passed, a strange illusion that added to the unnerving atmosphere hovering over the steel citadel. Other than the portraits, there was little else in the hallway, no decorative items, tables, or seating, nothing to muffle their approach. The sound their boot heels made on the stone floor echoed off the steel walls, causing a hollow reverberation to thunder around them as they walked.

Killenn opened the doors, motioning for them to pass. They emerged into a large shadowy, circular foyer. Dane assumed they must be inside the base of one of the numerous towers she saw from the exterior.

"Where are we?" Stevie asked looking around the room in awe.

"This is the Grand Hall," Killenn responded.

Dane understood now the carefully planned architecture of the royal citadel's main entrance. The entry hall, bare except for unsettling portraits of the royal family, and the Grand Hall, imposing in both size and impression—were meant to intimidate.

Drow headed directly for the large staircase to the right. The winding metal steps were suspended from the ceiling by thick steel cables anchored into metal support beams. A handrail snaked up the left side secured to the steps and the steel cables by a thin, sturdy wire. The effect, structurally, was impressive, a black metal sculpture that curved elegantly toward the second floor. In fact, the entire foyer was grand. A massive iron chandelier hung from vaulted ceilings, polished slate floors were inset with sparkling veins giving it a marbleized effect, and tall ornate metal pillars flanked the sides of each doorway.

As they reached the landing, Stevie moved in beside Killenn, engaging him in small talk. She appeared at ease in this new reality, intrigued more than overwhelmed. The prince upon hearing the animated whispers glanced back, his eyes flitting over them. Seemingly, uninterested in their interaction he continued to lead the small group through the citadel.

As they came to the first landing Dane noticed a single glass and metal door off to her right. Breaking from the group, she walked to the door. A strange pull guided her toward whatever was on the other side. Peering through the etched glass she saw it led outside to a suspended balcony. As the rest of them continued up the next flight of stairs, she opened the door and stepped outside.

The landscape stretching for miles in front of her was indescribable. As she gazed at its expanse her appreciation for the diversity of these realms increased. A familiar energy invaded her thoughts as Rafe came to stand behind her, his arms wrapping comfortably around her waist.

"Are those poppies?" She asked. Her eyes never left the acres of red flowers spreading for miles in the fields below as she sank comfortably back into his warmth. A sea of red petals swayed in the breeze as the tepid wind carried its sweet odor upward. Dane took a deep inhale of the fragrant scent and sighed.

"Yes," Rafe responded. "And I am glad to see them return in abundance, especially after the Great War damaged the fields so severely. Poppies were a popular commodity with many artisans and tradesman on Kaizi, but none more so than the alchemists. Poppy dust, made from grinding petals picked immediately after first bloom, was the main ingredient in a multitude of their elixirs and potions. Poppies have a magical property that is useful in many serums: medicinal, protection, power enhancements. It was also said that alchemists used poppies in many of their experiments when modifying the composition of base metals.

Rafe softly kissed the side of her cheek. "It is good the poppies have made a plentiful return. They may prove useful once again."

Dane stood in silence, gazing across acres of red. The poppy fields were a sight to behold, a vivid, red carpet of life blanketing the land as it disappeared over the distant horizon. Such vital growth in a place so bare and stark. Her brow furrowed as something Rafe said made her curious. "You mentioned the poppy fields were damaged during the Great War and from what you and Sebastian have told me, many of the realms suffered destruction as well. Why then is there no sign of this devastation here or on Dywen?"

Rafe smiled understanding her query. "The Great War was a long time ago and the elemental magic of each realm has repaired the damage. I doubt we will see signs of destruction on any of the realms."

"Even though the magic is in stasis the worlds are able to repair themselves?"

He nodded. "The power of the Thanissia Universe is

undeniably infinite. The realms and magic are immortal in a way we cannot explain. The essence contained within has always protected them, even the destruction caused by the ancient dark would never be permanent. It took a long time for the realms to heal, but time is all they need."

She thought about this as she stood with Rafe. The ancestral worlds still had many secrets to reveal, and she hoped, releasing the ancient magic from its slumber would provide answers as well as guidance.

Rafe touched the nick on her throat, his fingertip stained with the blood that still trickled from the wound. His muscles clenched as angry energy exploded inside him. It burrowed through Dane swiftly leaving her breathless in its wake. She knew Rafe had little control over these emotional onslaughts, but it was difficult for her to experience at high velocity. She knew it wasn't intentional but considering their binding, they were going to have to find a way to deal with his emotional instability.

Tipping her chin up she gazed at him. "Rafe," she said, taking the hand that was stained with her blood. "It's just a little cut. I'm fine."

The angry surge relented, the fury flickering in his eyes dissipated as he quelled the rage, pushing it back down into the depths of his being. They were still adjusting to the emotional overload of the binding, but Dane sensed Rafe's inability to control his rage went much deeper.

She turned to face him, tangling her fingers in his long hair and gently stroking the stubble that grew on his cheek. The sweet scent of poppies aroused her, and his closeness became difficult to ignore. Pulling his face toward her she kissed him. Passion exploded in the air as their energies combined. He pulled her closer. His kiss deepened as his hands explored the dip in her lower back and the outside curve of her thigh.

"Do you need a room?" Sarcasm dripped from the question.

Gabby, Dane thought, untangling herself from Rafe's embrace. She turned to face her friend who was standing in the doorway, arms crossed. A look of smugness shadowed her pretty face.

"Do you think we can get on with the reason we are here, or would you like us to wait for you to finish?"

Rafe smirked as he sensed Dane's anger rise, then dissipate as she thought better about engaging the celestial. Instead, she grabbed his hand and stalked from the balcony pulling him along with her and ignoring Gabby as they passed.

A few minutes later they were all gathered in a narrow room dominated by a lengthy, steel table and high-backed chairs. *An ancient boardroom,* Dane thought as she looked around. On the walls, large tapestries hung from iron rods, topographic maps of what she assumed were the other realms. Rafe caught her frowning and confirmed.

"The Five Realms," he said glancing at the maps. "This room was often used for diplomacy. The royal family hosted emissaries from all over. There were many problems solved within these walls. The Velkia enjoyed unrivaled peace and prosperity within their realm, which thrived on structure, so they often intervened if trade relationships fractured, a financial crisis loomed, or diplomacy was at risk. Gabriella would have you believe the people of Kaizi were undisciplined because of their power but actually, the Velkia and their people were the most structured race in our universe."

Rafe turned his attention back to Drow as he began to speak, gesturing for them to take a seat at the table. Killenn stood to the princes right, his rank and position had not ceased even though the entire Dragon Gypsy race was no more.

"I must apologize again for my less than welcoming introduction," Drow said directing his sentiment toward Dane. "It has been a long time since someone other than Killenn and me, has set foot on the charred rocks of our realm." He hesitated before looking at Rafe. "Oddly enough, the last was a warrior of your kind, but forgive me, his name escapes my memory."

A roar erupted in Rafe's ears as the prince's words connected the puzzle pieces of the past. "Brannon," he whispered.

The prince glanced at him, his face passive but his eyes curious. "Yes, I believe that was his name. You knew him?"

"I do, quite well. He is my friend."

The prince glanced toward Killenn a concerned look passing between them.

Rafe understood its meaning and pushed back his chair. He stood and approached the prince extending his hand. "I would like to thank you for saving his life. Brannon has recently returned to Dywen. When the portals closed he was caught in between worlds but reigniting the Druidstone allowed him to return home. He is well thanks to you and speaks with fondness of the man who saved him from the daemons. He owes you his life."

Drow's passive expression did not change, but the look he cast Killenn was one of relief. He clasped Rafe's hand and a slight smile appeared at the corners of his lips. "I am happy to hear he is well, but I am afraid the praise must go to Killenn. He was the one who found your friend and brought him back to the citadel."

"Then my gratitude is extended to you as well," Rafe said bowing to Killenn.

"I too am happy to hear of his recovery. At the time we were uncertain of his future. He was badly wounded, and infection had set in. I surmised his best chance at survival was to return him to his own realm where elemental healing specific to your kind could occur. We were afraid that keeping him on Kaizi would be a death sentence. I am glad to hear it was the right choice."

Rafe nodded, a mutual respect evident between the warriors. Dane smiled, at their interaction and at the wave of gratitude that overwhelmed Rafe.

"If you two are finished, I believe we have a Druidstone, to reactivate," Gabby said, fingers tapping incessantly on the iron tabletop.

"Yes," said Drow, taking his seat. Rafe did the same. "But if you do not mind, I would like to be informed of all you know with respect to the prophecy and the outside worlds."

"Of course," replied Dane. She began at the beginning —*her thirty-first birthday*—the night her ancestral legacy was discovered, which set in motion a sequence of events that led to this very moment.

CHAPTER 6

AN HOUR LATER, DROW AND Killenn were privy to all the knowledge the others possessed and understood the events as they happened. Their reactions were non-expressive. Each listened quietly as Dane spoke, nodding when appropriate or glancing at one another when something said piqued their interest. Gabby only spoke once and astoundingly it was not to admonish or insert sarcasm into the conversation. When Dane finished, Drow rose, his passive expression unchanged. With a nod of his head, he directed them to follow as he left the room.

Although the Temple of Fire was in the crypts beneath the royal citadel, Drow led them to the roof. The location of the only access point was an inconspicuous staircase built between the outer and inner walls. The dark, winding stairs were wedged between the metal with no windows or reference points to mark their specific location, so the descent became disorienting.

Eventually, they emerged into a shadow-filled room littered with royal objects. Remnants of a forgotten past were scattered over shelves, tables, and the floor. Dusty scrolls, tattered tomes, weapons, their blades tarnished or broken, and trinkets occupied the space. Like the marketplace shops, there was a heavy layer of dust covering the objects. It floated up into the air as they passed, their presence disturbing the quiet surroundings entombed in this shrine.

They exited into a long narrow hall. Metal doors lined each side, one after another, separated by a burning metal sconce. The flames cast shadows onto the walls that bent and stretched awkwardly. There was a slight chill emanating from the stone, a strange phenomenon considering the entirety of Kaizi was sweltering.

"What is this place?" Dane whispered to Rafe.

"I believe it is the family crypt."

Each of the doors was emblazoned with an iron plaque signifying the name of the occupant buried inside. Dane noticed Drow hesitate as he walked by one of the final doors. His shoulders slumped briefly before he regained his stoic composure and moved on. She slowed as she reached the same door, the name on the plaque revealed the immortal entombed inside was Bellisine Velkia.

"She was Drow's mother," whispered Stevie coming up beside Dane. "They were extremely close. He was devastated when she took her own life force during the Great War shortly after his father was killed. It's the reason he stayed here on Kaizi; he doesn't want to leave her."

"You seem to know a lot about this, Stevie."

"Killenn informed me of Drow's direct lineage during our walk here." She hesitated a moment, aware of Dane's curious stare. "And, I may have asked about the prince once or twice."

Dane was not surprised at how much information Stevie garnered during her journey through the royal citadel. She was very adept at getting people to reveal things about themselves and apparently others. Killenn was a loyal servant of the royal family, but Dane assumed his relationship with Drow extended beyond the confines of class structure. Since he knew so much about the prince personally, she suspected they were also friends.

As they came to the last door on the left, Dane noticed it was ajar, so she peeked in. The room itself was nondescript, four plain metal walls, one with a blank plaque hanging from it. The black metal coffin that sat in the room's center was a different story. It was another ornate and spectacular achievement in metalworking, the metal delicately carved into a multitude of images and strange words. On the face of the coffin lid, was a dragon its eyes set with two red jewels that sparkled brilliantly in the firelight. As her eyes flitted to the door, she saw the name engraved on the iron plaque—*Drow Velkia.*

"He is the last in the Velkia line," whispered Rafe as he reacted to the shock reverberating through her.

"I don't understand," she said turning to face him.

"It is a Velkia tradition, a way to honor the Dominion of the Dragons. After a death, a family member must forge the coffin for the deceased family member. The Velkia use ancient metal found deep in the belly of the volcano. It is impenetrable and seals so tight the body inside remains unblemished even after the life force returns to the dragonlands of their ancestors. Since there is no one left to honor the prince, he must have forged the coffin himself. I suspect Killenn will entomb him when his life force leaves this realm."

"And if Killenn dies first?"

"Knowing the efficiency of the Velkia royal family, Drow will have thought of something if that comes to pass."

Dane nodded, her eyes drifted back to Drow as he disappeared through the door at the end.

⸎

They emerged from the royal crypts into the Temple of Fire—a circular room of architectural brilliance. The walls stretched upward, their height hidden by the shadows. On the far side, panels of stained glass let in a subtle, eerie red light. Massive metal columns, their bulk thick and sturdy, supported girders and catwalks hanging from the rafters. Thick steel cables crisscrossed the ceiling. Hung at the center of the room was the most magnificent chandelier Dane had ever seen. It was an enormous metal box. Two of its sides were clear glass, the other two, flat metal sheets adorned with intricate filigree cutouts. A soft candescent light, cast from the fire burning inside, escaped through the filigree. The movement of the flames ignited the room in a kaleidoscope of sparkling golden-red light; a subtle luminosity that besieged the metal walls with a splatter of shifting patterns.

Metal dragon heads stared down from their placement on the walls. They were larger than the ones hanging on the entrance gate and their eye sockets bulged with a brilliant red gemstone. The flickering light from the chandelier enhanced their menacing appeal as it glinted off the dark metal.

An iron trough, about twenty feet, ran the circumference of the temple. It was lit by a vibrant fire. The flames licked the ceiling. The trough connected the dragon heads and provided the flame raging sporadically from their open mouths.

"Wow," she heard Stevie whisper. Killenn grinned in response, but he quickly rescinded when he caught Drow eyeing him with strong disapproval.

"Welcome to the Temple of Fire," the prince said, his face somber. "The heart of the royal citadel."

Dane felt the power that tinged the air. The room was filled with ancient magic even in stasis, it was detectable. Her eyes scanned the room. The fire and metal gleamed in contrast, one light, one dark. A massive metal altar stood in the room's center, a simple black box with rivets lining its edges. The altar was unadulterated. It did not reflect the metalworking bravado that was showcased throughout the citadel.

Drow turned to face Stevie, his dark eyes burning with an intensity and curiosity that surprised her. "The Druidstone," he said as he pointed to the large metal circle protruding from the top of the altar. Like Dywen's Druidstone it was plain, void of any scripture or embellishment. Its surface was smooth except for four small holes.

Stevie walked to the altar. Her hand shook as it reached toward the metal circle. She flexed her fingers, a conscious effort to calm her nerves. As her fingertips brushed the metal, an invisible pulse throbbed through the room. Startled she pulled her hand back and glanced at Drow who nodded in encouragement. Her Roma curiosity piqued in exhilaration as she reached toward the Druidstone again. It was cool to the touch, its surface smooth and blemish free. Her mind spun as she faced her destiny and the overwhelming sacrifice she was about to make, the price—*immortality*.

"How does this work?" She asked, her voice breaking as she trained uncertain eyes on Dane and the others.

Drow approached the altar, positioning himself beside her. He reached for her hand as he pulled a small object from his pocket. "The Claw Key," he said as he placed the item in her palm.

Stevie stared at the object. It was a foot, or paw, whatever dragons had for feet. Long, black, pointed talons protruded from the four toes. Burnished scales covered the foot, and she brushed her thumb over their surface. The leathery texture was rough and the skin taut. It wasn't real—*the foot*, just a miniature replica made of metal and painstakingly painted to enhance its realism. She flipped the dragon claw over searching for the key Drow had mentioned. He must have realized the source of her confusion for he gently touched her arm. His deep cabernet eyes held an uncharacteristic kindness as his eyes locked with hers.

"The claw *is* the key," he said, pointing to the four small holes in the front of the circle. "Use the talons."

She glanced back at the others. Dane stood beside Rafe shifting from one foot to the other, Gabby was impatiently drumming her long fingers on the metal column she was leaning against, and Killenn stood in the shadows his face distorted by the dark. Stevie's heart beat loudly in her chest, and she felt restricted by her own clothing. Her hand trembled, and she inhaled, a deep, calming breath. She moved the talons closer to the holes, shifting their position until they lined up correctly. Pushing the claw into the circle, she heard a click inside the metal as the talons found their alignment within the lock.

"Wait!"

The voice was forceful, and Stevie pulled her hand away from the Druidstone, startled.

All eyes were on Killenn as he emerged from his shadowy corner. "How will we know if we need to mark her?"

"Mark her?" Dane inquired, impulsively glancing at Drow's forehead.

Rafe also looked puzzled, which gave Stevie and Dane

little comfort. Killenn had directed his question at Drow, and she noticed a strange look pass between them before he answered. "I trust her journey to immortality will reveal her specific ancestry before she needs to enter the Dragon Flame."

"What is the Dragon Flame?" Stevie asked. Dane could sense the elevation of anxiety in her energy.

"The Dragon Flame is our race's gift of life. It is a magical flame that cleanses the internal soul, a process every Dragon Gypsy must go through shortly after birth." Pointing to the symbol scarred into his forehead he glanced at the others. "If Stevie is from the royal Velkia lineage, she would need to bear the mark of our bloodline prior to entering the Dragon Flame. This mark ensures the purity of the royal bloodline. No one who carries Velkia blood may mate outside their own. The royal marking ensures our bloodline stays untainted."

Dane's eyes widened as the reality of the prince's disclosure became clear; the Velkia bloodline was incestuous. She stole a quick glance at Rafe, whose face remained a mask of indifference. Gabby too seemed unfazed by this revelation but regrettably, Stevie was not. She'd turned a grayish shade of pale and was staring at the prince mouth agape.

"And I need one of those?" she whispered.

"Not necessarily," Killenn said. "One's place in the Dragon Gypsy society is imminent from the time of birth as each individual is born into a specific class. The Velkia bloodline is no different; a royal is born to a royal. The mark is not just an identifier it is also a magical barrier. It maintains the blood's purity. Since you were not born from a bloodline but descended from one, we are unable to determine if you require the mark or not."

"And what happens if Stevie is from the Velkia bloodline

and unmarked when she enters this Dragon Flame?" Dane asked.

Killenn's somber expression betrayed him. "She would die."

His words throbbed in her ears and a roar built in her head as she struggled to accept what he said. "Die? From the flame?"

He nodded. "Yes, the mark not only protects the bloodline from being tainted by another, it also protects the royal blood from the potent magic of the Dragon Flame."

"And only the royal bloodline is affected negatively by this magic?"

"Yes. The ancient magic of the Dragon Flame is integral to our people and has guided us since our inception in the universe. It defines our class structure; a hierarchy that dictates an individual's rightful place in the Dragon Gypsy society." His shoulders slumped. "At least it did."

Dane understood the enormity of Killenn's last statement and how deeply it affected both he and Drow. She felt the same conflicted emptiness surrounding Sebastian and Rafe; then again from Gabby when she first reverted—a deep sense of mourning and loss of identity. "Your bloodlines are connected to the Dragon Flame?"

"Yes, our race is derived from the four ancient bloodlines of the dragons. Our class structure was archetypal of that ancient hierarchy and each bloodline descends from one of the elder dragons—fire, smoke, ember, and ash. The royals or the ruling class were born from fire, the royal elite guard, or warrior class were descendants of smoke. Commoners made up the remaining two classes, the ember born skilled class: artisans, merchants, tradesman, and alchemists, and those descended from ash, known as the rearing class, responsible for molding and guiding the *whelplings*—commoners under the age of maturity."

"The royals? Why were they so different? And what does this have to do with Stevie and the Dragon Flame?" Dane asked, indicating Drow's marked forehead.

"The royals are known as the *Brevadant*—the untouchables. They are the pure-bloods, the ones whose bloodline derives directly from the fire dragon. This bloodline is the most powerful of the ancient kind, but it has one weakness; the Dragon Flame. The magical flame is one of the few things that can burn through dragon hide and because of their purity the royals are susceptible to the fire's wrath as their composition is the closest to the ancient dragons. Unless they bear the mark before entering its flame—"

He did not need to finish his thought as they all knew what Killenn meant. If Stevie was of the royal bloodline, and she entered the Dragon Flame without first being marked, her immortal life would be short-lived. Stevie looked shaken, her recent acceptance and bravado at her pending immortality had disappeared.

Dane felt Stevie's energy fluctuate. She knew she was worried about her birthright even more so now there was a serious unknown attached to it. She felt helpless for there was nothing she could do to ease her friend's anxiety. This was a journey Stevie must make alone.

Gabby's calm voice interjected. Her tone almost kind as she spoke. "Let us have this conversation after Stevie receives her birthright. There may be a clue provided by her ancestors that will help us determine her rightful lineage or something else revealed in her journey to immortality."

Stevie smiled weakly, casting a forlorn look Dane's way.

"Remember everything you see." Her eyes implored Stevie

to pay attention. She nodded. Turning back to the altar she grasped the dragon claw. Fighting the trembling in her hands, she pushed against the metal until the talons once again clicked into place. The claw warmed under her touch. A throbbing heat seeped through the talons and scales, spreading out across the metal of the circle. The Druidstone inflamed as heat radiated from its surface causing the circle to shimmer with invisible waves. Stevie let go of the claw, mesmerized by the red-hot circle. Cracks fractured the metal as magma pushed from the fissures. It oozed onto the altar surface and spilled over the sides, pooling in a bubbling mass on the floor. It hissed as it crept outward until a lazy, steaming river of lava swirling around Stevie's feet.

Dane and the others took a few steps back, mesmerized by what was unfolding in front of them. The temperature in the temple dropped as the heat from the lava sucked the air toward it. Oxygen fed the flames causing them to leap erratically from the thick magma. The molten river churned, spiraling upward to cocoon Stevie in a fiery embrace as the temple shuddered. Flames flared in the wall troughs as an indiscernible whisper filled the temple with an eerie chant. The magma surrounding her brightened, blazing slightly in reaction to an unseen energy rising from the realm's depths.

As the magma slowly encased Stevie, her face slipping beneath its throbbing thickness, her eyes locked on Danes. There, deep within Stevie's irises, she saw something unabashed—*pure ecstasy.*

CHAPTER 7

ER BODY WAS AFLAME, NOT with the searing heat of the magma engulfing her but with a primal sexual arousal. A passionate agony ignited her skin and left her utterly breathless. The heightened state of arousal was both pleasurable and cruel. Its intensity was exhilarating but without the desired release her body desperately craved.

The magma's crushing embrace loosened abruptly, and its thick density diluted until it flowed around her like silky red water. She was no longer encased but floating, warm magma caressing her skin provocatively. The flow began to move, pulling her forward in its seductive current. Although the magma had thinned, she still couldn't see outside its boundaries. Immersed in the red liquid she was relaxed, uninhibited. Her heart beat at a steady pace and her mind was calm. Neither panic nor fear existed in this place for the sexual intensity that battered her body was too overwhelming. Time drifted away as the endless barrage of carnal agony intensified. Liquid magma tantalized her skin. Every ignited fiber sent waves of sexual heat crashing through her—a torturous battery of pleasure without end. The current ebbed and flowed. The crimson water churned like a fiery mist lulling her with its seduction. Without warning the current changed direction, and she felt herself plummet straight down. A cascading waterfall tumbling into the abyss. She was helpless to stop her descent. The magma crashed toward the unknown with her helplessly caught in its tow.

Just when she thought the free fall wouldn't end the liquid fire vanished, leaving her standing at the center of an ancient throne room. Her intense breathing abated as the sexual tension that assaulted her body vanished. She turned in a small circle, engulfed by the haunting silence that saturated every corner of this massive room, a memory from another time.

Metal seats lined the room's length on both sides, their high backs covered in a tattered red leather. Cobwebs hung from the fixtures on the walls; iron sconces lit with a dull orange flame. Dusty, torn tapestries swung from the bottom of the grated windows. Two imposing iron doors stood closed at the far end, their height reached the ceiling of the wall they claimed. Both doors were adorned with large round shields. The runes etched on the metal surface were foreign but the image at the center she knew well—*a red dragon head.*

She turned back to the front of the room, her eyes scanning the space. A long black carpet runner ran down the center. Iron pillars, set apart about ten feet, flanked it on either side. The runner ended at the bottom of three steps that led to a magnificent iron throne.

Tentatively, she moved toward it.

The stale air was heavy with dust that made the back of her throat tickle uncomfortably. Shadows moved across the floor as the flames, burning in the iron sconces, hissed as she passed. At the bottom of the stairs lay a broken dagger, the blade shattered, at the top an intimidating throne. The metal structure eluded power but sitting vacant in a room suffocated by a hollow silence, it was a haunting reminder of a long-forgotten history.

In the wall behind the throne, a circular window, its etched glass cracked, allowed beams of light to cascade down upon the throne seat. The throne's design was simple. An armless chair with a tall back that splayed outward as it rose. Its metal frame was connected to girders and wires that crisscrossed behind it, constructing an elaborate backdrop. Wedged between the girders were chunks of molten rock, fusing the throne and backdrop together to create an imposing structure made specifically for a dragon king.

She bent. Her fingers brushed over the broken blade of the dagger. The silence in the room unexpectedly shattered when a voice spoke from the shadows.

"Impressive is it not."

Stevie stood quickly. Her stance defensive. Her eyes searching. The deep, gravelly voice echoed through the room again. Her eyes strained to peer into the darkness, but she could not detect the source of the voice.

"I have seen many kings sit upon that throne. Good, fair rulers who flourished under their responsibilities, forging relationships with allies and foe; and others who faltered, the burden of their task unbearable. This room, once a sacred place, is now a faded echo of a past long gone. A reminder of our own vulnerabilities."

The voice quieted again. The shadowed silence permeated the room as she shifted uncomfortably, her mind searching for a response.

"Who are you?" She asked. Her voice sounded small within the magnitude of this darkened room.

The sconces flared as a solitary figure appeared from the shadows stopping when he reached the throne. "I am Dornan and you Arcanist, come from my blood. A line that has stood beside this throne for generations." He took a step forward, emerging from the shadows completely into the light cast by the large etched glass window overhead. The man was tall with broad shoulders. His short black hair was streaked thick with silver at the temples. His long beard, the same. He was dressed head to toe in black leather, the familiar red dragon head emblazoned on the breastplate. He was a handsome man although his face showed signs of both age and battle. It was marred with welted scars that crisscrossed with creases and lines.

He walked to the top of the stairs moving down them deliberately until he stood one step above her. His dark eyes, the color of a deep cabernet, stared with intent into her own brown ones. "You are the future of my bloodline Arcanist, the only one who can ensure our kind never truly dies."

She gawked at him, in awe of the imposing power he eluded.

"Have you a name child?"

Her mouth was dry, and she swallowed hard. "Stevie."

His head tilted, the brow deepening as his mouth pursed in thought. The flames hissed in their sconces, flaring for a moment before some sputtered pitifully and extinguished.

Dornan's eyes squinted suspiciously at them. "This world is fading. Soon it will be gone and with it your legacy. Come, time is expiring."

"Where are we?" She asked, her eyes imploring him for answers.

"A place that exists only in time and space and built from memories of our past. A place known only as The Lair."

The Lair, it sounded so ominous. Looking around the throne room again, she could sense the silence shift. The past reached toward her, an echo that slipped seamlessly through the stone and metal.

She shivered.

The shadows darkened as the light from the window receded to dusk. Dornan stepped around her and walked to the middle of the throne room. Stopping he turned, his back to the massive doors. He beckoned, and she walked to stand in front of him. The metal pillars surrounded them, their bulk a protective circle. Grabbing her hand, he pulled her toward him until only a few feet separated them.

"It is time for you to become."

Stevie nodded but remained silent. Dornan was an intimidating presence, even more so because he was no longer alive. She was not sure where the Druidstone had sent her, but she was positive wherever she was it didn't exist on the same plane as the other worlds.

Dornan's strong, calm voice interrupted her thoughts.

"Once you receive your birthright, you must search out those who can train you in our ways. Learn how to protect, fight for, and honor not only our bloodline but the dragon. When you have given your sacrifice, your essence will be forever linked to our past. Use it as a vessel for knowledge. The magic of our realm will be inside of you, an elemental power that burns within our kind will be yours to wield. Listen to that power it will guide your magic. The fire element knows our souls. It will not fail you." Dornan's eyes searched hers. "But be warned, fire magic is extremely volatile. Without the ability to control it, the magic will eventually consume you. Do you understand?"

She nodded again, her mouth open but unable to speak. Anything she said at this point would be futile.

He removed a small knife from his belt, its silver hilt intricately carved in the shape of a daunting talon. He took her hand. His thumb rubbed the skin of her palm. The blade glinted in the firelight as he swiftly sliced through the flesh. She winced but remained silent. The sting abated quickly as her blood rose to the surface. Dornan repeated the act on his own palm. Blood trickled down his wrist. Droplets fell soundlessly to stain the stone floor at their feet. Clasping her hand, the warm blood of their open wounds mingled as he began to recite an incantation.

Dragon fire
Circle of light
Bless new blood
With smoke and flame.

A fire sprang from the floor, circling them in flames that licked maliciously at their feet. She tried to remain calm but the heat emanating from the flames was stifling. Dornan's grip tightened as he continued to chant. His eyes closed. He seemed oblivious to the fire that raged higher and higher around them.

Dragon fire
Blood of old
Ember burns
'til ash prevail

The fire was now a raging wall of flame, surrounding them on all sides. It crackled and spit. The heat was unbearable. Sweat ran in rivers down Stevie's skin, soaking her clothes until they clung like wet rags to her body. She coughed, as she tried to inhale much-needed oxygen, but the singeing heat tore at the back of her throat, scorching the skin as she gulped. Dornan could feel the panic swell inside her as the flames crept upward, suffocating the air and stealing the oxygen. He pulled her in closer, so the only thing she could see was his eyes.

Dragon fire
Flaming pyre
Seeds of wisdom
Covet thy own

As the last of the incantation echoed through the flames, Stevie felt a tightening in her chest. Flames licked at her skin and a smoke began to billow from the pyre.

Her eyes remained locked on Dornan, his presence quashing the rising panic. His dark irises reflected memories of a long-forgotten past, secrets hidden for millennia. A sense of peace engulfed her. A calm pulsated from the world she saw reflected in his eyes, the world of her ancestors. Heat sizzled in the air and flames licked and spit around them. Smoke choked her breath, but she felt only serenity.

As the ancient magic began to push toward her birthright, Dornan released her hands. The deep red of his eyes faded behind the engorged flames as he stepped backward and disappeared behind the smoke. She could no longer sense him or feel his presence. She was alone. Her life slowly slipping away. Stevie closed her eyes against the stinging smoke. As she breathed her lungs filled with the suffocating heat, but there was no panic, only tranquility as she listened to the deceleration of her heart.

It was uncanny, being cognizant of your own death, having a keen sense of awareness of the very moment you inhale your last breath. A chorus of whispers exhaled in the flames as her heart took its final beat.

CHAPTER 8

DROW WAS PACING THE FLOOR. His hands clasped behind his back, brow furrowed, eyes cast downward. Dane watched him from where she sat cross-legged on the stone floor, absently stroking Diego's fur.

After a few moments, she glanced back at the red cocoon of magma. It slithered silently around Stevie, its movement sensual and intentional. Her gaze strayed to Gabby, who had taken an interest in an old book she found on one of the shelves. She didn't look restless, merely bored as she flipped the pages mindlessly. Killenn and Rafe stood near the door, their heads close, whispering in hushed tones. Warriors born from fire and earth.

She rubbed the back of her neck kneading at the tight muscles. The transformation seemed to be taking a long time, and she was beginning to worry. Other than Drow's constant pacing, no one seemed concerned her friend was mummified by lava. Stretching her legs out, she pulled herself up. Diego rose with her. She ambled toward the cocoon. The heat from the magma strengthened with each step until sweat glistened on her exposed skin and her thin tank clung to her torso. She stared at the bright red lava, its provocative movement evoking a strange hypnotic lull. The heat emanating from the core was extreme, but as her fingertips grazed the surface, she realized it was only slightly warm to the touch.

Diego whined beside her shaking out his fur in frustration. She glanced down meeting his gaze. His golden eye imploring her for an answer.

"She'll be back soon," she whispered.

He bowed his head and yawned. Stretching his hindquarters he lay next to the lava cocoon. He rested his massive head on his paws, his eyes full of sadness.

Dane left him to watch over the cocoon.

She circled the altar coming up behind Drow. He had ceased pacing. His eyes were closed, and his head was tilted toward the cocoon as if he were listening to something only he could hear.

"Drow," she said softly, unsure if she was disturbing some ancient ritual. He didn't move. His eyes remained closed. If he heard her voice, he was unwilling to acknowledge her presence. She waited a few moments before turning to go back to where Diego lay.

"It is almost complete."

Startled by the sudden response, her head swiveled. He was facing her, his hands once again clasped behind his back. His dark red eyes focused directly on her brilliant green ones.

"Excuse me."

"I can sense one of my own has emerged. The transformation to immortality, to the world of the dragonkin, is almost complete." A nod of his head indicated the cocoon. "It should open soon."

"Thank you."

"You care about her. The Dragon Gypsy?" His stoic expression did not reveal much but the lift in his right brow indicated he was curious.

"She is a good friend."

"So even in your world, fire and earth are intertwined?"

"I'm not sure what you mean."

A shadow darkened his features. "The elements have a specific identity in our world: fire ignites, earth grounds, water sustains, air binds, and spirit is the one that balances them all," he said, motioning toward Gabby.

Dane smirked. The irony that Gabby was the balancing force.

"The elements work in unison but only fire and earth can exist within one another. Together they generate powerful magic." Drow backed away and raised his hand. His long fingers curled in toward his palm. He looked at his hand. His lips moved silently. Flames leaped from his skin, forming a rotating ball that flickered and danced in his palm.

Dane's eyes widened. "You have Warlician magic?"

"No, my power comes directly from the ancient fire Dragon. Only the Velkia blood has this power among my people. It is not a weapon, but a tool until it is infused with Warlician earth magic. Bring forth your energy."

She moved closer extending her hand toward his. The green energy surged beneath her skin recognizing her intent. An energy ball emerged, rotating leisurely in her palm, waiting. Drow placed his hand near hers. The red flaming ball flickered, its intensity brightened the closer it got to her energy ball. The two balls arced toward one another, melding together in a flash of sparks, forming a golden ball that flamed voraciously from its inside.

"How?" Dane stammered.

"Fire and earth magic are drawn to one another. Our ancestors discovered this long before the Great War, but it was never used until then. It was how we were able to defeat the hordes of daemons the ancient dark summoned to our lands." He pushed his hand toward the flaming golden ball and in response, it moved away from him. The energy morphed as he spun his hand. It flattened, spreading out until a small portion of the temple was draped with the flaming gold energy.

"Your energy makes the earth magic spread, thinning and expanding it to cover a large area." His outstretched hand flexed, his fingers clenching to form a fist. The blanket of yellow light responded, erupting in a flaming explosion. An incinerating fire burned up the yellow energy and everything in its path.

Dane watched in awe as the remains of a small table and chairs collapsed lying in a smoldering heap of ash and embers on the floor. Turning her head, she caught Drow's gaze. The stoic expression had returned but a subtle glint in his eye remained.

"It can be extremely effective when our magic is intertwined."

"I would say. This could be helpful in defeating the ancient dark."

Drow shook his head. "Unfortunately, as the last royal, the scope of this combined power is limited. I have no confidence that it will be of any use in the battle to come."

"Unless Stevie is from your bloodline and has the same power."

"Even then it won't be enough. During the Great War, my entire family was alive, and we had hundreds of Warlician warriors. The area over which we could disburse this magic

79

was extensive. We had the ability to strike down hundreds of daemons at once giving our warriors a fighting chance. With one or two royals and a handful of Warlicians, the combined power will be weak and limited." He pointed to the burning furniture. "If the ancient dark unleashes a dark army again, we will be infinitely outnumbered, and our magic will not be of much help."

"Then why show me this?"

"As a way for you to understand the intensity of the magic your friend will possess. Fire magic is passionate but often erratic. Dragon Gypsies must learn to control their power when they are young, but even the best of us lose control now and then. Earth magic grounds all our magic, not just the magic energy that the royals possess. I suspect our new Dragon Gypsy will require your help once she returns." He motioned toward the lava cocoon. "If she already trusts you, it will be that much easier."

Dane opened her mouth to respond but Drow had already retreated. His hands clasped firmly behind his back as he returned to pacing. Her gazed drifted back to Gabby who was still mindlessly flipping through the leather-bound tome. Leaving Drow to his thoughts she walked to where Diego lay, taking a seat on the concrete floor beside him.

The scent of charred wood drifted from the pile of smoldering furniture in the corner as the last of the embers sputtered. She thought about what Drow had said. If Stevie had no control over her new powers when she emerged, she doubted any advice she offered would help. It made more sense that Drow and Killenn be the ones to offer guidance. She gazed at her hands, the green energy still simmered under the surface, waiting for her intention.

A cold breeze crossed her face its wisps tinged with a wet

mist. The cocoon above her hissed. Diego rose, hackles raised, teeth bared. A guttural growl escaped from his throat as he pawed nervously at the ground.

"What's happening?" She yelled, jumping up.

The others came quickly surrounding the cocoon. The swirling lava began to petrify turning from a bright, red, malleable substance to a black, encrusted rock. Steam rose from the cracks that formed on the surface as the cocoon began to fracture.

"She is returning to us," Killenn said, just as the cocoon groaned, shattering like a fragile egg.

Ash and dust drifted into the air.

Dane coughed, as she inadvertently sucked in the particles. The air surrounding them was thick with residue making it difficult to breathe or see. Her irritated eyes stung. Tears seeped from the corners, and she wiped them away with the back of her hand. As the ash floated languidly toward the floor, Stevie emerged from the dust.

"Stevie, are you OK?" She stood with her head down, eyes closed, her breathing was shallow, her skin pale. She didn't move or respond to Dane's inquiry. Dane shrugged, as she glanced at the others her expression marred by concern. Drow's calm eyes found hers and he bowed. A simple gesture but one she took to mean, *wait*.

Stevie gasped. Her head and shoulders shuddered as she took in a considerable amount of air. She blinked wildly, her eyes darting from one person to the next. Dark cabernet irises had replaced her brown ones. She rotated her neck and shoulders, shaking out the stiffness. "Intense," she whispered.

Dane exhaled when she realized that she had been subconsciously holding her breath. She grabbed her friend in a hug. "Hi," she said as tears welled in her eyes, the stress of the last hour finally releasing.

Stevie hugged her back a smirk appearing at the corners of her mouth. "Hi yourself."

Dane released her and grasped her hands, looking deeply into her eyes. "Thank goodness you're all right. How do you feel?"

Stevie smiled. "Honestly, the same but with a sense of confidence, like I'm infallible. Is that what immortality does to you?"

Dane laughed, relieved that Stevie Jacobs was back and thankfully not as transformed as Gabby. She glanced at the celestial who was standing behind the others, her face in the shadows. The magic of the ether pulsed around her as she moved out of shadows. Her black wings unfurled as she strode forward.

"Welcome back Dragon Gypsy," she said, bowing her head in greeting.

Stevie didn't reply. The tentative look on her face indicated she was waiting for Gabby to continue with a snide remark or insult. Neither came, as Gabby turned on her heel and headed back to wait by the temple door.

Drow moved to stand beside Dane, his gaze intently focused on Stevie. "Your birthright was passed?"

"Yes, I believe so."

"And you remember how it happened?"

Stevie's face darkened, remembering the suffocating fire. "He said we were in a place called the Lair."

Drow's eyebrows raised. "Who did?"

"He said his name was Dornan."

Upon hearing the name Killenn stepped forward, surprise

and astonishment visible on his face. "Dornan, you said? Was he of the royal elite guard?"

"I believe so, he wore the same uniform as you."

Killenn's face was a mask of disbelief. Drow shot him a look of disbelief. Dane could sense the surprise rise in them both.

"So, Stevie is not of royal lineage?" she asked.

Killenn shook his head, his brow deepened. "No, she is of my blood."

CHAPTER 9

"WELL, I GUESS WE WILL not have to worry about her burning up in the Dragon Flame," Gabby said, from her position by the temple door.

All eyes turned toward her, most not amused.

"That's a good thing," she said, unfazed by their irritated stares. Shrugging she leaned against the wall, her iridescent eyes sparked defiantly.

Rafe returned his attention back to Killenn. "What do you mean, 'your blood'?"

"Dornan was my father," he responded. A shocked silence resonated through the room.

"Your father?" Stevie whispered. Her dark red eyes implored him for more information.

Killenn nodded. "He served as commander of the royal elite guard for both Drow's father and eldest brother. He died when I was just a boy leaving me an orphan as my mother had already perished in childbirth."

He glanced at Drow. "The Velkia family took me in and raised me as their own. I was schooled in the art of the warrior. Trained to follow in my father's footsteps and one day lead the royal elite guard."

"Killenn is like a brother to me," Drow said, a surprising softness in his voice.

"And I owe the Velkia, my life."

Dane now understood why the bond between the prince and his servant was so strong. How they knew so much about one another. They were family and the only person each had left.

"If my father was the one to grant Stevie her birthright, it must confirm she is of my blood."

Drow put his hand on Killenn's shoulder, addressing Stevie as he did. "You have inherited the magic of a powerful line of warriors. Killenn's family legacy is eminent among our people. His bloodline has a long and storied history of serving in the royal elite guard. If you possess the skill and powers of this family, you will be an invaluable asset to the fight that is to come."

Drow hesitated as his eyes met Killenn's and a strange look passed between them. Dane noticed it immediately, sure there was something the two of them were not disclosing. "Come," Drow said. He strode toward the temple door. "It has been a long day. The new Dragon Gypsy must cleanse her soul in the fires of the Dragon Flame or the magic inherited will be useless, but that part of her journey can wait until morn."

After dinner, Drow showed them to the citadel's largest bedrooms. As Dane and Rafe walked the shadowy halls towards theirs, she hesitated.

"Drow told me our combined magic will be ineffective against the ancient dark."

"I agree, it is most likely not powerful enough."

"He said he wanted me to know how earth and fire magic intertwine in case Stevie needs help to control her magic. But I don't know how I can help her."

Rafe smiled. "He is speaking of how earth magic can be disbursed through the natural elements. It is an aspect of your power I have not yet shown you."

Dane scowled. "Don't you think I need to know?"

"Earth magic grounds and witches have the ability to use other elements to disburse their power to other magic if it needs to be stabilized. It is temporary, but it can help another supernatural whose magic is erratic." He raised his hand and brought forth an energy ball. "Warlicians disperse their energy the same way, with intent."

Dane could feel his emotions shift as he concentrated on his magic. It flickered momentarily before dissipating into a thousand small strands of green energy that floated up into the air.

"You must separate the warrior from the witch otherwise, the intent may be grievously misinterpreted," he said. "As a warrior your intent is aggressive, it is battle magic, but as a witch, your intent must be focused solely on your intent to aid." He walked over to the candle that sat on the hall table. From his pocket, he pulled a small vial of liquid. He poured a small drop on the flame and it ignited into a chaotic burst of sparks and fire. "Calm the flame," he said taking a step back.

She brought forth her Warlician magic, concentrating on the fiery flame. She willed her energy ball to infuse the flame, calming its sizzling fury. Her energy ball flickered as it spun, jumping from her hand and splitting in two. Both halves hit the candle at the same time sending wax flying in every direction as the energy destroyed the candle and extinguished the flame.

"Apparently, I need some work controlling that aspect of my magic," she said sheepishly.

Rafe wiped candle wax from his clothes, nodding. "Come, we will try again in the morning." He took her hand and led her into their bedroom.

Although none of the rooms had been used since the portals closed, underneath the dust and cobwebs the furnishings still displayed a sense of regal beauty. As Rafe began to snuff the candles on the walls, Dane stood at the center admiring the room. High, vaulted ceilings sloped gracefully upward. Iron beams, anchored into the top of the walls, crisscrossed the room's girth creating a spoke pattern. Hung from the center was a large square metal chandelier. Candles, unlit for centuries, were at each corner. Long silk draperies framed two glass and steel doors leading to the balcony beyond. The walls were covered with silk tapestries and gilt-framed maps, but it was the four-poster bed that drew her attention. The bed frame was made of solid iron and four bedposts, as thick as tree trunks, stretched at least ten feet toward the ceiling. Connecting each of the four posts were red gauzy strips that blew gracefully in the breeze when Rafe opened the balcony doors.

"The night air is perfect on Kaizi," he said, smiling as he placed a candle on the bedside table. The fragrant scent of poppies drifted through the door, the scent wrapping around them seductively.

"The poppies smell amazing," she said, as her body began to react to Rafe's closeness.

"It's the pheromones. Poppies are also an aphrodisiac." He

winked and walked to where she stood, encircling her waist with his arms and pulling her close.

"Is that why you opened the balcony door?" She murmured.

He smiled mischievously, gently brushing his lips against hers, teasing her with his touch before he pulled away. Playfulness flashed in his eyes as he sauntered to the far side of the room. Dane bit her bottom lip, her eyebrow raised in protest as her eyes followed his movement. She watched as he undressed. Her body ached as candlelight cast dancing shadows across his tattooed skin. His muscles flexed as he peeled the cloth from his torso. She licked her lips. The intensity of their binding erupted inside her as his desire mixed with her own. Tossing his shirt to the floor, he undid his jeans. The waistband gaped open as he walked back to where she stood, a small tuft of hair visible above the denim. He lifted her hand and placed it on his bare chest directly over his heart.

He lowered his forehead to hers. "For you," he whispered.

She could feel his heartbeat, a rhythmic pulse vibrating from his chest. Magic swirled around them, invisible energy creating an unbreakable bond. The essence of their ancient binding—a syncing of minds, hearts, and souls.

He kissed her forehead as he swooped her up in his arms and carried her to the side of the bed. His lips tantalized her skin as he removed her clothes. His fingertips traced a deliberate path down her stomach coaxing a sensual heat to erupt inside her. Her tongue explored his mouth hungrily as she encircled her hands around his back. Her nails dug into the skin on either side of his spine, and she threw her head back moaning as he brought her to a quick release.

Collapsing into him, Rafe picked her up and placed her

gently in the middle of the large bed, blowing the candle out simultaneously. With the flame extinguished, the room was blanketed in a soft darkness, hued by the light of the red burning moon illuminating Kaizi's night sky. Somewhere in the distance, she could hear the wind whisper as it carried the sound of crackling embers on its breath and the sweet intoxicating scent of poppies. He hovered over her as he moved in between her legs. His eyes locked on hers as he entered her, thrusting deeper. His sexual energy flowed through her as their innate connection intensified their passion and desire, her need for him, insatiable.

They moved in unison, each acutely aware of the cravings of the other. Lost in the heat and energy that crackled around them they succumbed to their hunger. At this moment there was no one else in the world, just the two of them, and the palpitating longing that existed between them.

"Rafe," she whispered, as she felt the familiar wave.

The fragrant scent of poppies floating through the room heightened the crescendo and brought them both crashing breathlessly to the satin sheets in a sweaty, exhausted pile. They lay without speaking, limbs tangled, enjoying the aftershocks vibrating between them. Their hearts once again beating in unison.

As she lay naked in Rafe's arms, Dane felt herself drift. Her eyes closed as the quiver from their lovemaking waned. She felt him move beside her and her eyes fluttered open, smiling as she focused on the ruggedly handsome face looking down at her. His green eyes shone with lust and love.

"Sleep," he whispered, gently kissing her eyelids.

It had been an exhausting day and as she snuggled up to his warm body, she gave in to her fatigue.

CHAPTER 10

AS THEY EMERGED FROM THE royal citadel the next morning, the red sky had already begun to crackle, and sheet lightning flashed in its midst. The scent of burnt ash no longer filled the air, replaced by the sweet, spicy scent of incense. The hot, hollow breeze still blew, chasing its own wisps through the streets and alleys, but a cool mist tinged its edges. Like Dywen had done before it Kaizi awakened, its energy gaining strength as the Druidstone pushed ancient magic through the realm's core. It shook off billions of centuries of sleep as magical fibers ignited and released an essence that long lay dormant.

"The armory is in an open quarry about a mile from the citadel," Killenn said, as they began their trek through the steel city.

"Is this where the Dragon Flame is?" asked Stevie.

Killenn shrugged. "It is where we need to go first."

The armory was built into the quarry's rock wall. A steel vault buried deep into the side of a steep plateau. Its entirety was covered in thick quartz and shale. A steel-plated door, locked tight by massive iron bolts and locks, was the only accessible entrance. Killenn produced a large key from inside his breastplate and pushed it into the lock. A grating sound echoed through the quarry as the unyielding key penetrated the unused lock. It reverberated loudly, amplified by the high rock walls and the absence of anything that could muffle sound.

Stevie winced, her hands flying to her temples. Killenn leaned in and whispered something in her ear. She nodded, closed her eyes, and took a ragged breath. Their interactions were different since Stevie emerged from the cocoon, the blood of his ancestors now a part of her. Dane wondered if it was a magical connection or just Killenn being overprotective of his family bloodline. There were definitely secrets between him and Drow, and she wondered if Stevie would be drawn into their private world.

They entered the armory. A fire trough sputtered to life above their heads illuminating the inside. The steel walls were lined with metal grates from which hung a multitude of swords, knives, crossbows, and whips. Even though all that remained in the armory were vestiges from the Great War, its contents were still vast.

Killenn turned to Stevie.

"Do you have a preference?" His hand gestured toward the weapons.

Frowning, her gaze searched the walls. Shaking her head, she said, "I have never used any of these before, make-up brushes are more my thing."

His face clouded at her response, even Drow looked at her and scowled. Dane snickered and glanced at Gabby. The corner of the celestial's mouth turned up in a smirk as she too acknowledged their lack of understanding with respect to Stevie's sarcasm.

Sensing Killenn's disapproval, she shrugged. "What do you suggest?"

He walked over to the second wall grate where a group of katana swords hung; their curved blades encased in thin red sheaths of leather. Their guards and long grips were a masterful display of metalworking and each was decorated with an ornamental cord. Killenn selected one, weighing it before handing the sword to Stevie.

"This should do."

Stevie took the katana, holding it tentatively. Dane knew she had never held a sword before and the awkwardness showed in her grip.

"Relax," Killenn said, moving in behind her and adjusting her grip on the weapon. He pulled the sheath off the blade and helped her raise the sword, moving her hands back and forth in sweeping motions until he felt the blade's momentum become part of her own. The steel glinted as it swung, its razor-sharp edge catching the firelight that flickered overhead. As Stevie moved the sword, Dane could see the detail on the katana's handle. It was sculpted like the wing of a dragon. The indents for the fingers mimicked the skin that stretched between wing bones. Like much of the architecture and décor of the steel city, delicate metal filigree covered the surface of the handle and grip.

"I've never held a sword before let alone used one in battle," Stevie stated.

Killenn grinned. "It will not matter."

Stevie gave him a confused look.

"Dragon Gypsy weaponry are all forged here. Like the steel city, the metal used in its construction comes from the quarry's rocks. The entire surface of Kaizi is embedded with veins of dragon steel, an impenetrable substance that is infused with our world's magic. Once you have been cleansed, the skill set of the royal elite guard, our warring class, will be instinctive. You will become one with the sword and know how to wield it."

"Come," Drow said, his voice fettered. "We must make haste."

He moved beyond the armory through another door and into a small enclosed space. There was nothing in the room except an open shaft in the floor and a metal ladder that descended into its inky depths. There was no light in the shaft and Dane watched as Drow was quickly swallowed by a darkness so black even shadows did not exist. She hesitated before following him, her instincts questioning the intelligence of descending into unknown depths. As she carefully followed the ladder down, she could feel Rafe's calming energy careen toward her through the darkness. She relaxed, concentrating on the careful placement of her feet as she searched for the next rung with her toe. Her eyes were useless in the pitch dark and only her other senses kept her from plunging into the abyss.

She could hear boot leather on metal somewhere in the dark above her as another person descended into the shaft. The occasional swearing and annoyed flap of wings identified that person as Gabby. Smirking, she continued down the ladder until she detected a faint glimmer in the distance, a pinprick of light somewhere far below. Focusing on the minuscule amber glow she increased her speed moving down the ladder at a steady, confident pace. The light expanded with each step and the crushing pitch-black became shadows.

Eventually, the ladder ended, and she found herself in a

small crevice. Rock walls surrounded her on three sides their rough surfaces shimmered with dampness. The amber light flickered from somewhere down the cavernous passage to her left. Drow was nowhere in sight and although she could still hear Gabby's boots echoing above her, she didn't wait. She entered the passage and followed the beckoning glow.

She emerged into an immense cavern far below the surface. No natural light penetrated its interior. Dark rock walls, their surfaces pocked with holes and marred with thick black soot, surrounded her. Huge stalactites hung from the ceiling dripping tiny drops of lava from their tips into the molten pond below. At its center, on a small stone platform rising prominently from the bubbling lava, was the Dragon Flame. Its luminescent glow cast orange and red shadows across the walls and lit the entire cavern with a faint flickering glow.

"What is this place?" She whispered, instinctively lowering her voice as it echoed through the hollowness.

"A place where dragons used to lay."

"Dragons?"

Drow nodded, motioning to the impressive flame at the cavern's center.

"In the time before my people, many dragons were born of that fire and just as many died by its flame. This cavern was sacred to the dragons, a place where they attained life and succumbed to death. Like the dragons before us, the people of Kaizi were born from that flame. Their magic and power infused by the bloodline to which they belonged. Entering the flame is a cleansing of sorts. It gives our lifeblood meaning and ensures one's sacred position within the Dominion of the Dragons. This cavern is infused with the ghosts of our ancestors both dragon and gypsy."

Before Dane could inquire more, Gabby and the others filed into the cavern, each having a different reaction to the magnitude of the sacred place.

"You keep your most sacred object in a hole beneath the ground?" Gabby complained, brushing soot and dirt from her leather coat.

"I think it's beautiful," said Stevie, eyes wide in awe. Killenn stood silently behind her. He watched her response to the sanctity of the cavern carefully.

Rafe came to stand on the other side of Dane, his hand brushing hers as he did. Energy spit fervently between them causing her to smile. Looking past her to Drow he said, "I have heard of this place, the dragon tombs, but the stories do not do it justice."

Drow met his gaze, his deep red eyes glistened. "Stories are nothing compared to feeling the echoes of the memories that reside here, for only then can one truly appreciate its majesty." Turning, he walked to where Stevie stood. "You must walk through the Dragon Flame, it will cleanse you of your past life, purify your energy, and ignite the blood of the dragons. You are now one of us and the process must be complete."

She nodded, looking toward the flame. It pulsed erratically at the center of the lava pond as if it sensed her presence. "How do I get to it?"

"Trust that it will recognize the blood of the dragon."

She glanced at Killenn, who nodded encouragement.

The flowing liquid swayed back and forth as she walked toward the pond. Heat rose from the surface and produced a sizzling steam that drifted upward into the darkness of the cavern ceiling. The ground began to quake the closer she got to the edge. A rumble erupted from the earth and reverberated off the cavern walls. Dust and debris fell from the surfaces of the stalactites and small fissures appeared in the walls. Stevie halted her progress, holding her arms out to steady herself from toppling into the lava pond as the next quake shook the ground. Dane moved forward fearful that Stevie would fall into the molten lava but Rafe stopped her, his strong arm blocking her path. "Let her go."

The rumbling intensified. The shaking disturbed the intentional flow of the lava, sending it splashing chaotically in all directions. Bubbles erupted on the surface bursting into flaming pyres that flared before burning out. The tremors subsided as quickly as they started, leaving an eerie silence in its wake. The lava pond stilled its glass-like surface reflecting the light of the Dragon Flame. Slowly, and with much less fanfare, a metal walkway emerged from the depths of the pond connecting the edge where Stevie stood with the platform at its center. Tentatively, she touched the first part of the platform with the toe of her boot, ensuring its stability before putting further weight on it. With caution, she started across the walkway, her eyes downcast, ensuring each foot was placed securely on the metal beneath her. The lava pond remained calm as she walked across to the platform on the other side.

Drow glanced at Killenn and without a word exchanging between them, instructions were given and received. Dane, now aware of their past, could see the strong bond the two shared and how easy it was for them to understand the other. Their bond transcended their status because it was firmly grounded in mutual respect and trust.

Killenn followed Stevie across the walkway. Drow placed himself at the end so that no others could cross. Diego followed laying at Drow's feet, placing his massive head on his paws to wait. Dane, still restrained by Rafe, shot Gabby a concerned look and in return received a stare of indifference. "Let it happen, Dane," Rafe said quietly in her ear. His energy floated around her, cocooning her in a warm embrace. She relaxed into him as his arm encircled her, pulling her close. "Stevie will be fine. This is her destiny."

Nodding Dane watched, as Stevie and Killenn spoke in hushed tones, their heads close. After a few minutes Stevie turned, and without hesitation walked into the pyre of the Dragon Flame.

CHAPTER 11

DANE WAS DEEP IN THOUGHT as they walked back to the citadel. The air was warm, the stifling heat fading as a stiff breeze blew over the lands. Stevie had emerged quickly from the Dragon flame; no worse for wear and apparently no different from when she went in. Whatever magical cleansing had taken place, it clearly did not manifest externally.

She glanced at Stevie who walked comfortably beside Killenn. An unspoken connection had drawn them closer. It was odd to see her friend so at ease with a virtual stranger. Even Diego seemed comfortable with him as he bounded ahead of the group confident that his master was fine. Her concern was obviously unwarranted and chided herself for thinking it. Hadn't she been drawn to Rafe the same way? Stevie's relationship with Killenn was different though. It was natural, respectful, and caring yet it didn't seem to reach the intensity of two people who were romantically drawn to one another.

"It's not what you think Dane," Rafe whispered, squeezing her hand.

"And what is it you think, I think?"

"That Killenn and Stevie are destined, like us."

Dane rolled her eyes and scowled. "Stop analyzing me."

"Dragon Gypsies do not bond like witches. They are ruled by the element fire which is volatile and passionate, not grounded like earth. They do not settle down and fall in love. Dragon Gypsies are too free-spirited for that." He winked and quickened his pace, catching up with Drow, leaving Dane to consider just how much Stevie's mortal life mimicked her destined one.

They made their way through the barren streets of the steel city to the gates of the royal citadel. The portal, that would transport them to Gabby's world, was in a courtyard just to the side of the back entrance. Drow led them through a small iron gate, its steel bars covered in a thicket of thorny vines. Their black stalks and crimson burnished leaves crawled haphazardly over the stone walls on either side of the path. A faint scent of charred wood drifted from the thicket. Emerging into the courtyard, Dane spied a large water fountain. It was like the one in Dywen's village square but was crafted from metal instead of stone.

She pulled Drow to the side as the other's ventured closer to the fountain.

"I need you to tell me what is going on with Stevie."

His gaze intensified, his somber face giving nothing away. "I am not sure what you are asking."

"You and Killenn. The looks that keep passing between you. There is something about Stevie you are not telling us."

Drow's gaze softened. "It's nothing really, not yet anyway."

"I need to know everything that you and Killenn suspect about her transformation. I can't help her if you keep secrets."

Drow turned slightly to look over his shoulder. Again, his gaze fell on Killenn who responded with a nod. Turning back to her, he leaned closer, his voice quiet. "As you know the Dragon Gypsies of Kaizi are born from the ancient bloodlines of the four origin dragons: fire, smoke, ember, and ash, but there is much more to our ancestry. Our legend says that the origin dragons each held a specific power. Those powers, when passed to their human descendants, would manifest in a way specific to the ancient bloodlines. My ancestors, descendants of the fire dragon, are all pale-skinned and ashen hair. Our active power is the power over flame. We can manipulate it to our will even bring it from within as you saw. Killenn's bloodline, that of the smoke dragon, yields the power to raise and control the dead. More specifically, call upon the spirits of the four origin dragons."

"Are you saying that Stevie can raise a ghost dragon?"

"That is currently unknown. The power of the smoke dragon often skips a generation or two. Dornan, Killenn's father, possessed the ability but alas Killenn does not. Killenn is the last of the bloodline from our time. If the ancient gift is to be passed on, it is possible that your friend may be the next to wield it."

Dane glanced at Stevie, her demeanor still so relaxed and comfortable.

"And how will we know if she possesses this power?"

"It will manifest when it is ready. Until then, we must be patient."

They joined the others at the base of the fountain. A red, hazy mist flowed lazily inside its basins, cascading over the sides of the metal the way water would.

"Kaizi's magic is strong enough to activate the portal," Killenn said, gazing around the perimeter of the courtyard at the variations in the environment.

Dane had been in deep thought as they returned from the dragon tombs so hadn't really noticed the changes surrounding her. Glancing around she noticed the magic awakening as everything displayed, to some degree, the effects of the fire element. The metal of the royal citadel gleamed as if recently polished to a high sheen; the dull red of the sky seemed brighter as it flickered with golden sparks; even the black crust of the cooled lava rock gleamed.

"I'm staying here," Stevie announced abruptly.

"What do you mean?" Dane snapped.

Stevie ignored her friend's tone. "I'm going to train with Killenn and Drow. I need to understand my powers and connect to the knowledge of my ancestors, and Kaizi is the best place to do that. I will meet you in Brighton Hill in a few days."

The warrior and the prince remained silent as Dane glared at them.

"She's right Dane," Gabby said. "There is nothing for her in my realm, in fact, our presence there will be uneventful. Activating the Druidstone is a simple task as it is not connected to a descendant."

"I agree," said Rafe. "Stevie is more valuable if she learns how to fight and control the powers she now possesses. I am sure that Killenn and Drow will see to her welfare."

Dane did not like the idea of leaving Stevie alone in a strange realm in another dimension, but it seemed her choices were limited. Sensing her apprehension Stevie walked over and took her hands in her own.

"I love you like a sister, Dane, but I'm not asking your permission. I don't need it. You must trust me. This is for the best."

There was a confidence in Stevie's eyes. A profoundness that hadn't been there prior to her transformation. She accepted her destiny and was more comfortable with her immortality than Dane had been initially.

She sighed. "Just a few days."

Stevie nodded. "I will meet you back home soon." Hugging her friend tight, she whispered, "I'll be fine."

"I know."

The red mist in the fountain swirled ferociously as the portal was called. Sparks spit erratically as the opening to the ether emerged from the mist, crackling with intensity as it grew.

Gabby nodded toward her. "It is time."

As Dane took a step toward the fountain, she turned to Stevie. "Be safe."

"I've got this."

Smiling, Dane nodded. "Yes, you do."

Rafe put his hand on her lower back as they followed Gabby through the portal. She glanced over her shoulder one last time as the portal closed in around them and for a brief second, she thought she saw a gray, smoky mist hover over Stevie.

CHAPTER 12

THE LEYLANDS WERE AN EXTENSIVE stretch of flat rock and grass. Rafe stood atop a large pile of boulders, one of the many that dotted the countryside. His eyes scanned the horizon.

"I do not see Mt. Elderon," he said. "Are you sure we are going in the right direction?"

"I think I know my world warrior."

"Why the hell would the portal open up in the middle of nowhere?"

Gabby's eyes narrowed, contemplating the question. "That portal was inactive even before the Great War. I am unsure as to why the Kaizi portal even recognized it. We should have emerged inside the Hall of Elders."

"So how far are we from the Druidstone?"

"Half a day, maybe more."

Rafe shook his head and climbed down from the rock pile. "We better move before we lose what little light we have."

Gabby's eyes turned skyward, nodding in agreement.

Etheriem's firmament was a dark purple, its seething

depth periodically interrupted by the static that crackled and flashed above them. The unusual sky created an eerie ambiance and Dane felt a shiver of anticipation as she followed Gabby and Rafe toward their destination somewhere in the distance.

The trek through Etheriem's expanse was uneventful, and the trio moved efficiently and without delay. A stark contrast to the dark purple sky, the white mountain glistened on the horizon as it finally came into view. Its bulk emphasized by the static that bolted overhead. Framed by the enormous purple and silver moon that peeked from behind it, Mt. Elderon was an awe-inspiring sight. Their pace quickened as a slow rumble ripped through the sky. Static electricity arcing erratically over the mountain as the firmament exploded in anger.

"What was that?" Dane asked.

Gabby shook her head, gesturing to the sky. "The ether is unstable. It is reacting to the sudden flow of ancient magic coming from Dywen and Kaizi. Without the magic of the ether being at full power, it does not have the strength to provide balance to the other elements, so it tries to reject it, unsuccessfully."

Another rumble erupted overhead, static flashing in its wake. "It will settle once the Druidstone has been activated."

The scope of Mt. Elderon was impressive. The mountain reached high into the cloud bank that hovered over its mass. Its width stretched for miles in each direction and the wood and stone bridge they stood before was equally daunting. Dane gasped as she looked down into the chasm that encircled the mountain. The ether that filled its depths was equally unstable and the same static flashed and crackled erratically in its depths.

The bridge to the other side boasted five stone arches,

race symbols carved into each of their surfaces. Three of the symbols were devoid of the light that normally burned behind them but Dywen's and Kaizi's flickered with elemental magic.

"Soon all the races will again be represented," Rafe whispered.

Dane smiled, her fingers caressing the stone arch of Dywen as they walked under its frame. The stone emanated warmth from its surface and it tickled her fingertips. The symbol glowed brighter as it seemed to recognize the blood of the ancients that ran through her veins. As she passed a shiver crept over her skin and her mind darkened as the forgotten past whispered.

"Are you well?" Rafe asked, noticing the frown on her face.

"Yes, fine," she said as the feeling dissipated. "It's nothing."

"Hurry," Gabby said pointing to the sky. "We must stabilize the ether."

The sky had begun to churn as dark purple clouds raced past them. The static was volatile, sending sparks outward as it cracked through the atmosphere. They ran across the remainder of the bridge slipping through the entrance doors to the Hall of Elders just before another rumble exploded overhead, the sound thankfully muffled by the thick stone of the mountain.

The Druidstone was in a chamber near the council room. It was a simple room, small and clean with minimal décor. Unlike the simple Druidstones of Kaizi and Dywen, this one was remarkable in its size. It sat at the center of the room on a white, solid rock pedestal. It was a clear crystal sculpture of Mt. Elderon. Its peaks reached almost to the ceiling. There were numerous sigils etched into the surface, all throbbing with an iridescent light.

Gabby moved forward placing her hand at its center. Her voice, barely a whisper, drifted through the small room as she began to recite an incantation. As she spoke the glow of the sigils intensified, throbbing as her voice elevated. Light sprang from the sigils, beams of sparkling lilac crisscrossing the small room as the magic escaped from the Druidstone. The entire crystal blazed as the powerful magic pulsed outward. She raised her wings, the black tips infused with iridescent light. The lilac-hued magic swirled, wrapping itself around her as a melodic hum swelled inside the room. The light spun around her, the intensity increasing until only a faint blur of her outline was noticeable through its sparkling essence.

Rafe pulled Dane back through the door aware of the power that was now whirling around Gabby.

The vortex lasted a few minutes; then altered its direction. Swirling back into the Druidstone where it pulsed momentarily before exploding out the top in a violent eruption. At an astonishing speed, the light magic funneled straight through a small hole in the ceiling and out into the atmosphere.

Gabby shook her wings as the last of the lilac light disappeared, the Druidstone quiet once again.

"It will not be long now. Come."

They followed her to the council room. The emptiness overwhelmed them as they entered. A haunting ache pulsed through the quiet. A large table sat vacant at the front surrounded by high backed chairs its surface covered with a thick layer of dust. Gabby walked to the windows, released the bolts, and threw open the shutters, giving the room access to the outside world.

Dane moved to one of the open windows, curious as to the

changes that Etheriem would experience now the Druidstone had released the ancient magic. Surprisingly, it looked the same, no sign of the sparkling lilac light emitted from the Druidstone visible. The sky was still an angry deep purple, split by the static electricity flashing overhead. Another rumble erupted, and static bolted in multiple directions. As the energy dispelled, Dane felt a calm fall over the land. There was something forming behind the chaotic sky.

"It's happening," Gabby noted, pointing to the east.

Dane's eyes followed the direction of her finger. The firmament in the distance morphed as glistening lilac flowed from the mountain and spread over the entire realm. In its wake, it left a layer of iridescent magic. The energy covered all the surfaces momentarily in a sparkling sheen until it too faded leaving Etheriem bright and breathtakingly beautiful. Vibrancy emerged from every inch of the realm, the colors deep, their contrast significant. The white mountain glistened under the velvety lilac sky. A shimmer that pulsed just under its surface, no longer chaotic, the static gone. The landscape stretched out for miles intensifying into a brilliant carpet of lush green.

The ancient power of the ether seeped over the lands stabilizing the magic that flowed from the other realms and creating a unity of balance, beauty, and strength. Standing at the window, Dane could feel the realm expel its uncontrolled tension. The chaotic power ripping through the sky earlier settled into a peaceful tranquility. Unlike on Kaizi, she could feel the magic of Dywen here. It intertwined with the other magic, intensifying her senses and engaging the ancestral magic that flowed through her blood. She felt invincible.

"It's an intoxicating experience," Rafe said, moving in behind her. "But unfortunately, one that is not sustainable.

Inhabitants from other realms cannot stay on Etheriem for long. Proximity to the purest of magic will eventually overwhelm our own powers, and we will be driven mad."

Dane frowned as she looked at Rafe and then to Gabby.

"The warrior is correct. Etheriem can be a dangerous place for those who are not created directly from the ether. We must make haste back to your world. The power of the ether is not pliable and cannot be absorbed by those of a race different from celestials. It is too much for your kind."

Rafe's eyebrows raised. "Another reason celestials deem themselves to be far superior to the other races of the Five Realms."

"It is merely fact. My kind is connected to the ether in a way the other races are not. Take it as you will but the power of the ether is only for those who are born from it and exist within it." Expanding her wings for emphasis and giving Rafe a stare that rendered him quiet, she moved around them.

A golden door appeared at the back of the room. Invisible to the naked eye until the blood of a celestial released the magic concealing it. Turning the large handle, Gabby pulled the heavy door open to reveal a steady swirling iridescent light. Instinctively, Dane threw up her hand to block its brilliance, squinting as she came closer.

"The portal," Gabby stated moving back and gesturing for Rafe and Dane to pass through. "I will follow momentarily."

Watching until the sparkling light swallowed them, she turned and scanned the council room. Without hesitation, she hurried to a barred door to the left. Her skin pulsed brightly with her realm's magic. The energy vibrant and alive churned around her. She grasped the bars easily bending the metal and separating them from the wall.

Her strength was back.

Prying open the narrow door she entered the shadowy hallway. Moving with a graceful ease, Gabby hurried to the far end emerging into a large space. The sconces on the wall ignited at her presence. A hissing purple flame cast a pale light over the room's contents. Smiling mischievously, she turned in a circle appreciating the multitude of swords and daggers that lay before her. She selected her weapons carefully before walking over to a glass case near the center of the room. Inside the case was the ancient symbol of her people. The lid lifted without resistance, and she took the pendant from where it lay. Beads clattered together as she held it in her hand. The crucifix dangling from a separate string of crystals swayed methodically. She touched the metal disc above them, calming the beads before hanging it around her neck and tucking the crucifix beneath her jacket.

With a wave of her hand, she extinguished the flaming sconces and exited the way she entered. Closing the door, she bent the barred bolts back in place. She paused and inhaled deeply, her wings trembling behind her. She had one more thing to do now that Etheriem's magic was once again at its peak. Hurrying through the council room and a network of vacant halls, she emerged from the Hall of Elders into a large courtyard. A glistening pond sparkled at its center. White weeping trees, their boughs drooping, sluggishly brushed the grass as the warm breeze blew them in multiple directions. The scent of jasmine drifted through the air.

Gabby hastened her way to the far side where a beacon stood, waiting. Her hand shook as she placed it on a panel at its base. Closing her eyes, she recited an incantation until the beacon glowed with the shimmering lilac essence of the ether. The large sigil protruding from the beacon sparked. Iridescent light throbbed from its edges. She pushed it inward until it clicked. A whirling sound emanated from the beacon as it powered up. After a few moments, a beep sounded followed by a faint tick. It repeated incessantly, a strange monotone melody that pulsed through the ether.

Turning away from the beacon she returned to the Hall of Elders. As she stepped into the portal back to the new world, she felt the familiar awakening. An ethereal power shuddered through the ether surrounding Etheriem. A distinct presence that she recognized immediately.

The Seraphs had heard the call.

CHAPTER 13

AS GABBY STEPPED THROUGH THE portal, the scene greeting her was not what she expected. Dane paced back and forth, her anger upsetting the tranquil aura that normally encircled her.

"Calm down, Dane," Rafe said, as Sebastian tried to still her movement.

"I'm going to kill her!"

Rafe was leaning against the tree, his face a mask of emotions.

"What is going on?" Gabby inquired.

Sebastian turned at the sound of her voice, his brow furrowed. "The dark witch has taken Dane's familiar."

Gabby's head tilted to one side at this news. "Tyson?"

Sebastian nodded.

"A witch stealing another's familiar. That is certainly crossing a line. What is her purpose?"

"I believe she is trying to get Dane's attention."

Gabby motioned to Dane's erratic pacing. "By the look of things, I think she has succeeded. But what does she want?"

"That is another mystery. If Dane would calm for a few minutes, I can explain what has transpired since your exit to the other worlds."

He paused briefly scrutinizing the area. "Where is the Dragon Gypsy, Stevie?"

"She is staying on Kaizi, to train with the royal and his elite guard commander," Rafe said.

Sebastian turned to look at him. A curious expression crossed his features as he contemplated the meaning behind Rafe's words. "It seems that you too have a story to tell."

Nodding Rafe glanced at Dane. Her ire crackled in the energy encapsulating her. The ancient magic throbbed under her skin as the green energy threatened to explode to the surface. Rafe leaned back against the tree and continued to channel peaceful energy toward her, keeping her magic at bay. Their binding made it difficult to separate emotional responses, and he was exhausted. "You first," he said.

Sebastian walked over to Dane, placing himself directly in her path. She stopped abruptly and eyed him with a stern look.

"Will you listen now?"

She shrugged, the meaning behind her silent attitude not lost on him.

"Since you left yesterday, the dark witch has been active. At first, she just funneled the power from the energy around the mill, but eventually, I sensed a shift in the magic she was invoking. It was much darker, more sinister. There existed a presence in the magic. It was fleeting. I sensed it only for a moment before it was gone, but it evoked an immediate change in her. The dark witch became erratic, her magic chaotic like she no longer had control. I have never experienced a shift in magic like this before."

"Do you think she has somehow tapped into the dark sphere?" Rafe inquired.

Sebastian lifted a hand. "The entire mill is doused with evil. An unstable darkness is consuming the energy. The imprints are understandably confused and frightened. I fear the dark witch may have opened a door to a power we will not be able to contain."

"That's impossible," replied Gabby. "The dark sphere is only attainable by those that possess the power to consume evil. There was only one from our time with that power."

"Adaridge."

"Yes, but he ascended during the Great War."

"Ascended?" Dane asked. She could feel Rafe's energy flux at the question.

"Adaridge was a Druid, the last of his kind. Druids maintain multiple forms of existence. Their beliefs, magic, and powers are deeply intertwined with nature and the All Soul; the sphere of existence to which they are tethered. It allows them to manifest physically in a specific realm. When they pass through the physical world, they ascend into the All Soul through a place they call, the Druid sanctuary. The All Soul is the source of Druid magic and when the physical life they are living ends it is where they ascend to await their rebirth.

"Could Lilith be a descendant?" She asked.

Gabby shook her head. "Unlikely, the Druid bloodlines ended long before the Great War. Even if a descendant existed, a Druid as powerful as Adaridge would never be able to hide his powers from a mortal world. Those who possess magic in your world would have insight. A Druid would be known to your kind."

"And this dark sphere?"

Gabby looked at Rafe. "Have you not taught her how to bring forth the Warlician knowledge?"

"We have been busy with other matters."

"Knowledge is power warrior. She must attain this part of her legacy before it is too late."

"How?" Dane said flatly.

Sebastian held up his hand, silencing both Rafe and Gabby.

Turning to Dane he said. "Use your mind, feel the magic that flows inside of you. Listen to the whispers of your ancestors and will their knowledge to your consciousness." He took her hands. "Close your eyes and concentrate. Let the magic go."

Dane did as he directed, clearing her mind and focusing on the familiar throb of the magic in her veins. Her mind swirled as a new magic mixed with old. She released the tension. Letting go of the control she so desperately clung to when it came to her magic, she submitted to the power existing in another time and place. As her mind emptied, she felt a twinge ripple through her energy. The ancient magic pulsed within her. Concentrating on its essence she allowed it to consume her own magic and as she did the whispers of a thousand witches erupted. The knowledge of an entire race of magical beings flowed into her. The onslaught was abrupt, leaving her gasping for air as she was overwhelmed with names, places, ideas, emotions, and information.

Sebastian smiled, giving her a moment to compose herself. "What is the name of your family coven Callathian?"

Dane felt the remnants of the ancient link dissipate leaving her mind sharp. "Shindoriah Covina. The Eternal Coven."

"And what is the dark sphere?"

"It's a place outside time and space that exists only in an

infinite realm. A place where no light penetrates the darkness and no good exists to challenge the evil. It is a place where only emptiness dwells and where malevolent energy manifests, tainting the darkness. The dark sphere cannot be penetrated by magic. Only those who freely consume its energy and give themselves willingly to its infinite power can access its dominion." Dane scowled, surprised at her recall.

"Good. I believe you know who Adaridge is as well."

Dane nodded. "The last Druid of Thanissia."

"Correct." He turned to Rafe. "We must ensure the witch has not tapped into the dark sphere or the ancient dark will not be the only entity who inflicts their wrath on the mortal world."

"I will go," Dane said stubbornly.

All eyes turned toward her. She could feel the apprehension rise in Rafe.

"She has Tyson. I *am* going."

Rafe glanced at Sebastian who nodded in response. "Go then."

"We will meet my house. The key is under the pot on the back porch. Please keep out of sight." Dane said as she ran out of the clearing, Rafe following close behind.

Sebastian waited for them to disappear before turning to Gabby. "Did you set the beacon?"

She nodded.

"Will they come?"

"I am unsure. Although they fought in the Great War, I am afraid the prophecy will keep them from interfering in the Second Coming. I believe they will instead let the destinies of the Arcanists unfold. If they are truly needed, if we are losing the battle, they may intercede." Her iridescent eyes looked deep into Sebastian's bright green ones. "I suspect we are on our own. I do not think we should count on them."

"Then we shall not. The powers of the Arcanists must be enough."

"If they are not, then this world will fall to the same defeat as ours, only this time neither the Seraphs nor the Guardian can save us."

CHAPTER 14

IF SHE HURTS TYSON IN *any way I will kill her,* she thought, pushing the pedal further toward the floorboard. The Wrangler lurched forward in response. She could feel Rafe beside her and knew he was reading her thoughts. She didn't care, getting Tyson back unharmed was her only focus.

About a quarter mile from the mill, she pulled over.

"This is close enough."

"I think I should go with you, Dane."

Her anger elevated as her patience waned. "She said to come ALONE! I agreed to let you come because I knew how worried you were. Please, Rafe, get out and wait here."

He ran his fingers through his long dark hair, his eyes locked on to hers. "I'll be here if you need me," he said, opening the door and climbing out.

She nodded and put the Wrangler into gear. Gravel spewed as she drove off.

An abnormally heavy air encircled the mill, saturated with a stifling chill. She shivered as she emerged from the warmth of her vehicle. Goosebumps appeared on her skin as the night wrapped its icy fingers around her. The starless sky pressed down; a sheath of black ink hovering over the mill's bulk, waiting. An unbalance atmosphere greeted her.

Dane could feel a presence in the chill, a dark evil lurking just beyond its fringes. She walked quickly to the mill's side door. The hinges creaked as she pulled. As the door gave way, a putrid smell escaped the mill's confines and assaulted her nostrils. She held her breath against the pungent fragrance as she entered the mill.

A strange hum drifted through the dark, the sound out of place in the abandoned building. Turning on the flashlight she swept the beam back and forth, gasping as she saw what hid in the darkness. Strange slimy pods covered the entire bottom floor of the old mill. Cocoons pulsing eerily with a yellowy-brown light. They lay scattered on the empty floor situated between unused grinders and millstones.

There must be hundreds! She thought, as her eyes scanned the building.

Her sudden shock alerted Rafe, whom she could feel moving closer to the mill.

What is it? His voice in her head was tinged with concern.

I'm fine, she thought, removing her cell phone from her coat pocket. Waking it from sleep mode she snapped a few pictures of the pods. Careful not to touch any she tiptoed through the maze, heading for the stairs leading to the second floor. The humming increased as she navigated through the pods. The sickly glow pulsated as if they were acknowledging her presence.

This can't be good. Her heart beat faster, and she felt the familiar itch in her palms as her ancient magic took notice.

Immediately Rafe was in her head. *Dane, what is going on?* Before she could answer, she heard Sebastian's calm voice asking the same.

She found it unsettling and rather annoying to have others linked to her thoughts. Specifically, two overprotective ancient warriors. She ignored them both as she made her way through the pods. She could feel their presence in her mind questioning, probing.

You two are driving me nuts! Get out of my head! I'll let you know when I need either of you. I'm trying to concentrate, and you are making it very difficult. I am heading upstairs now to deal with that witch and get my dog back!

Assuming her annoyance and anger translated telepathically, she was confident they got the message when neither responded.

Halfway up the creaky, rotting stairs, she heard him. His low, anxious whine tore at her heart. Running up the remaining stairs, she headed toward the sound of her distressed dog. Her anger built, and her palms began to itch. Without taking take off her leather gloves, she knew the green energy simmered just below her skin's surface.

Calm down! Rafe commanded. *You must not lose control.*

As irked as she was, Dane knew he was right. Lilith was up to something, and they needed to find out what. Which meant, she needed to focus and remain in control. Sebastian's concerns were warranted as the mill's atmosphere had changed significantly. Dane felt the funneling effect of the imprints when she pulled up and still sensed the disorder they emitted. The imprints were being pulled into a void, a hollow space inside the mill. Their energy manifested in different ways: terror, rage, and disbelief as they were sucked toward whatever lured them. Dane wished she could help but unless she identified the dark magic Lilith summoned, counteracting it would be impossible.

She crept down the dark corridor toward the room at the end. A faint light seeped out from the door which stood slightly ajar. Large, terrified eyes met hers as she peeked into the room. Her bullmastiff, Tyson, cowered in a corner on a dirty blanket. The thick chain tied around his neck was anchored into the wall. The chain so heavy he could barely lift his head from the floor when he saw her instead, he acknowledged her presence by thumping his tail on the floor.

"I am glad you came," Lilith said, her back to the door. "We really need to talk."

Pushing the door wide Dane walked into the room her eyes reassuring Tyson. "And you thought stealing my dog would be a good way to get my attention?"

"I have the attention I seek, do I not?" Lilith whirled. Her dark eyes exuded hate and envy, a strange penetrating grip that locked onto Dane. Her crimson lips pulled back into a defiant sneer as she relished in her perceived victory over her nemesis.

"I guess you do Lilith," Dane answered, her voice barely a whisper.

She shot Tyson another comforting look, pushing calming energy toward him. He laid his head back down on the dirty blanket and watched, one final whimper escaping him before silence.

Lilith began to pace. Her stiletto heels echoed against the old wooden floorboards and a creak penetrated the tension as her foot hit a loose one. She seemed distracted like her mind was concentrating on something or someone other than Dane.

There was a distant emptiness in her eyes, vacant eyes rimmed with dark circles. She continued to pace, lost in her own thoughts. Her mouth moved as if mumbling under her breath as she wrung her hands. Finally, she stopped, her glazed eyes finding their way back to the present.

"Do you know who I am?" she asked. The sneer finding her mouth once again. She glared at Dane her eyes seething with defiance.

"I have an idea."

"I don't think you do," she hissed.

"Then why don't you tell me, Lilith."

She whirled again, pulling her shoulders back as she walked quickly toward where Dane stood, stopping when they were inches apart.

"Your worst nightmare."

Dane had a difficult time stifling the giggle that threatened to burst from her mouth. "Bit dramatic don't you think, Lilith."

The slap was unexpected. The sting left on her skin sent a warm heat across her cheek. Her palms sizzled in response sensing a threat. Sucking in air, she attempted to calm herself and her warrior magic before turning back to look at the angry redhead in front of her.

"What is it that you want?" Dane said through gritted teeth.

"I want revenge," she replied, moving away from Dane. "I want you to know what your family did to mine and how it affected me. I want you to feel the same pain."

"My family doesn't even know you."

Lilith's eyes burned with hatred. "Not your family on Earth, Dane, your ancestors, the ones who lived long ago on Dywen."

Dane was stunned at the dark witch's revelation. *How could she possibly know!*

"You look surprised." She laughed, pleased at the impact her statement made. "Don't be, I have known for a long time where you and I come from, our bloodlines and the ancient realms. I've been biding my time until the day we would meet. It took me a while to track you down. Your scent is not easy to follow. You hide well witch."

"But you managed."

She smirked. "What my ancestors left me was informative. My family grimoire detailed much. Unfortunately, it wasn't until I learned to harness my powers that I was able to reveal some of its hidden secrets. It made finding you a lot easier after that." She turned and walked to the back of the table. "Join me."

Dane walked cautiously to the front side.

The table was set up like an altar. Thick pillar candles burned at different points on the surface, a black powder spread between them. Carved into the wood top were strange markings, sigils or runes of some sort, splinters and sawdust surrounded them. At the center of the makeshift altar was a thick, leather tome, its surface marred by cracks. The faded leather, peeling in places, had a strong odor of mold and dirt permeating from its pages.

Lilith leaned down and grabbed the old tome by its edges, turning it in a circle until it faced Dane. "The family grimoire."

Looking down at the cover Dane noticed a large symbol embossed at its center—a cross emblazoned with a moon and intersecting a scythe. *The same symbol on the coin she picked from the fountain floor in Dywen's town square!*

"You are a descendant of Vertigan Tierney."

This time it was Lilith's turn to be surprised, but the shock on her face did not last long before she regained her stoic composure.

"Very good. You seem to know more than I thought you might."

"I'm sure I don't know everything. What are your plans?"

"My plans have been the same since the day my family history was revealed to me. To enhance my powers, find you, and seek revenge for the curse put on my bloodline."

"Curse? That is not the way I understand it. Your ancestor, Vertigan Tierney, was consumed by dark magic. He had broken the code of The Order and murdered others in the brotherhood. He was stripped of his magic because of his crimes and banished to this world as punishment. No curse was put on him."

"Being banished to this forsaken world was the curse. You see, when your ancestor stripped him of his magic, he was left with nothing. A shell of the formidable immortal warrior he once was. His days on Earth consisted of one failure after another. He eventually died alone, penniless, disgraced. The only legacy he left was the family name but with that came more failure, heartache, and pain. The bad luck continued through every generation, each member of the Tierney bloodline falling into the same pattern of despair, an endless cycle."

"And you blame my ancestor, Claaven Callathian, for your family troubles."

Lilith tapped the tome with her index finger. "My entire lineage did. This book has found its way through generations of Tierney's, each passing it to the next as their birthright. The book came to me on my twenty-fifth birthday. As a Tierney, I had already experienced my fair share of misery. Beatings as a child from an alcoholic step-father, constant bullying from kids my age, abuse at the hands of someone who said they loved me. Pushed to the very bottom of society, I have seen the depravity that tarnishes humanity. I lost almost everything, my dignity, strength, my self-worth, but one thing I never lost was the will to survive. Your family gave me that."

Dane searched Lilith's eyes as she spoke. The dark irises held something else deep within, past the obvious contempt. A flicker of something powerful, a darkness that didn't belong.

Lilith sneered. "This book revealed the truth about the past and the treachery bestowed against my ancestors by yours." She stopped speaking and her eyes glazed as once again something only she could see distracted her.

"Lilith?"

At the sound of her name, dark eyes turned to glare. "You can take your dog and go," she said. Her voice was tight, and she ignored Dane as she began digging her nails into the skin of her hand, scratching absently at the surface. The repetitive motion caused bloody lines to appear, but Lilith seemed unaware. Her eyes darted back and forth. "I have things I must prepare. Things to do. What needs to be done? I must do them now."

Dane watched as Lilith receded into a strange madness, her senseless words mumbled as she spoke only to herself. Reaching across the table she grabbed Lilith's hands. "Lilith what are you planning on doing?"

She laughed as her eyes focused on Dane.

"I wanted to kill you once," she giggled. "It was so important that it consumed my very existence. But now…"

Her mind drifted as she trailed off. Her glazed eyes flitted back and forth, and her hands began to shake. She yanked them from Dane's grip and clawed at her hair, pulling strands from her scalp as she muttered. Unexpectedly, she let out a scream. An agonizing tortured feral sound that filled the stale air and reverberated through the cold darkness. "LEAVE!" she yelled as she ran around the table, careening at Dane like a madwoman.

Shocked by the sudden change Dane stood frozen, unable to react to the sudden onslaught or remove herself from Lilith's path. With surprising speed Lilith flung herself at Dane, knocking her to the ground, the air escaping from her lungs as their combined weight hit the floor. Gasping, Dane covered her face as Lilith's hands clawed and scratched. Her incoherent screams mingled with Tyson's agitated barking as he pulled desperately against the chain restraining him.

"LEAVE," Lilith shrieked again. Her crazed eyes rolled back as spittle flowed from the corner of her mouth.

The dark witch writhing on top of her was not the calm, controlled woman Dane had met numerous times in the past, this was someone else entirely. As she continued to block Lilith's attack, she felt Rafe's energy draw near at a significant pace.

Stop!

As if Lilith heard her thoughts, the fevered onslaught ceased. Dane peered up at the redhead, whose eyes now shone with something else—*panic!* Jumping to her feet, she grabbed the grimoire from the table and ran from the room, leaving Dane on the floor exhausted.

Tyson whimpered.

"I'm okay, buddy," she said. Surging magic rifled through her veins, its essence full of emotions not her own. She could feel Rafe's panic. He was close—too close.

I'm okay, she's gone.

You need to get out of there. NOW! His panic wrapped around her. His voice in her mind dripped with it.

She lifted herself up carefully ensuring nothing was damaged. A twinge indicated the force of the impact most likely bruised her back, but there didn't seem to be anything serious. Getting to her feet, she hurried to Tyson who tried desperately to lift his head in greeting. The heavy chain pulled at his neck keeping him from standing. She grabbed the chain, looking for a way to disconnect it. The far end was bolted into the wall by a thick anchor, the other tied tightly around his neck and closed with a massive iron padlock.

She searched the table in vain for the key.

Desperate, she returned to Tyson and pulled off one of her leather gloves. Gripping the padlock in her bare hand she thought back to her lessons in the courtyard. How Rafe said there was nothing more he could teach her that she didn't already know instinctively. Inserting her gloved hand between Tyson's neck and the links of the chain, she closed her eyes, concentrating. She visualized the energy ball seeping out of her hand and into the padlock. It grew in her mind as it found its way into the metal, the iron expanding with it until it broke. The pressure of the chain on her hand diminished and the clank of metal filled the air as the padlock fell in pieces to the floor. Gently, she unwrapped the thick chain from Tyson's neck, coaxing him up onto his wobbly legs.

"Come on buddy, let's get out of here."

Wagging his tail, he followed, his head nudging her leg in reassurance. As they reached the first floor, she noticed the strange hum from the pods had diminished. An eerie silence draped itself over the entire mill. Rafe stood in the middle of the pods, his jaw clenched as his eyes flitted from one to the next.

Dane moved in beside him. "Do you know what they are?"

He tensed at her voice, a film of sweat appearing on his top lip. His hands trembled, and a feeling of déjà vu washed through her as his memories triggered an emotional response deep inside his being. "Unfortunately, I do."

"What are they?"

"Nothing good," he responded, grabbing her hand and pulling her from the confines of the eerie mill.

CHAPTER 15

"**D**AEMON PODS?" SEBASTIAN SAID. "ARE you sure?"

Rafe nodded. His jade eyes flashed with certainty.

"But how?"

"Magic," Gabby responded. "Very dark magic."

"It is not possible for a dark witch to summon magic of that magnitude, not even with the knowledge of the ancient Tierney bloodline. A specific type of archaic alchemy is required to grow daemons, and it is extremely difficult to master that type of power. It is a rare gift." Sebastian scowled. "Where in this world could she gain knowledge to accomplish something so archaic?"

Gabby stretched her wings, a habit she had come to relish now that she was back in her rightful form. "Sebastian is correct. There must be something else, something we are missing."

"Lilith does have her family grimoire, maybe the pod spell is in there," Dane stated.

Gabby shook her head. "There is no spell that can create a

daemon. To specifically birth one from a pod is a type of sorcery. It requires a skilled alchemist with an extensive knowledge of base metals, transmutation, and archaic solvents and solutions. You cannot just call on the quarters or invoke a goddess." Her brow crinkled as she paused. "Surely, no one existing in this world possesses such knowledge."

"What about the dark sphere?" Dane asked.

Rafe shook his head. "I did not get any sense that the dark sphere had been penetrated. The aching hollow evil that leeches from its darkness is not tainting the mill or the pods. This dark magic is coming from somewhere else."

Dane could feel Rafe's frustration. An anxious and distressed energy surrounded every immortal in the room as they tried to make sense of the daemon pods sudden appearance.

"Was there anything else in that mill? Anything that would give us some idea of how this happened," Sebastian asked, his voice low his gaze penetrating.

Dane shifted uncomfortably as she recalled the drastic changes in Lilith's behavior. Before she could respond to his inquiry, the doorbell sounded, and she hurried from the kitchen, glad to be out from under his piercing stare.

"Dane are you OK! Where is Tyson?"

Kai burst through the front door, heading into the kitchen before Dane could stop her. Mr. Parker gave her an apologetic look as he followed his daughter into the house. Dane shut the door and took a deep, cleansing breath.

As she entered the kitchen, Kai was checking Tyson over and mumbling about the kind of person who would kidnap a dog to get the owner's attention. When she was sure Tyson had no lasting trauma from his ordeal, she turned to face the group standing around Dane's kitchen island. Her gaze drifted over each of them, stopping on Sebastian who was still dressed head to toe in his shiny, black armor. Shaking her head, she looked at Dane.

"Where is Stevie? And who the hell are those two," she demanded, her blue eyes flashing with boldness as she pointed at Sebastian and Rafe.

"Stevie is on Kaizi, learning to wield her new powers and these two are warriors from another time," Gabby said nonchalantly.

Shocked, Dane fixed her with a disgusted look. She glanced at Kai and Mr. Parker her mind churning, desperate to defuse the curiosity she saw simmering on Kai's face.

"You seem different Gabby," Kai stated, more focused on that than the facts she just revealed.

"We are all very different since last we saw you."

How long has it been? Dane's mind searched for the answer. She had lost track of time since going back and forth to Dywen and the other realms. What was the date?

"It's been two weeks," Kai huffed. "You can't be that different. Will someone please tell me what the hell is going on? Where have you been, why all the secrecy, and who the hell is that bitch who took Tyson?"

"I know you want answers Kai, but can we talk about this later?" Dane asked. She didn't need Kai to reply, the look on her face told her that she wasn't going to be ignored.

"You know, do you not?" Gabby asked, her eyes directed at Kai's father. "What she is?"

Once again, Dane shot her a dirty look. "Gabby," she hissed, turning toward the corner where Mr. Parker stood.

"Yes," he whispered, his face drawn and pale.

"Gabby what are you doing?" Dane whispered. She was

acutely aware of the volatile situation Gabby had created but was helpless to halt it.

"We no longer need to hide our true selves from Kai, for she is one of us." And with that statement she unfolded her large black wings, stretching them out to their fullest.

Kai jumped backward. "What the hell!"

"I believe there is something your father needs to tell you about your mother."

"What is she talking about dad?" Kai said, her eyes never leaving Gabby.

Mr. Parker's skin turned ashen. A thin sheen of sweat covered his face. He looked at Gabby in awe, shock evident on his face. His hands trembled as he stared at the woman who stood in full celestial in front of them.

Gabby's iridescent eyes sparkled as the light of the ether glowed brightly beneath her skin. Panic rose inside her as Dane looked to Sebastian and Rafe for help, but neither seemed fazed by Gabby's spectacle. Kai shifted her weight perplexed. Dane knew her mind churned as Gabby stood flexing her wings with that damn look of indifference plastered on her face. She couldn't think of anything else to do or say to defuse the situation, so she moved quickly to the cupboard. Removing a glass, she filled it with water and handed it to Mr. Parker.

"Come," she said gently taking his hand and leading him to the counter stool. He didn't look well, and she was afraid he may faint. "Sit down."

Confident that her point had been made, Gabby folded in her wings and returned to her mortal form. Kai remained transfixed. The disbelief contorting her face had turned to morbid curiosity.

"What are you?" She asked.

Gabby stretched her neck, rolling her head back and forth, seemingly working out the knots. "A celestial."

"An angel," Kai corrected.

"That is a man-made title for my kind and I wish not to be addressed as such."

Kai turned to Dane, casting her the same look Stevie had when she first experienced the new Gabby.

"You will have to get used to her. It doesn't get any better," Dane said defeated.

Kai just glared.

The color had returned to Mr. Parker's face. He looked around at everyone, his eyes taking in manifestations of things he seemed already familiar with. "My wife told me about your kind, but I never expected to meet anyone from her world."

"Dad, what are you talking about?" Kai's voice squeaked as anxious energy encircled her.

"Your mother was supposed to tell you when the time was right, but then she got sick, and it never happened. I'm sorry Kai, I just never knew how to tell you."

"Tell me what?"

His shoulders sagged, and his eyes filled with tears.

"Your mother was a mermaid," he whispered.

A hush fell over the room as all eyes fixed on Mr. Parker. He fidgeted uncomfortably glancing down at his hands before giving Kai an imploring gaze.

Kai burst out laughing, a reaction no one in the room, including Mr. Parker, anticipated. Dane glanced at the others and shrugged. Finally, Kai calmed herself and spoke. "Seriously, dad."

A somber shadow darkened Mr. Parker's face. "It's true Kai, just look around you. Everything she told me about, it's all right here—*your mother's world.* His hand swept through the air, a gesture that took in all the immortals standing patiently waiting for Kai to process what her father was trying to tell her.

Her gaze found Dane. Her eyes hardened as the smile faded from her lips. "Tell me the truth."

Truth, Dane thought, the one thing she had never been good at.

"Your father *is* telling the truth. Although I didn't know about your specific heritage until now, there is much I do know, which confirms what he is saying." Taking a deep breath, she decided to forge on, as at this point there was nothing to lose. "Like Stevie and I, you are part of a destiny written long before our time, in a world that exists only to those that possess magic. Your birthright comes from your mother and her ancestors."

Raising her hand, palm up, she willed her magic forth. A slight crackle hissed through the room as the green ball of energy appeared, spitting and spinning in her palm.

Kai once again pulled back. Her eyes narrowed but never wavered from the magic that flickered in Dane's hand.

"My powers come from the earth, Stevie's from fire, and yours apparently from water."

"And her?" Kai croaked, pointing at Gabby but keeping her eyes locked on the glowing energy Dane held in her hand.

"Gabby is a celestial, a fallen angel if you will. Like Sebastian and Rafe she has always been immortal and is from the same universe as they. She was never from our world."

Kai frowned. "It's why she has no past."

"Excuse me?" Dane said.

"Gabby. It's why we could never find anything about her before the day you and Stevie found her on the road. She didn't have a past because she didn't exist here before that day."

Dane's eyebrows raised in surprise as she nodded in agreement. She hadn't really thought about the connection to Gabby's missing past once her identity had been revealed, but Kai was right she never had a mortal past to find.

"You are correct," Gabby noted. "I fell to Earth as part of the prophecy, as I too am destined."

"Destined?"

Gabby looked at Dane, her iridescent eyes shimmering under the kitchen's fluorescent lights.

"You better sit down."

CHAPTER 16

I T HAD BEEN DECIDED IN the wee hours of the morning,
Sebastian would escort Kai to the Druidstone on her
realm in the morning. The discussion had been long
and arduous but by the end, Kai was up to date on Lilith, the
prophecy, and her ancient heritage.

Her ancestral realm, known as Viccinius, was the smallest
of the five and the trek would be simple, so they agreed splitting up was the best solution. Gabby would stay at the house
and continue to try to detect the other two Arcanists while
keeping an eye on the old mill and Lilith. Rafe and Dane
would head back to Dywen to retrieve Brannon and Tauria;
then take the portal to Kaizi to retrieve the others. Sebastian
deemed the situation at the mill untenable. With Lilith's
erratic behavior and the evil essence detected in the mill's
atmosphere, he thought it essential to have all the immortals
come to this world.

The sun peeked over the horizon. The early morning rays
spread across the backyard and reflected off the icicles
hanging from the eaves. Dane stood at the kitchen window

contemplating her new life. Since she was thirteen, she had lived in constant fear of being discovered as a witch, keeping people at a distance, and never staying in one place too long. None of that mattered anymore. She no longer needed to hide who she truly was, at least not from those she cared about for they too were like her. Amidst all the chaos, fate had given her one very valuable thing—*hope.*

"It's time."

Dane smiled at the sound of his voice.

And it had given her Rafe.

Turning she nodded. "Is Kai ready."

He smirked. "She is the skeptical one, yes?"

Dane laughed. "Maybe a little."

He kissed her forehead and turned to go.

"Wait," she said.

Rafe paused, his brow furrowed. "What is troubling you?"

"Time."

He laughed. "We are back to that concept again."

"I was thinking about something Kai said. How we have been away for almost two weeks. Sebastian said time moves more slowly here, and we were only in the other realms for a few days. How then has almost two weeks passed here on Earth?" She checked the calendar on her phone. "Today is February 10th."

"You know that means nothing to me, but I do understand what you are asking. We entered the portal to Kaizi from the Elder Oak which connected your world to ours. But we did not return to your world prior to moving through a different portal to Etheriem; thus, severing the link. Time as you know it, therefore, does not exist and the two worlds move through space separately. There is also an energy gap between the

Thanissia realms. They do exist in a parallel sphere, or as you would say, at the same time."

Dane raised her brow and put her phone back in her pocket. "Never mind."

An hour later she was saying goodbye to Mr. Parker at the front door. He had offered to take Tyson with him to the marina, and the bullmastiff squirmed excitedly as Dane put his leash on. She handed it to Kai's father with a bag of Tyson's supplies.

"Thanks for looking after him."

"It's the least I can do."

"She will be OK."

Mr. Parker's eyes filled with tears. "Her mother would have handled this better."

Dane took his hands, squeezing gently. "Kai is strong. She will know how to handle this. Once Kai has accepted her birthright, she will understand everything about who her mother was—*before*." She hesitated unsure if now was the time to inquire. "When did you know about Mrs. Parker? What she was?"

Surprisingly, he smiled as memories of his late wife surfaced.

"I was on the sea more than I was on land back in those days. We were off the coast of Oahu on a training mission when a rogue wave capsized our skiff. I was at the helm and as the boat flipped, my ankle got caught in a line. My men were all safe, but I became trapped under the vessel unable to free myself. I was losing consciousness, the dark water crushing the breath from my lungs when I heard the most beautiful song. The waves overhead carried it across the ocean. It was mesmerizing and soothing. It calmed me and made me feel safe. I thought I was dead. Then a glint of light flashed in my peripheral vision. I turned toward it, my lungs bursting for air. She floated in the glowing light, her long blond hair gently waving in the current—she was beautiful."

He wiped away the stray tear sliding down his cheek. His eyes haunted as the past overwhelmed his senses.

"I thought I was hallucinating, my body's response to the last of my life leaving me, but the feel of her lips on mine as she pushed air into my lungs was so real. I gazed into her beautiful blue eyes where both sadness and determination seemed to mingle. I don't know how long I was under the capsized boat, but I do know Kai's mother saved my life that day. The navy divers found me two hours later, on a deserted beach. I remained in the hospital for a week but once I was discharged and cleared for duty, I returned to the same spot. Over and over I searched the area until I found her. She gave up everything for me, including her life."

"What do you mean?"

"A mermaid's magic allows them to walk on land, their tail only appearing when they are in the water. But a mermaid can only be on land for a short while before their magic reverts, and they become human."

The way Mr. Parker emphasized *human* was very telling. Mrs. Parker had not only given up her immortality, she had given up her invincibility and eventually her life. Succumbing to a human disease—cancer.

"So, you knew from the beginning she was a mermaid."

He nodded. "Yes, and I knew from the first moment I was in love with her."

Dane smiled.

"She was grateful Kai found such wonderful friends, but she always sensed something in you Dane—in all of you. She

138

suspected, in some way, you were bound for prominence." Mr. Parker kissed her on the cheek. "See you when you get back."

Dane hugged him tightly, feeling the sadness engulf him. "She will be fine."

"I know," he said taking Tyson's leash as he walked to his car. "You all will."

She watched him drive away, absently playing with the bracelet on her wrist he made for her thirty-first birthday. Closing the door, she thought about Kai's mother. She had always made them feel like family, protected and safe. Mr. Parker's words surfaced in her mind—*she always sensed something in you Dane—in all of you.* Gasping, she ran to find Gabby.

"I think I know who the other two Arcanists are," she blurted.

Gabby raised an eyebrow, waiting.

"Destiny has a way of finding those who share the same one."

"And."

"It was something Sebastian said to me." She thought for a moment. "Like Diego found Stevie, doesn't it make sense the bloodlines from our ancestral homes would find each other here, in this time? What if we found each other long before we even knew we were destined?"

Gabby sighed, her exasperation heavy. "Is there a point coming?"

"You, me, Kai, Stevie." She hesitated to take a deep cleansing breath. "And Marlee and Elyse."

"You think Marlee and Elyse are the other two Arcanists."

"It makes sense, doesn't it? The strange way we all met and how close we have been since. We've stayed connected over the years even after Stevie and I moved out of town. Fate always seems to bring us back together."

Dane could tell Gabby was assessing the information for viability.

"There is one way to find out for sure, Gabby."

"How?"

"I think you should pay them a visit, not in your true form of course in case I'm wrong. Since you can detect the blood of the ancients you would know immediately if they have ancestral ties, right? You haven't seen them since you reverted to your true self, so it is possible."

Gabby nodded. "Alright witch, let's see if your intuition is as strong as your magic."

Dane smiled and turned to walk away, stopping as a thought occurred. "If you do detect the blood of the ancients, you better wait until we get back to tell them."

"Why?"

"Let's just say your people skills need a little work."

⁂

She knocked quietly on the spare room door. "Kai, can I come in?"

There was no answer, but she could hear movement on the other side and sense her unbalanced energy as it seeped under the door. Pushing open the door, she entered. Kai was sitting, fully dressed, at the end of the bed. Her head was down, and she held a small picture in her hands. Kai's purse lay open beside her as did her wallet and Dane knew instantly the picture she held was the one of her mother she kept tucked behind her license.

"Are you OK?" She sat beside Kai, their shoulders touching. Tears stained her face, and she shuddered as she spoke.

"I don't know what I am."

Dane put her arm around her friend. "That's understand-able Kai. What is happening to you, to us, none of us could have imagined. Not even me and I've been a witch my entire life."

Kai looked at Dane and crinkled her nose, her sad eyes sparked with interest. "That is quite the secret you kept from us Dane, and one you should probably elaborate on at some point."

Dane signed. "I know, and I will. It wasn't easy keeping that part of me from any of you, especially Stevie, but it was necessary, at least at the time. Now I guess, not so much." She winked at her friend and they laughed.

"Are you having reservations about going to Viccinius?"

"No, not really. I just needed some alone time to try to figure it all out. Process this new reality. You know I don't believe in this stuff."

"You mean magic?" Dane asked, lifting her hand and flip-ping Kai's wallet to the floor.

Kai shook her head in feigned disgust as she bent over to pick up the wallet. "I hope I gain a power I can irritate you with."

Dane grinned. "Imagine, Kai the realist with a magical ability."

"Yeah. It's more a Stevie and you thing."

"I always wondered why someone like you would want to be friends with Stevie and me."

"I give you two cred. A sense of normalcy," Kai responded, shrugging.

"Yes, that's it."

Kai inhaled deeply wiping her tear-stained face. "OK, if I'm truly going to become a believer in magic, other worlds, immortal beings, and the fate of the universe, I guess I should see it with my own eyes."

"So, you're jumping in with both feet?" Dane smirked.

"Did you just make a joke about my being a mermaid?"

"I think I did."

"At least you haven't lost your sarcastic sense of humor." Kai quipped. "Maybe immortality isn't so bad." A shadow crossed her face. "What am I going to tell Ethan? I have been ignoring his calls all morning."

"You have to tell him something."

"Dad offered. He says he has some things of mom's that will help convince Ethan we are not all crazy."

"You need to speak with him as well Kai. He loves you as much as your father loved your mother. He will understand."

"I'm not even sure I do." She tucked her mom's picture back into her wallet and pulled her phone from her purse. "Tell Sebastian, I'll be down in a minute."

Dane stood. "Take your time."

Kai laughed nervously, "Apparently, time will be all I have soon."

CHAPTER 17

"WELCOME TO VICCINIUS," SEBASTIAN SAID as they emerged onto the edge of an ice embankment. As they exited, the bright blue portal began to swirl, funneling and disappearing like water down a drain. Kai looked around, stunned. A landscape of frost and snow lay before them. The icy ridge they stood upon bordered a small sea. Ice chunks floated aimlessly in its midst. The water was dark blue. Waves crested into whitecaps as they broke the surface, but the sea's depth was unknown as the naked eye couldn't penetrate the darkness.

"You've got to be kidding," Kai groaned, shivering at the vast amounts of ice and snow.

Sebastian fixed her with a strange look.

"I hate snow. Ice. Being cold. Everything about winter."

Sebastian smirked, seeing the irony.

"Your kin are cold-blooded Kai. This type of environment is suitable for your kind. You will understand once you have obtained your birthright."

"I doubt that."

She shivered as the breeze blew a damp mist toward her. "The Whispering Ice Sea."

Kai frowned. "Excuse me."

Sebastian pointed to the frothing water. "Listen."

Glancing back at the dark, churning sea, she said. "I don't hear anything."

Sebastian raised his hand to silence her. Closing his eyes, he repeated, "Listen."

Following his lead, she closed hers, focusing on what her other senses detected. Waves crashed on the ice followed by a splash as the water left the sea. The wind whistled and there was a crack as ice, somewhere in the distance, split. The smell of brackish water assaulted her nostrils, and she could taste the salt as she licked her dry lips.

As her senses adjusted to her loss of sight, her hearing became acute detecting a faint sound rippling just beneath the waves—a melodic chant, a tantalizing hum, a lulling whisper. Kai's eyes flew open surprised by the intimacy of the murmurs.

Sebastian watched her his green eyes full of curiosity.

She understood now why it was called The Whispering Ice Sea. The water had its own energy, a specific essence that flowed through it. She could feel its lure.

"Come."

Her gaze wandered once more across the sea's rough surface before following Sebastian.

For all its bitter cold and snowy landscapes, Viccinius was breathtaking. Sheer white clouds floated aimlessly around a large moon that hovered majestically in the pure blue sky. Spears of light protruded from the moon's center, sent a shimmering glow across the landscape. The far end of the sea was surrounded by a tall ice wall, hundreds of feet high. Multiple waterfalls thundered down its side, spraying shards of ice outward as it erupted into a foaming froth in the sea below.

Shivering, she pulled up the collar of her coat in a feeble attempt to gain additional protection from the frigid wind. They made their way carefully down a sloping path, trekking across the ice shelf surrounding the water. The walk was treacherous as splashing water and newly fallen snow combined to create a slick sheet of ice.

"Where are we going?"

Sebastian didn't stop, just waved her onward.

She huddled deeper into her coat as the spray from the water intensified, the wind casting it sideways across the ice shelf. Small pellets of ice combined with the freezing spray ricocheting off her exposed skin. Groaning she swore to herself, silently cursing the fateful joke that this frigid place was the home of her ancestors.

When they finally reached the ice wall Kai's mood had darkened, but she experienced a sense of relief when she realized the cold was less bitter here. The fierce wind blowing without impediment across the open sea did not blow as viciously near the wall.

"Just around the corner," Sebastian said, disappearing behind a massive block of ice. Kai followed, a strange sense of curiosity and adventure spurring her forward. As she reached the other side, Sebastian was waiting at the foot of a staircase. The steps were embedded into the side of the wall and like everything else, they were solid ice. They glimmered under the moon's light as it reflected off the filmy sheen of soft snow covering their surfaces.

"We need to be at the top," Sebastian said, pointing to the pinnacle that in Kai's best estimation was hundreds of feet straight up.

With assurances from Sebastian that it was safe, she began to ascend the staircase. Finding her footing on the slippery steps was easier than anticipated and before she knew it, they reached the pinnacle. She could feel Sebastian's penetrating eyes upon her, but she didn't look his way, she was too mesmerized by the sight that stretched before her.

Atop the wall sat an ice castle. The entire structure shimmered in the hazy light of a million stars gracing the sky above. Beyond its mass lay a city of ice, a cornucopia of structures surrounded by water. Sparkling canals ran through its core. Ice bridges and paths connected one section to another. The city was whimsical yet evoked a quiet power as it sparkled under the moon's silvery light. The moon, much larger now, seemed to be the only light source for this world.

Kai held her breath and blinked, sure that the spectacle before her was not real. Closing her eyes, she waited a moment, but when she opened them, the castle and ice city remained. "It's unbelievable."

"The realm of Viccinius is an extraordinary place. Although small, it certainly maintains a certain grandiosity."

"Does the moon always stay out?"

"Yes, it dims greatly for an extended period during its cycle but continuously maintains its luster."

"It's amazing. I've never seen a moon so close."

"The realms of Thanissia are revered for their moons. Every world, regardless of the element governing it, has a moon providing its own ethereal beauty to the environment."

"And the city."

"The city is known as the Frost Isles because your ancestors built it on top of the water and each building is accessible by water and land."

"What about the castle?"

"The castle does not emulate those found in your world. It is not a place of hierarchy, more a place of commune. The Druidstone and all magical items that belong to the mermaid race reside inside those walls. It is the center of magic, trade, warfare, and exists for everyone, equally."

Kai turned back to the city. Beneath its ethereal beauty emanated a haunting silence. She could feel the stillness. The echo of a past hiding under layers of ice and snow—*waiting.* Dane told her about this poignant silence, for apparently, it leached from the surfaces of the other realms, as well.

From where she stood she could see the entirety of Viccinius. It wasn't very large. Other than the city and the sea, there was nothing visible beyond its edges.

"Breathtaking, yes."

Kai nodded even though it was more a statement than a question.

There was a static in the air, a strange energy dousing her in a bizarre coolness. She was finding it difficult to focus as the odd sensation took over her senses. The intimacy of it leaving her visibly shaken.

"Are you well, Kai?" Sebastian asked, noting the pallor spreading over her features.

Kai ignored him as the sensation intensified. Her skin vibrated as the blood in her veins throbbed impulsively. She felt faint. Her head began to spin as the moisture vanished from her mouth. Sure, she was about to collapse she reached out toward him hoping he would catch her if she did.

Everything went black.

She could feel herself falling. Instead of landing quickly on the cold icy ground beneath her feet, the falling seemed endless. Trapped in a free fall, the surrounding blackness comforted her as she floated slowly downward. As the sensation of falling ceased, and the blackness dispersed, she found herself surrounded by water, cool and blue. A glint of light caught her eye, and she swam toward it, fighting the pull of the current. A small school of fish darted around her, their colorful scales twinkling under the light penetrating the water's surface. She could hear the swish of their tails as they swam. Everything under the water was clear, vibrant and calm, all her senses sharpened by the cold fluid motion of the water.

The glint of light drawing her toward it continued to beckon. She swam until she reached the source, unaware of time or distance, and unburdened by fear. At the bottom of the sea, buried in the white sand was a trident. The prongs reflected the water's light and created a sparkling halo. As she neared, a low hum sprang from its depths, reverberating in the surrounding water. Reaching out she grazed the prongs with her fingertips. A tingling vibration pulsed through the metal. As her energy mingled with the trident's magic, the water began to churn. Bubbles erupted from the sandy bottom and for a minute her vision was obscured. When the water cleared, Kai could see a woman standing in front of her. Her long blonde hair floating languidly. Pale blue robes twisted around her body, the loose fabric cascading outward as it drifted in the current. She watched in awe as the woman turned toward her, a powerful tail where her legs should be.

Kai gasped as she saw the mermaid's face.

A face she knew well.

Mom, she thought, knowing instinctively there was no need for verbal interactions.

Kai, how I have missed you, my darling girl.

I don't understand. How?

There is much for you to learn but now is not the time. You must awaken the trident. It holds the secrets of our kind and you will need that knowledge and our magic for what is to come.

Kai looked back at the spear protruding from the sandy bottom. The humming vibration intensified as the aura surrounding it grew brighter.

It recognizes the blood of the mermaid. It senses your inner power. Take it, Kai, and return to the surface. Your destiny is fulfilled.

Kai reached toward the trident. Her hand shook as it wrapped around the spear. Pulling it from the seabed she held the trident close. The humming rang in her ears, growing louder until she realized it was a song—a bewitching melody.

It's the song of the siren. A call to your ancestors. They will forever be with you as will I, my daughter.

Kai smiled at her mother, knowing this would be the last time she would ever see her face. *I love you,* she thought as the current pulled her mother away from her until she disappeared behind the shimmering water.

And I, you.

⋰⋰

Sebastian reached out his hand and pulled her from the icy waters.

"What happened?" She asked.

"I am not quite sure. One moment you were standing beside me, the next you had walked backward off the cliff."

"I fell?" She asked looking at the ice wall above her. "From up there."

"Yes, but it was more a float than a fall."

Kai's brow furrowed unsure of what he meant by that.

"How do you feel?"

"Okay, I guess."

Sebastian extended his hand and pulled her up to a standing position. "I meant, are you cold?"

"Surprisingly not," she answered, looking down at her soaking wet clothes.

"It seems receiving your birthright does not require reactivating the Druidstone."

"What do you mean? I fell in. I don't remember anything except feeling strange up there." She pointed to the top of the ice wall some couple hundred feet above them. "Then I blacked out."

"Put your feet in the water."

"Why would I want to do that?" Kai queried, not wanting to douse herself with even more freezing water.

"You said you were not cold."

Kai hesitated, again looking down at her wet clothes, wondering why she wasn't.

"So."

"Please, just do as I ask. If I am correct, you will have your answer."

Kai shook her head but sat on the edge, lowering her feet carefully into the frigid sea. As the toes of her boots touched the water, she felt a twitch slither under her skin. The further she pushed her legs into the water the more intense the twitch became. She looked back over her shoulder at Sebastian who had a strange smile on his face.

"As I suspected," he said motioning to her legs.

She turned back. Her legs were only submerged in the water up to her knees, but the scales appearing already reached her mid-thighs. As she watched, more scales emerged.

Kai gasped as she realized what was happening.

She was growing a mermaid tail.

CHAPTER 18

THE COOL WATER HAD A silky texture as it flowed over her bare skin. She was sensitive to every ripple and current as she dove deeper. An ethereal glow came from the depths of the seabed, a light shimmering below. It illuminated the water making it easier for her to find her way along the bottom where fish, seaweed, and coral gathered. She spun in a circle creating a vortex that spun upward. Kicking harder she turned, propelling herself quickly away from the bottom and back up toward the shoreline.

Sebastian was waiting when she surfaced.

"I see you have taken to your ancestry quite well." His brilliant green eyes shone with amusement.

"It's incredible," Kai responded, "And so natural."

He held out his hand which she gracefully accepted, helping her from the water and onto the ice shelf. Within seconds her tail morphed back to human legs, and she was no longer in mermaid form. She watched the transformation in awe.

"The change happens so quickly."

"Mermaid magic is very potent. It has no boundaries as it derives from the element water. It is fluid, constantly changing, and therefore extremely fast."

"I guess I have much to learn."

Sebastian nodded. "You really do not recall anything from your fall into the sea."

Kai shook her head. "No, it's just blank."

"That is strange. But, the mermaid race was very enigmatic."

"Tell me about my ancestors."

Sebastian gave her a long hard look. "Come."

Kai followed him up the ice staircase once again.

"Viccinius' people were a small clan and extremely private. Of all the races, the mermaids preferred solitude more than any other. They kept to themselves, were a peaceful race, and only interacted with the other supernaturals when necessity demanded it. I did not have much contact with any of your ancestors, but your mother was known to all of us. She was the envoy for your people."

Kai held her breath at the mention of her mother. Her eyes glistened as tears welled up. The memory ignited fresh emotions.

Sebastian paused, allowing her to gain control of her grief before continuing. "The mermaid race was a female-dominated one, but there were a few males. To keep the mermaid line pure and intact."

Kai gaped at his words and Sebastian nodded in confirmation.

"Mermaids normally do not fall in love, they procreate, and the males of the pod are shared among the females appointed as birthers. What your mother and father had was not only extraordinary but very rare. After the Great War, the remaining mermaids lived in the oceans of Earth, but they never interacted with humans for they did not trust them. This is where your mother differed. She saw the goodness in mankind. Saving your father from drowning was something only she would have done."

Kai smiled as memories of her parents' love surfaced.

"Giving up her immortality for him was an act of selflessness. Unfortunately, it came with extreme consequences. The pod your mother led for billions of centuries did not approve, and she was shunned, banished to live a mortal life. Eventually, her magic diminished, and she became human but her connection to the sea never left her. It is why you are so at ease with it."

Kai stared at the sea, its dark blue waters churning under the chilly air. She felt a kinship with this place, her mother's home, something she had never truly felt in her own world.

Sebastian cleared his throat, interrupting her thoughts. "I am afraid time is not on our side, Kai. You must activate the Druidstone. Come, let us continue to the castle."

Kai agreed, following him down the icy path toward the gate. She glanced back at the sea, the sparkling stars reflected in its dark surface. A mist swirled lazily a few inches above the water, its movement causing her to squint as shadows appeared within it. Something broke the surface, distorted by the mist. A dark shape bobbed in the water. The clouds in the sky parted. The moon's rays pushed out from behind them igniting the water in a silvery glow casting away the dark shadows. Just for a moment, before the light retreated, and the mist thickened, she thought she saw her mother—*smiling*.

As they crossed the ice bridge, Kai looked down at the frozen moat below. The ice formed over its surface was cracked and jagged, broken into a million shards and jammed into one another. It looked dangerous but stunning. Each exposed edge glistened in the silvery light, the whiteness of the ice intensified by the clarity of the blue sky. She was in awe, consumed by Viccinius' visual intensity. It was mesmerizing and slightly disconcerting—the way the entire realm's immeasurable power lay hidden under a whimsical facade.

One of the front doors of the castle stood ajar. She paused to inspect the foot-thick block of clear ice. It was carved with intricate symbols and a strange light encapsulated within rebounded back and forth behind them, emitting a small intense sparkle before moving to the next. The hinges and door handle were metal, but nothing like Kai had ever seen before. The metal was warm to the touch, extremely shiny, and embedded with a strange metallic thread that seemed to pulse with a faint blue light. At the center of the door, a massive blue jewel sparkled, a perfect oval entrenched in the ice and surrounded by a multitude of smaller purple stones. The stones caught the light and reflected it outward in a kaleidoscope of color.

They walked through the front hall. Huge ice pillars stretched to the ceiling. A three-tiered fountain sat at the center, the water once flowing, now frozen. Cascading icicles draped over the basin's sides and a dusting of snow blew haphazardly through the open door carried in by the salty breeze. Kai could feel the pull of the sea's current as the wind gusted. Its soothing flow wrapped around her. Her birthright connected her to the sea, and she could intimately sense its movement. It was a part of her now, and she would forever be lulled by its strength, power, and majesty.

Kai recognized the Druidstone immediately—it was a trident, and it held a certain familiarity like she had seen it before.

But where?

It sat silently in an ice pedestal. Instinctively she touched its prongs, her fingers grazing the three points. The metal was cold. There was no energy encompassing it and the air around it lay stagnant. Being this close to the trident she could not feel the sea, the fluidity of its essence no longer distinct. An emptiness hovered around it, a haunting reminder of the finality of the past. She stepped closer. Her hand gripped the shaft, but nothing happened. She glanced back at Sebastian and shrugged.

"I don't know what to do."

"Relax. Allow the knowledge of the past to guide you."

Turning back to the Druidstone she placed both hands on its shaft. Closing her eyes, she inhaled, allowing her mind to soften and go blank. Somewhere, deep in her subconscious, she felt a twinge, a subtle awakening of the ancient knowledge of her ancestors. Relaxing deeper into her breathing, she listened. Whispers surfaced in her mind. A chorus of voices flooded her with their past. A rush of water encompassed her as a coolness swept over her skin sending a chill through her very being.

The trident began to vibrate in her hands. The whispers elevated in volume.

Coolness spread down the shaft, wrapping effortlessly around every fiber of her being. The connection created a conduit for the magic of the ancients to flow back into this world. In her mind's eye, the sea reared up. Its power and majesty infinite. The sound of waves crashed around her and the taste of salt water, bitter and dry, assailed her mouth. The silky-smooth coolness of seawater slid over her skin, down her arms, and back into the trident.

Sebastian watched as the water element once again ignited its power in this realm. He could see the liquid flow of its essence coursing through Kai—a silvery-blue current of magic and knowledge ignited the ancient trident. In response, it began to glow and tremble. The prongs sparkled with a silver light and the metal shimmered. The sound of rushing water filled the room as the walls began to drip with condensation. As the energy built, Sebastian felt the deafening silence, the eeriness that precedes the ferocity of the element's power —the power of the sea and the ancient magic of Viccinius.

The room trembled as it built. The energy surrounding Kai became chaotic, like a stormy sea. Suddenly, water exploded from the trident. The force of its release threw her backward as she was caught in its vortex. Slammed against the back wall she slumped, unconscious to the floor. Sebastian waded to her side, fighting the surge of rushing water as it poured from the trident. Lifting her onto his shoulder he carried her through the door, slamming it shut behind them, as the room filled with the sea and submerged the trident in its raging surf.

"Kai."

Her eyes flickered at the sound of his voice.

"You must wake up."

Her eyes fluttered open. "What happened?"

"The water element is a forceful one. The magic and its essence flooded back into this world quickly. Unfortunately, you were caught in its path."

She rubbed the back of her head, allowing Sebastian to assist her in standing.

"I'm okay," she assured him.

"Are you sure? Your pallor is grave."

"A little lightheaded maybe, but I'll be fine."

Sebastian did not look convinced. "I think you should rest awhile before we return to your world."

Kai began to argue, but as her sight blurred and the room started to spin, she decided maybe a quick rest was warranted.

Sebastian helped her through the castle and out into the fresh air. A crisp breeze blew through the courtyard, and she closed her eyes, breathing in its refreshing scent. Her senses sharpened as she inhaled the awakening magic. It ignited her skin. A cool and comforting tingle flowed under the first layer of the epidermis. She relaxed into the feeling, allowing the ancient magic to course freely through her. After a few moments, she opened her eyes. The clarity of her vision had magnified. She could see everything with pinpoint precision for miles. The entirety of Viccinius crystal clear.

Raising her hand to her face she studied it, every wrinkle, freckle, and imperfection well-defined. "I can see everything, perfectly."

"Mermaid sight. It is extraordinary. It provides a unique clarity when under the sea."

"So, I can feel and hear the sea at all times and I now possess exceptional sight. What magical powers does my ancestry provide me with?"

"Mermaids have only one. They can freeze space."

"Like stop time?"

"No, only Timestoppers can manipulate the time continuum. That is a very ancient and rare power and not one that is enacted without consequences. Bending time or stopping time means changing the vortex around something undefinable, the area where time and space connect. Mermaids can only freeze the space that time dictates. The things within the space are stopped while time is not."

Kai shrugged. "So, I can freeze people, things, or objects from moving but not time as we know it."

"Precisely. Time itself will continue moving forward."

She pulled herself up to stand unsteadily on her feet. Her head still ached, and she felt dizzy.

"I think you should continue to rest."

"I'm fine, and we are running out of time are we not?"

Sebastian nodded.

"Then let's see what I can do."

Walking over to the bridge, Sebastian plucked an icicle from the thick corded cables.

"Let's start small," he said, waving the icicle at Kai and sauntering to the open space at the center of the courtyard. "Concentrate on the icicle as it moves through the air. Stop its trajectory."

"Do I need to do anything special? Throw up my hands? Wave? Say a magic word?"

Sebastian smirked. "No. A mermaid's power is control of the mind. You just need to think."

"Okay." There was an uncertainty in her voice.

"Trust the ancient magic." Sebastian held out the large icicle, vaulting it high into the air. The clear ice reflected the rays of the moon as it twisted and turned skyward.

Kai held her breath. Her eyes never leaving the twisting icicle. Constantly tracking its trajectory as it sailed through space.

Freeze, she thought, willing the icicle to stop. Its momentum slowed as gravity worked against it, pulling it back toward the ground. Frustrated, she again concentrated, pushing the cool sensation washing over her skin outward. It flowed from her, pushing her magic through the cold air. An invisible current reached for the icicle.

There was a startling pop as exploding ice fragments scattered through the air, landing with a clinking thud on the ground.

"What happened?" Kai asked.

Sebastian stared at the shards littering the courtyard. "It seems your powers may be slightly different from your ancestors or currently uncontrolled. What was in your mind?

"I was thinking freeze, but the icicle kept falling, so I concentrated instead on the cool sensation flowing constantly over my skin. I pushed it out toward the icicle and willed it to stop."

Sebastian's face contorted. "That cool sensation is your connection to the sea. It is the ancient magic defining the water element. It seems, unlike your ancestors, you can manipulate that magic into an active magic, a weapon of sorts."

"Let's try again."

He retrieved another icicle instructing her to only use her mind this time. She did as he requested pushing out only her intention. This time the icicle spun momentarily before it froze, hanging motionless ten feet above the ground.

"Shit," Kai said.

Sebastian bowed his head in approval.

"Now what?"

"Release it."

"How."

"The same way. Use your mind to will it."

Kai looked back at the icicle still frozen in mid-air. It quivered. She thought about it hurtling through the surrounding space to catch up to the passing time. The icicle careened to the ground, smashing into a multitude of fragmented pieces.

Kai smiled, proud of herself.

Sebastian cast her a stern look. "You will need to practice. To control and use your power decisively without this being the result." He waved his hand at the shattered ice fragments. "For now, we need to get back to your world. The others will be waiting for our return. We can use the portal in the village center. It will take us back to the Elder Oak."

Kai sulked as she followed Sebastian toward the bridge linking the ice wall to the Frost Isles. *How was she to know he wanted her to put the icicle down gently? He really needed to learn to communicate better.*

As they reached the suspension bridge, the wind picked up. Metal cables creaked in the icy squalls blowing across the sea. The bridge swayed violently in the gusts. The Frost Isles were at sea level and the bridge crossed a vast chasm that connected the sea to the canals. A raging waterfall flowed just to the left of the bridge, thundering straight down into the canal mouth below.

Kai looked down. Her stomach wrenched at the distance.

"The bridge is safe, just be careful on the ice," Sebastian said, sensing her apprehension.

Kai began to move across the bridge, her steps tentative and her grip on the metal hand cable tight. Spray from the descending waterfall iced the metal floorboards. Wind gusts furiously battered the bridge sending it swaying precariously sideways. Her heel slipped, the awkward momentum sending her toward the edge. Her other hand grasped for the handrail but missed as a second strong gust lifted the bridge, tipping it. She felt her heel slip off into nothingness as she was propelled forward into the abyss. Her arms flailed as she desperately tried to grasp anything that would stop her fall. Her fingers grasped leather. A strong grip wrapped itself around her hand, but only for a moment, until gravity pulled her away. Sebastian's hand was the last thing she saw as she plunged toward the raging waters below.

As she fell, the cool sensation flowing over her skin intensified, exploding all around her in a cocoon of briny water. She heard the rumble of the waterfall escalate as she plummeted.

It was getting closer.

Unexpectedly, her feet righted themselves as if they had landed on something forgiving. Her fall slowed. Her trajectory shifted, and she was pushed back up toward Sebastian who peered over the bridge, his face a palette of disbelief.

The roar of the waterfall encircled her, and she could feel the gentle movement of the sea caressing her in its rocking motion. The ancient magic hummed in her ears as she drifted back from where she had fallen until she was level with Sebastian's curious expression.

"It would seem that you possess another power," he said, indicating the massive wave she stood upon. "You have the ability to manipulate the sea to your bidding."

Kai looked down at her feet, but they were not her feet at all. Her tail, the fins moving back and forth in the wave's surge were holding her upright. She had subconsciously summoned a wave to stop her fall.

In her terror, her magic had responded, and the sea had saved her.

CHAPTER 19

THE PORTAL TO DYWEN LED them directly to the courtyard. Dane was correct. The Elder tree standing at its center was a portal on this side. They searched the barracks but did not find Brannon nor any sign of Farrimore.

Moving through the corridors toward the training grounds, Dane wondered how Kai and Sebastian were. After Kai spoke to Ethan this morning, she seemed a little more at ease, but a sense of uneasiness still surrounded her as she went through the portal to Viccinius.

"I should have gone with her."

Rafe stopped. "Why? Sebastian is perfectly capable of handling the task."

Dane grinned. "I'm more worried about Sebastian being able to handle Kai."

The sound of laughter interrupted their conversation as it echoed through the corridor. The door at the end stood open and bright sunlight beckoned. As they emerged, Dane could see Brannon at the far end. His caramel skin glistened with sweat as he wielded a large sword. He swung the blade overhead driving it forward toward his opponent who quickly moved to avoid its path.

She could feel Rafe beside her, his energy exploding with love and pride.

"Tauria," he yelled.

She turned at the sound of his voice, a huge smile appeared on her face.

"Brother," she squealed, dropping the short blades she held in her hands and running toward him. She leaped into his embrace, her laughter exploding.

"Oh, how I have missed you."

"And I you," Rafe said putting her down.

He turned his attention to Brannon, who stood feet away.

"How long has she been awake?"

"Brother, I am right here. You can ask me," she huffed as she placed her hands on her hips and stuck out her bottom lip.

He smiled affectionately. "Then you may tell me."

"Brannon said it happened a few days after you left. Have you really been to the new world?" The excitement in her voice was undeniable.

"I have."

"What is it like? You must tell me everything. Does it have magic? When do I get to go?" She was almost breathless as the questions flew from her mouth.

"Easy, Tauria, first I need to know about your journey from stasis and how you have been since."

"I'm fine," she pouted.

Rafe looked at Brannon for confirmation.

"The first thing she did when she woke up was to eat three days' worth of food."

Everyone laughed including Tauria. "I was famished."

Farrimore's musical bellow erupted overhead. The large black bird soared in circles, dipping, and swooping. The sun reflected off its black feathers, sending a tinge of green sparkling outward. It continued to circle, getting lower and lower with each pass until with a melodic screech he landed gently on Rafe's shoulder.

"Hi, boy."

Farrimore responded by cocking his head, his eyes shining with what Dane could only glean was happiness at his master's return. He nudged Rafe with his head and pecked gently at his hair—a definite sign of affection.

"I think Farrimore missed you," Dane said.

Rafe smiled, stroking the large bird lovingly, "And I him."

Tauria snickered, turning her attention to Dane. "And you must be the prophesied Arcanist? The last of the Callathian bloodline?"

"Just Dane," she replied extending her hand.

Tauria grasped it heartily in both her own.

"Apparently you are much more than that," she whispered, eyeing both her and Rafe mischievously.

Rafe glared at Brannon who shrugged in response. "She is very persistent with her inquiries, and still very annoying."

Dane noticed the affectionate way Brannon looked at Tauria when he teased her. She wondered if Rafe knew how his best friend truly felt about his sister.

"It was meant to be a secret."

"Nonsense," Tauria retorted. "A binding should never be kept a secret. It is a huge honor." She paused, a shadow passing over her features. "But for my own flesh and blood to have found this connection with someone not of our time or place, well that is curious indeed. Fate must have much in store for you both."

"Do not read too much into it Tauria," Rafe scolded. "I see your eternal sleep did nothing to dampen your fantastical imagination."

"I only see what is right in front of me, brother. A binding of two worlds is a destiny far greater than any of us could imagine."

Dane looked deep into Tauria's eyes as she spoke. Although she was billions of centuries old, like her brother, she was frozen in time as a young woman of about nineteen or twenty. The ragged wisdom she held in her eyes hinted at a girl who had experienced much tragedy and been forced to grow up quickly.

"Well, now that is out in the open, there is something we need to show you." Brannon moved toward the gated side of the barracks, motioning for them to follow. He led them to the base of the guard tower. Opening the barred door, he gestured for them to enter before following them up the winding stairs to the top. From here they could see for miles in each direction. To the north, the peaks of Ardrin Gorm towered in the blue sky. To the southwest, the waterfall glistened under the sun's early morning rays, but it was what they saw in the far west that Brannon referred to.

The sky over the Dead Lands churned. Storm clouds gathered on the horizon as lightning flashed in their midst. Behind the dark pewter sky, a sickening greenish hue hovered. It surrounded the storm clouds and cast an eerie pale over the already unappealing landscape. The chaotic sky seemed to be gathering to the north of the Dead Lands above the underground caverns.

"It started two days ago and has been building ever since," Brannon said. "Something has infected the Dead Lands.

Dywen's magic is fighting back but whatever is out there, whatever is causing these storms, is ancient and evil."

"The ancient dark?" Dane asked, watching the storm clouds batter the horizon.

Rafe shook his head. "More likely, something the ancient dark has conjured up. With the magic of the Five Realms awakening, the ancient dark will harness its power and use it to try to release itself from its tomb."

"But if it is entombed below the earth, why would it be causing a disruption on Dywen?"

"That is an answer I do not have." Rafe frowned, looking at the portentous sky hovering over the Dead Lands. "But maybe the caverns do."

"Brannon and I were going to trek out there today," Tauria said.

Rafe glanced at his sister; then back to the threatening cloud bank. "We will all go. Brannon retrieve the portal ring. Just in case."

Brannon nodded and headed down the tower's steps followed closely by Tauria.

"Portal ring?" Dane asked.

Rafe's gaze broke from the distant horizon.

"Now Dywen's magic is awakened, and the Druidstone has been reactivated in Kaizi, we have the ability to use portal rings. Magically infused objects that create instant portals to other realms, negating the need for us to return to the main portals.

"And you can use this portal ring to open a portal anywhere?"

"Yes."

"Convenient."

"Unreliable," he countered.

"Excuse me?"

"Portal rings are erratic, an unstable magic and often unreliable."

"Then why use them?"

"Their use is only relevant in dire circumstances. Finding yourself in a realm different to where you wished to go, is often more favorable than the reason you used the portal ring in the first place."

"So, when you say unreliable you don't mean dangerous."

He smirked. "Only if you emerge on the other side in a precarious place. Come, we must leave soon before we lose more daylight." He squeezed her hand and disappeared into the shadows of the tower.

Dane turned her gaze drawn to the darkening landscape. A dread welled up inside her as lightning flashed menacingly behind the gray clouds hovering low over the Dead Lands. There was something out there, something connected to the ancient dark. She could feel its presence in her mind. It was waiting. The temperature in the air dropped as a chill slithered over her skin and the rattle of its laughter echoed briefly in her mind. The dark sky roiled and flashed in anger as a bone-chilling cold and the bitter taste of decay reached her senses.

"We need to hurry," she whispered.

CHAPTER 20

T HE FOUR OF THEM CLIMBED down the metal stairs into the cavern. A cold chill emanated from the walls as an icy sheen wrapped around their skin snuffing the heat from their bodies. They could hear Farrimore, somewhere in the sky above them as they descended. He too sensed the unstable energy and the Hawkitete warrior bird's melodic cry deepened. As he circled above his forceful and alerted tone followed them down into the shadows.

"There is something down here," Brannon whispered, his hand tightening on the hilt of his sword as they reached the floor of the cavern.

The cold was biting, the air deathly static, and a putrid stench drifted from the depths of the murky tunnels. Dane gagged as it filled her nostrils. The taste of rot soiled the back of her throat. Exposed skin, hot from the burning sun only moments ago, was now clammy and chilled. Sweat turned to frost.

Rafe hesitated as a hissing sound echoed from the depths of

the blackness filling the tunnels. He tensed at the noise, immediately turning to Tauria. Concern etched his features. Stretching out his hand toward her he said. "Take the portal ring and go, quickly. Straight to the royal citadel, you know the way. Find the others, bring them back here. Whatever is disrupting the energy of the Dead Lands is ruled by dark magic, and we may need the magic of more than one element to contain it."

Tauria moved forward and took the ring he offered, her eyes imploring him to let her stay.

"Please Tauria, for once, do as I ask."

Nodding she put the ring in her pouch and turned back toward the stairs.

"Get to the green lands before you open the portal. We are unable to determine how far this infestation of the Dead Lands extends, so be careful."

"I will not let you down brother."

Rafe squeezed her hand. A faint smile crossed his face as he looked at his little sister. "I know." His gaze flicked to the cavern opening. "Go now."

Without another word she turned and sprinted up the iron stairs. The sky above rumbled as she exited, churning in anger as the dark cloud bank snuffed out the warmth of the midday sun.

Rafe watched her ascend the ladder until she was out of sight. Reverting his attention back to Dane and Brannon he said. "Dark magic has been awakened and something down here is tainted by it. We must be vigilant."

They took the tunnel that led toward the room where he and Dane had found the Book of Realms. As they moved through the tunnels, she noticed more sigils of dark magic stained the walls.

"What do you think is down here?" She whispered to Brannon.

He shook his head and concern furrowed his brow. His eyes found hers in the dim light. "I do not know, but the energy pulsating from these caverns for the past few nights has been unstable. It is dark, archaic. Something is being awoken, and it is not of this world. Whatever is waiting in these caverns will not welcome our arrival."

Rafe signaled for silence as he stopped, raising his hand to halt their progress.

They were near the end of the tunnel, hidden in the shadows near the opening. She peered around Rafe's shoulder into an empty room. Sigils on the wall were sizzling, burning once again. Tendrils of fire cascaded down the walls and across the room's floor. The flames burned a path through the dirt and disappeared into the darkness of a tunnel on the far wall.

They moved silently through the charred room, tiptoeing over the flames as they followed its trail into the shadows. Dane could feel Rafe tense. His senses alert and searching for signs of trouble. His warrior magic surged under his skin as hers responded in kind.

They hadn't ventured far into these tunnels when they were here last, so she was unsure of where they were heading and what they would find.

"Should we wait for Tauria and the others?"

The lack of response from either warrior told her what she already suspected. These two never waited for anything, instead, running headlong into the unknown without fore-thought or fear. After years of battle, she assumed they would be ready for anything. Moving silently behind them, she hoped they knew how to handle whatever was waiting in these tunnels.

The air turned sour; a rancid stench of rot and decay. The smell intensified as they moved deeper into the tunnel, and she was forced to breathe through her mouth, using her hand as extra filtration. It didn't seem to bother Rafe or Brannon as much, but she noticed they inhaled less often.

Without warning, the tunnel began to shake. Dust and debris fell from the ceiling.

"Get down!" Rafe yelled, turning back to pounce on Dane, pushing her to the floor and using his body to shield her.

The shaking continued, accompanied by a splitting sound. The thud of falling stone echoed from somewhere further up the tunnel. A shudder rippled through the cavern as small rocks fell on top of them as they lay huddled on the floor. Eventually, the shaking ceased, and the dust diminished leaving only the putrid scent of decay and wet dirt to linger in the cold air. Dane untangled herself from Rafe and Brannon and stood, wiping her clothes of debris. They were only a few yards from the tunnel opening, and she could see a strange glow penetrate the dusty darkness from that direction. Slowly, she moved toward it, she could feel Rafe and Brannon close behind. As she reached the end of the tunnel, she pressed herself against the cavern wall, peering from the shadows into the cavern room. Her breath caught as she pulled back and pinned herself against the wall.

"What do you see?" Rafe asked.

"I'm not sure."

Rafe peered around her. There was a sickly yellow glow pervading the room. The light and the overwhelming stench were coming from open fissures in the cavern floor. The room was expansive and surrounded by jagged, rock walls. Moss clung to the damp stone as dirty water trickled from small cracks in their surfaces. Numerous fissures had split open the cavern floor. Some were only small crevices, but others were large openings that steamed and hissed. From these fractures, a yellow glowing mist rose.

Rafe moved around her and into the room inching his way to the edge of one of the fissures. Dane and Brannon followed, careful to test the ground before advancing around the smaller fractures.

"The energy here is dark."

Rafe nodded at Brannon, "I have felt this before."

"When?" Dane asked, her eyes never leaving the wide crevice at her feet. The foul yellow mist obscured the depths below, and she squinted trying to see farther down.

"It smells of the ancient dark, the foul stench that saturated these lands during the Great War. I have not smelled it since its defeat."

Suddenly, a gnarled hand appeared from the mist reaching over the side of the crevice and grasping the edge with long bony fingers. Cracked fingernails, soiled with centuries of dirt, clamored for a hold. Strands of peeled flesh hung from the finger bones, flapping with every clawing motion. The knuckles were grotesquely large. Gray withered skin stretched taut across them. The fingers clawed at the earth as they pulled whatever was attached upward.

Dane backed up slowly, her eyes unable to look away from the steaming fissure as the creature dragged itself up from the depths. One hand, then two appeared followed by bony, unnaturally long arms. A head emerged, the skull misshapen and cracked. Two large bone spurs protruded on either side like horns, the same withered gray skin so taut over the bone it was translucent.

The creature continued to pull itself up until its bony pointed chin reached the surface. It wore a gruesome smile of decaying teeth permanently plastered to its face as whatever skin had been part of its mouth had long decayed. Its nose and eyes were nothing more than sockets, hollow black holes of nothingness.

Dane held her breath, paralyzed by both fear and curiosity. The creature continued to rise from the crevice as other bony hands began to appear around the edge of the other fissures. Multiple creatures clambering from the open fissures as they dragged themselves from the cavern depths. Vacant black holes, which once held eyes, turned toward them. Gaping mouths moved noiselessly.

She heard Rafe whisper in her head—*daemons*.

As the word reverberated through her mind, her unyielding trance was broken as Brannon yelled—*RUN!*

The three of them bolted through the tunnels, jumping over the debris littering their path and running up the iron steps as fast as they could.

The sky above them was pewter gray. Thick clouds rolled in anger as flashes of lightning lit up the darkening horizon. The normal scorching temperature of the Dead Lands had dropped considerably as the storm threatened from above. The sky rumbled as the storm bank moved quickly, encasing them in its fury.

As they emerged from the shadowy cavern, they could hear the echo of chaotic scurrying below. Making their way through the tunnels behind them were daemons.

"Over there," Rafe said pointing to the largest of the rock formations.

Farrimore screeched overhead. The Hawkitete dipped low toward the cavern opening, talons stretched menacingly toward the danger he sensed below. He veered at the last minute as he caught sight of his master fleeing, his strong wings pushing through the air, propelling him forward until he was flying protectively over Rafe.

By the sounds emanating from the cavern depths, they were most likely outnumbered. Their chances of making it back to the green lands before they were overrun were slim. Their only chance was to find cover and do their best to hold the daemons off, hoping Tauria and the others would make it back in time. Even with their combined powers, they probably wouldn't last long against an unknown number of daemons summoned by dark magic.

Dane ran behind Rafe and Brannon, her legs burning as she pushed them to move faster. Her skin prickled as the magic inside her warned of the danger emerging from the cavern behind. She could hear the wailing. A terrible screech magnified by the emptiness of the Dead Lands and the increasing cloud cover. Instinctively, she glanced over her shoulder.

The daemons scrambled over the edge of the cavern, a chaotic mass falling over one another as they climbed from the hole. They were unlike anything she could imagine, a hybrid of skeleton, rotting corpse, and alien. Some loped along on all fours, others wobbled unsteadily moving on limbs and feet barely attached by ligaments and bone. Some were faster, others more intact, but many were a decomposed, mangled, pulp of sunken eyes, withered muscles, and sallow, oozing, gray skin. They were never human, just decaying skeletons raised from their dark tombs by an archaic power.

She ran faster as daemons poured from the caverns in a

comical mad scramble. Some fell backward into the hole while others were trampled underfoot.

"Dane over here."

Tearing her eyes away from the grotesque mob she quickened her pace, following Rafe and Brannon as they darted around the large rock formation. She leaned against the backside, her breath labored as she tried to speak.

"There are so many," she gasped, her hands finding her knees as she struggled to catch her breath.

Rafe peeked around the edge. The storm had hastened its advance, angry dark clouds sunk lower in the sky. The wind swirled up dust from the Dead Lands dry, cracked surface. Lightning flashed behind the cloud bank, creating an ominous backdrop for the large herd of daemons careening toward them.

"We need to go up. We need the vantage point."

Brannon glanced toward the top of the rock formation. The only foothold was about ten feet up. Beyond, he could see nothing, as the rock wall narrowed.

"We can get Dane up there," he said, moving to a spot beside the rock, motioning for Rafe to join him.

Rafe looked up at the rock face and immediately knew what Brannon was suggesting. He joined him and together they formed a foothold with their hands.

"We need to throw you, Dane. You must grasp that ledge."

She nodded, eyeing the position of the rock shelf before climbing onto their hands. Before she could tell them, she was ready, she felt herself vaulting upward. Their combined strength easily lifted her toward the ledge. She reached out, her fingertips grazing the rock as she felt her momentum begin to fall back toward the ground. Fingertips found the ledge, desperately clawing for a hold as she crashed into the side of the rock. The force made her gasp as ribs collided with stone. Her fingers began to slip, the dirt and sweat on her skin betraying her as she scrambled to find a foothold before she fell. The toe of her boot hit a small divot in the rock face. She pushed it in, the stability allowing her to steady her momentum, regain control of her flailing body, and catch her breath.

"Hurry Dane," Rafe yelled. "You need to control the onslaught, attack at the center. Force them to either side of the rock formation."

Her aching muscles screamed as she pulled herself upward. The ledge was wider than she thought, and she rolled onto it. Her ribs ached from the impact, but she got to her feet and searched desperately for a way to the top. The ledge disappeared around the side of the rock face. She followed it, hoping it would lead up. As she rounded the boulder, the ledge sloped back down, ending abruptly. Her eyes scanned the rock face as the screech and howl of the daemons echoed through the stormy air. She noticed a series of indents in the rock face, and she used them to haul herself up the rest of the way.

From the peak, the entire Dead Lands spread before her. She guessed she was about thirty feet above Rafe and Brannon. She scanned the sky. The storm was almost upon them. A band of rain distorted the horizon to the northeast and dark clouds rolled in fury all around them. Glancing back toward the cavern, she saw daemons still emerging from its depths, the horde quickly multiplying in size.

There were hundreds or more—and only *three* of them.

CHAPTER 21

D ANE WATCHED THE DAEMONS ADVANCE toward the rock formation. They were slow, clumsy, and fragmented, half-crazed daemon corpses, infected by the dark magic that created and controlled them. Their chaotic movement made it difficult to be certain of their numbers, but the horde emerging from the fissures was impressively large.

As she watched them stumble across the dry earth, she wondered how long they had been concealed under the caverns.

Were they buried there during the Great War?

The sky rumbled, bringing her back from her thoughts. The clouds rolled with anger, belching out flashes of lightning and exacerbating the horror moving at a steady pace toward them. Her eyes scanned the horizon hoping for a sign that Tauria had found the others but there was nothing, only miles of cracked earth.

They were on their own.

The screeches from the daemons drew closer. The horde

was a mass of sunken eyes and shriveled bodies. She held out her hands, the energy of the Warlician sizzling and spitting in her palms as she readied herself to attack. When she was confident they were within range, she fired, aiming at the ones in the middle first, and splitting the horde in two at its center.

She threw energy balls, one after another, her intention causing the energy to strike its target and instantly rebound back to her. The daemons were weak, and the impact sent them scattering, one knocking down others as it fell. The energy was disruptive and destructive and the daemons fragile, decomposed bodies fell apart under the power of her weapon. Limbs flew in the air, flesh ripped further off the body, as bones cracked and broke. A thick black sludge squirted from new wounds as the daemons shrieked and wailed in pain or anger, she could not tell which. The bone-chilling howl mingled with the roar of the wind and blanketed the Dead Lands in the sound of death.

As she obliterated the middle of the mob, the daemons instinctively moved outward, away from her destructive path. Like a ghastly river, they flowed toward the sides of the rock formation where Rafe and Brannon stood waiting to attack. She could see a subtle green glow from below as they too joined the fight, more daemons disintegrating into piles of decaying, sludgy rot.

Farrimore flew near the middle of the herd diving from the sky directly into the daemons. His claws tore flesh from bone then immediately he soared skyward with gore hanging from his long talons. As he turned for another attack, his wings flapped furiously, and a distinctive melodic caw pierced the sky, drowning out the painful wails of his victims. The daemons seemed oblivious to Farrimore's presence, none looked skyward or reacted as he struck, their focus solely on the three warriors.

Churning clouds hovered low over the area reflecting the bright green of their magic and turning the entire battleground into an eerie phantasmagoria of horror. It also amplified the deafening shrieks piercing the air as the three of them continued to hurtle energy balls in quick succession.

The daemons did not stop their onslaught, even as their numbers were decimated by the Warlician weapon. Those that lost limbs found a way to crawl forward. Others continued mindlessly until they too fell under the powerful magic. The daemons weren't organized, they didn't have a battle plan, they were pawns brought back from the grave by dark magic with only one purpose—*destruction*.

The sky opened, and rain began to fall. Slowly at first, then faster until a sheet of water blurred the landscape and turned the dry, cracked earth into a muddy wasteland.

She kept firing energy balls at the mob, but as one fell another clamored forward to take its place. Their efforts thinned the herd, but they could not all be stopped. They were outnumbered. The daemons not rerouted to the sides of the rock formation clawed at the stone below her. Dead black eyes stared upward. She continued to assault the back half of the herd, but torrential rain blurred her targets. Wiping water from her eyes, she glanced over the edge. The green glow below had ceased, the sound of energy balls whizzing through the air, gone. Only the screech of the creatures, the eerie skittering noise they made, and the pounding rain echoed below. She couldn't sense Rafe or Brannon. The torrential rain and tortured evil stained the air suffocated their energy. She searched desperately for any sign of them, but the rock's foundation was too wide, and she was unable to see all the way to its base.

Suddenly, the sound of clanging metal echoed through the air, indicating that at least one was still fighting. Someone yelled and another replied. A sense of relief washed over Dane.

They are both OK.

Movement drew her eyes toward the far end of the rock as long bony fingers appeared, gripping the edge. Pulling her sword from its sheath, she watched as the creature pulled itself up and over the side. This one was stronger and more intact than the others. Although covered with the same taut, gray, withered skin, it was mostly unscathed, the decay limited to only a few small sheaths of flesh hanging from its body. Sticky black blood oozed from its wounds but was quickly washed away by the rain. One eye, fused shut, had sunk into the socket, the other a large black globe protruding grotesquely from the skull. The small circle of white sclera surrounding it was marred with red veins and the yellow glow of dark magic throbbed intensely behind the engorged socket. Slowly, it turned its gaze toward her.

The daemon seemed disoriented at first, wobbling on its shriveled feet, seemingly confused by its surroundings. The slick surface of the rock made it difficult for it to find its balance and it slipped a couple of times.

With a macabre curiosity, Dane watched it flounder.

It turned in circles grunting until whatever facilities it possessed sensed her. Its head jerked as it tried to screech. Black ooze ran from the cavity at the center of its face where a nose should be. Its mouth nothing more than a small round hole of rotten flesh that muffled any sound it attempted to make.

The wind picked up swiftly as the storm front blanketed the Dead Lands. Rain lashed at her skin as she waited for the daemon to draw near. As it moved toward her, she could feel the chaotic sting of dark energy and the putrid decaying scent wafting around it.

"Here boy," she taunted, raising her sword. Green sparks flew from her hands as they grasped the hilt, the ancient magic igniting the blade in a pulsating light. Timing her blow she careened forward leaping sideways as she swung. The blade sliced through the rain-soaked air before it connected with decaying flesh.

The daemon howled, a piercing screech that resonated through the chilled sky. A chorus of howls erupted below. Daemons mimicked one another, their pain and suffering one. As she followed her momentum, she glanced quickly at the scene below. Daemons clamored forward, climbing up the rock face by using the body parts of their fallen brethren as a macabre ladder.

They will be up here in no time, she thought, swinging the sword through the air as the daemon advanced toward her.

The sword cut deep into its rotting torso. Black sludge spilled from the wound. Maggots fell to the ground in its wake as the blade severed flesh and bone.

She followed the sword's momentum, spinning and driving the blade forward for another blow. The daemon's neck tore, the sharp steel severing it almost all the way through. Its final scream was a gargle of blood and mangled flesh. Its head lolled to one side before completely ripping away from its body and rolling silently to her feet as the rain pelted down on its distorted features.

Kicking the head away, she turned to defend her position from the others making their way up the side of the rock. The rain began to diminish and the mist that seized the Dead Lands started to disperse. She could hear the clash of metal below and the shriek of daemons as they were felled by the blades.

Behind her, a bellow erupted. The loud, raspy roar reverberated through the dark, thunderous clouds. Her head jerked upward, eyes searching for the source of the noise. The clouds were low and thick and whatever was making that sound was above them.

Another roar erupted, closer this time.

It shook the ground, and she stumbled. Steadying herself she glanced skyward just as a stream of flame blazed from the clouds. The fire scorched a trail across the dried earth, incinerating the daemons caught in its path. A large shadow crossed overhead, hidden by the black clouds and strobe-like flashes of lightning. She watched as it turned and at an impressive speed move back toward the battlefield. The clouds ignited again in a fiery orange glow, a brilliant eruption behind the thick gray barrier. This time, the shadow broke through the cloud bank, blasting flame across the barren landscape as it dipped and soared toward her.

As it drew near, charring a scar across the encrusted earth, she could see eyes of fiery orange. They were embedded in a dark, wispy cluster of translucent smoke. Tendrils streamed from its massive wings as it flew overhead. Its long smoke tail left a trail of blazing embers as it cut through the dark sky.

A dragon!

A dragon yes, but this one was not real, not flesh and bone, nor a living breathing entity. This was a specter, a phantom image of a dragon made of wispy smoke, embers, and blazing fire. An apparition. Its entire form translucent and fluid. Its wings, tail, body, and head morphed as the wind caught the smoke, swirling it around until it found its way back to its original form. The dragon was enormous, its roar deafening, the blaze dispelled from its mouth —destructive.

Stevie. Dane thought, searching the dark, smoky battlefield for any sign of her friend.

Another roar bellowed through the sky as the dragon passed overhead. Its enormity made her duck instinctively as she covered her ears attempting to block its deafening roar. It swooped lower as it circled the dark sky, scorching the earth and engulfing crowds of daemons in the fire it expelled from its lethal breath. They shrilled as they burned, their corpses collapsing upon one another in a massive pyre. Smoldering embers littered the Dead Lands as billowing clouds of dense black smoke streamed skyward.

She ran to the edge, sword at the ready but the daemons climbing the rock were gone. As she stared at the chaos in front of her, something in the distance caught her eye. She squinted toward the far horizon where the Dead Lands bordered the lush green lands. Emerging from the smoke-filled mist were four figures—faint shadows on a darkening horizon. They were moving quickly toward the rock formation, running toward the danger. A brilliant flash of lightning exploded overhead, illuminating the entire landscape and their faces.

Dane felt a surge of relief as she saw them—*Tauria had succeeded.*

She scrambled from the top of the rock, finding her way quickly to the lower ledge. Dropping onto a pile of black oozing daemon corpses she looked around. Rafe and Brannon had been busy. Severed body parts littered the area. Dead daemons, the yellow glow extinguished from their dead black eyes, lay scattered. Their bodies displayed the wounds inflicted by the warrior's blades.

Hurrying around to the front of the rock formation, she caught sight of Rafe. His long hair flew around him as he slashed his sword in an arc, cutting through three daemons in one blow. Brannon was to his left, trying desperately to remove the corpse of a daemon from the blade of his sword. Its body was limp and heavy, and the sword had wedged sideways between its ribs.

Dane ran toward him, her sword plunging into the daemon coming up behind him. The tip of her sword narrowly missed Brannon as he turned to defend himself, a smaller blade in hand.

"Thanks," he said, his bright eyes dancing with glee as he used his boot to dislodge the daemon from his sword.

"Having fun, are we?" Dane inquired.

"Nothing better than being in battle. I've missed it."

Winking, he raised his hand, summoning an energy ball and hurtling it forwards. It exploded against a daemon the size of a giant who was emerging from the thick smoke still stifling the area. The energy ball burnt a hole right through the middle of the daemon's chest, but it did not fall, instead, it only enraged it further.

"Uh-oh, not good," Brannon said as he retrieved the rebounding energy. Raising his sword, he charged toward the giant daemon.

Dane followed.

As she ran, she saw Killenn and Drow emerge from the haze, weapons raised. Tauria and Stevie appeared seconds later. Tauria aimed her arrow at a daemon, piercing its skull directly in the middle of its forehead. Stevie ran behind her, no weapon in hand, her katana still strapped to her back. Her hands were raised in front of her, a dark gray smoke, weaved its way back and forth between her palms. Diego was pacing, circling his master, teeth bared, ready to attack any stray daemon that threatened her.

As she and Brannon reached the giant daemon, a ghastly roar erupted overhead as the dragon circled the battlefield. Dane looked back at Stevie. *She's controlling the smoke dragon!* She thought, noticing Stevie's hands circling one another, the gray smoke between them a swirling ring.

She averted her attention back to the enormous daemon in front of her. Its rage seethed as black sludge spilled from the hole in its chest. The daemon's mouth was sewn shut by strips of scarred skin, raw strands stretched from lip to lip. The sounds it made as Brannon slashed its legs were guttural, an anguished growl. It flailed, long clawed fingers swiping at Brannon who ducked, whirled and plunged his blade into the daemon's leathery skin.

"Its knees and ankles," Brannon yelled, "We need to get it to fall."

She nodded, running quickly to the back of the giant while Brannon kept his attention. She held her sword with both hands, the length of the blade at shoulder height. It dripped with sticky black blood, but the green energy still throbbed fiercely through the blade.

The razor-sharp edge sliced through the giant's ankles severing flesh, tendons, and bone. The daemon howled, its glowing eyes turned back, its sharp claws reached for her. It was like watching the felling of a tree. The ankles snapped, no longer able to hold the weight. Its knees buckled in response and its momentum tilted downward, arms thrashing in a weak attempt to stop its descent. The giant daemon toppled. Unable to stop itself from falling it bellowed, a horrible, ear-shattering and booming wail that reverberated through the battlefield. Other daemons joined in, their moans and shrieks combining into a disturbing chorus of horror.

The torrential rain had left the Dead Lands saturated with large puddles unable to pierce the dry hard terrain. The giant daemon landed in one, displacing water in a large splash. It struggled to get back up, but Brannon reacted quickly leaping onto its back and driving his sword through the back of its head. The daemon was silenced instantly.

Dane looked around, wiping the sweat and blood from her brow. The smoke had dispersed and although a heavy mist covered the battlefield she could see Rafe, Killenn, and Tauria standing together at the center of the massacre. Their backs were toward one another, their stance defensive, as daemons advanced from all sides. The yellow glow of the daemon's eyes cut through the gray gloom—they were surrounded by dozens of daemons.

Brannon had also noticed their predicament and was running toward the back of the herd slashing and cutting but there were too many. The daemons gathering around them had cut them off from the others.

Stevie was standing off to their right with Drow. The smoke between her palms still swirled like a vortex as the dragon circled the sky overhead. She locked eyes with Dane and shook her head. Dane knew she couldn't send in the dragon, the risk to Rafe and the others was too dire. She looked back at the advancing herd, closing in from all sides. A panic welled inside her. She could feel the ancient magic surge through her blood, its essence swirling under her skin. Her mind raced, trying to come up with a solution.

Drow had moved in to help Brannon, slashing at the daemons in the back but neither was making headway.

She caught Rafe's eye.

I love you, whispered in her head as she watched him raise his sword slashing at the daemons as they closed in.

Helplessness consumed her, followed by fear and grief. A myriad of emotions battered her as she stood watching him fight for his life. A tear ran down her cheek as an unnerving sense of calm came over her. The magic inside was changing. The ancient energy morphed into something else as it surged through her blood with a determined focus, an eruption of power waiting to be released.

Instinctively she knew what to do.

Bending down she lay her hand flat on the surface of the muddy, rain-drenched ground. In response, a seismic pressure built in her body, thundering through her blood toward her hand. Within seconds, it bolted through her arm and into the earth, causing a rumble that spread outward through the dry, cracked surface. Concentrating, she envisioned the earth, the daemons, the bowels of the caverns, and she willed them back to where they had come from.

The mud beneath her hand began to tremble. The water on its surface rippled, then sloshed upward. A crack appeared in the barren ground beneath her palm then raced outward toward the edge of the herd. It widened as it stretched, the earth collapsing into the large crevice, pulling shrieking daemons into the bowels of the Dead Lands.

The cavernous split engulfed the area in front of her, the daemons succumbing to its trajectory. Brannon and Drow turned as the crevice raced past them. They leaped over the crack to safety as it continued its destructive path, circling the horde and mercilessly sending daemons into the abyss.

CHAPTER 22

T HEY STOOD IN THE RAIN as blood and mud ran in rivers around their feet. All the daemons had perished. Some fell to their deaths into the bowels of the Dead Lands, others were incinerated by the powerful fires of the smoke dragon or sliced to pieces by blades and arrows.

Corpses littered the area. The stench of black blood overwhelmed Dane's nostrils as she watched Rafe put his sword through the skull of the last remaining daemon still moving.

A black shadow seeped through her mind followed by a rattled scream as the ancient dark recognized its defeat. A piercing, anguished, and guttural noise filled her mind with its ire. She smiled at the fury she felt arcing through its still imprisoned soul, a searing rage bore from disbelief. She had learned quickly to control her connection with the entity. It was still in her mind, but it no longer affected her as it first had and that alone was a victory. The scream faded as the ancient entity retreated into the shadows of the dark realm where it was still trapped. It would regroup, use its rage to gain more power and find those in these worlds that it could manipulate and control. It would continue to try to kill them before they reached their full power but for now, the battle was over—*they had won.*

Dark smoke curled skyward from the pyres of daemons still burning. A fetid odor wafted through the air in its wake. The Dead Lands were covered with black blood and decaying corpses. A low, gray mist shrouded the battlefield after the storm but now a blue sky could be seen peeking through the billowing smoke.

Dane and Brannon clambered over the carcasses as they worked their way to the others.

"Are you alright?" Rafe said, his eyes showing his concern even though his voice was even.

She caressed his cheek in response, the familiar heat of emotions washing over her as relief flooded through her. "I'm fine."

Turning she smiled at Tauria, who stood at the edge of the charred bodies picking her arrows from their corpses. Her sword hung from her hip, the tip dripping the black, oily sludge leaking from the daemons severed limbs.

"Thank you," she mouthed, a knowing look passing between them.

Tauria nodded in response then turned and walked over to Brannon. Dane watched as he put his hand gently on her lower back, his head leaning down to whisper something in her ear. She turned to see if Rafe had noticed the intimate moment between his sister and best friend, but he was speaking in hushed tones with Killenn and Drow. She walked over to Stevie. The smoke dragon was gone but the red dragon emblazoned on her leather breastplate was marred by daemon blood and soot. "You good?"

"Of course."

"What were you doing?" Dane asked, her mouth curving up at the corner as she raised a brow. "The smoke between your hands."

Stevie shook her head and smiled. "I could ask you the same thing." She picked up Dane's hand and brushed her fingers over the palm where the green energy still flashed below the surface.

Dane smiled. "Seems we both have secrets."

"Apparently not anymore," Stevie responded, her gaze drifting to the corpses scattered across the Dead Lands. Smoke drifted up toward the sky and the smell of decay and burning skin lay heavy in the air. "I conjured a smoke dragon."

"It was impressive."

Stevie shrugged. "I'm still getting used to the magic. I was lucky that I controlled it for that long."

"It seems Drow was correct."

She nodded. "He told me you spoke of my family powers. It seems to not only skip generations but also to exist through time and space."

"How did you know? I mean, that you had this power."

"It was not long after you left. Killenn and I were training in the quarry when I had a vision. The Dragon Flame called to me and suddenly I stood before it. Whispers echoed off the cavern walls and the lava pool began to bubble as four dragons rose from it. They were the origin dragons, and they told me I could conjure their spirits whenever I needed."

Dane thought about the strange gray smoke she had seen

hovering around Stevie as they entered the portal. *Was it her power already manifesting?*

"How do you do it?"

"Honestly I'm not sure. I just clear my mind and envision the magic in my hands, willing the spirit dragon forward. I have only been able to conjure Sar, the smoke dragon to this point. Killenn says it is always easier to connect with the blood from which you were born, but in time, the others will come."

Dane laughed looking around at the devastation. "I think the Sar will do just fine for now."

Stevie nodded, smiling. "There is something else."

Dane looked at her friend.

"I can manipulate and control the fire element like you did with the earth."

"What do you mean, like I did?"

"The ground, causing it to crack open underneath the daemons."

"I don't know how I did that."

"We are born from the elements and our magic is ruled by them, but only we can control the element itself."

Dane cocked her head and frowned. "You seem to know a lot about our powers."

Stevie motioned to Killenn. "He is a wealth of information. It seems Killenn has spent many centuries unearthing information about the prophecy and its meaning."

"And he believes what I did is because I can control the element earth?"

"Yes, just as I made the volcano on Kaizi erupt."

Dane's eyebrows lifted in surprise. "You did what?"

Stevie grinned. "It started with candle flames and fireplaces but within a few days, my connection to fire was intrinsic. I could bend it to my will, even summon it from nothingness. The volcanic eruption was an accident. Killenn had irked me and it seems my magic like Gabby said, is unrestrained."

Dane thought about how panicked she felt right before her new power flowed through her. The jumble of emotions that surfaced at the thought of losing Rafe. Did intense emotions activate an ability to manipulate their elements?

"You and I have much to discuss," she said, throwing her arm around her best friend's shoulder.

"I've missed you," Stevie said. "Let's go home."

A shiver crawled up Dane's spine as she glanced back at the daemons, wondering if this is what would come from the pods at the old mill.

CHAPTER 23

LILITH STARED AT THE PODS as their sickening color gained intensity. The ominous glow they emitted doused the entire interior of the mill in a strange yellowish-brown candescent light. She closed her eyes, rubbing her forehead as a headache began to throb.

How long had it been since she had seen the witch?

She couldn't recall. Her days were hazy, her nights a blur of rituals and spells, none of which she could remember in detail the following day. She awakened each morning to paraphernalia scattered across the mill, symbols carved into surfaces, and the scent of sulfur lingering in the air.

Pacing back and forth across the dusty planked floor of the old mill, she tried to collect her thoughts. Small inklings of memory surfaced but disappeared into the dark recesses of her mind before she could grasp them. She pulled on a strand of long red hair, twisting it around her index finger. Her hands shook—another thing that started in the last few days she had no control over.

The witch, the witch, the witch, Lilith thought as her pace increased. She thumped her forehead with her palm trying desperately to keep the focus on the reason she was in this mill, this town.

She wanted revenge! *Yes!*

A shrill cackle escaped from her throat and echoed off the shadows of the mill's interior. It mingled briefly with the monotone hum resonating from the strange pods before it disappeared into the night. Wringing her hands, she began to mutter as once again her mind drifted.

She stopped pacing and turned toward the pods. The light pulsating underneath their surface reflected off her sallow skin, and she cocked her head and frowned. The humming had gotten louder and there was a strong scent of decay wafting through the mill. Hesitantly, she approached the pods, her breath shallow as she tried not to gag at the disgusting scent. As she walked in between them, her trembling hand touched their surface. It was warm and slightly moist but not wet like water, slicker with the consistency of petroleum jelly. She glanced down at her fingertips. There was nothing apparent on her skin. Her fingers grazed over the texture of the pods surface. It was a thin and grainy membrane covered with a glossy substance that didn't transfer from its host.

She stopped at a larger pod. The light from inside throbbed metrically, and she leaned over, her curiosity pulling her toward its innards. There was a soft mist hovering just inside the skin of the pod. It clouded her view, but as she leaned closer it parted, and saw a hint of what lay beneath. Startled, she leaped back, colliding with the pod laying behind her. Its innards throbbed in response. Her mind spiraled at the image of its contents, and she ran. Her feet pounded the floorboards and her breath heaved as fear spurred her forward up the stairs and away from the horror below. She didn't stop until she entered the room she called home. Closing the door tight behind her she leaned on the wall, trying to catch her breath. Her heart pounded in her chest and her skin was coated with a cold, clammy sweat.

Lilith clawed at the scarf tied loosely around her neck, yanking it from her throat and gasping in a lungful of stale, dusty air. Her pulse quickened as a terrified chill slithered over her skin.

What are those things?!

Her mind was constantly draped in haze and because of the blackouts, she'd been having there were large periods of time unaccounted for. Blindly she searched her mind for answers, any sort of recognition as to what those horrible things were laying below the membrane and mist.

Where had the pods come from? They were not here before her last blackout, or were they? Was it her? Had she used magic somehow to create these things?

She lifted her shaking hands up in front of her. They looked so different now. The blue of her veins was easily visible through the pale, loose skin. Her hands were wrinkled and covered with a discolored mottle, but it was the tips of her fingers that worried her. They were scarred with small criss-crossing lines, thin cuts that had healed into raised welts. The tip of each finger had turned gray. Her nails were broken, dry, and cracked, the cuticles darkened by a garish red that oozed bloody pus.

Lilith rushed to the table frantically pushing bottles of elixirs and tonics aside. Scattered across the table's surface were numerous dusty, old tomes, and she flipped feverishly through their pages. Finding nothing that would ease her panic she reached for the family tome.

It was not on the pedestal where she kept it.

Her eyes scanned the dusty table but the large, thick book was not among the contents. The panic began to rise, a suffocating tide of stifling terror that threatened to consume her sanity, worming its way closer to the surface.

She screamed silently in her head. *Where is the book?*

Her eyes darted back and forth around the room until they spied it open on the floor and hidden by the shadows. She lunged at it. Falling to the floor she yanked the dusty and tattered tome toward her. As it emerged from the shadows, she noticed it was open to a page she could not recall seeing before. The page fluttered, and a strange black dust drifted upward from the gutter.

She studied the words on the page and the image that accompanied the next. The black ink and the ancient scrawl were unlike anything she had seen before. Her fingers grazed the fragile page. A bolt of electricity rifled through her, searing a path up her arm and into her darkened soul. An overpowering anguish expanded in her heart and her breath halted in her chest. Tendrils of time splintered in her consciousness as she found herself slipping into a memory not her own. A vision of a dark, distant place wrapped around her mind as the memory pulled her into a time and place not her own.

She stood, an invisible sentinel in a world burning. Time fluctuated around her, pulling her through its threads; then pushing her out the other side. Her conscious mind was aware, but her physical body was detached, useless in the memory of a past long gone.

Pain and suffering leeched from the surface of this world. The scent of decay and seared souls floated past her on a warm wind. Besieged by revulsion she felt a presence, a darkness cast from the light of this world, yet embedded in its very fabric. It was all around her; flowing through the blood rivers tainting the dry earth, submerged in the magical essence as it flickered to its end. It existed in the wind as it carried the scent of death and in the agonizing screams penetrating the silent echo of time.

A crippling fear ran through her blood as the darkness consumed her. It slithered inside her mind, cold malevolent tendrils ravaging her thoughts unimpeded. She cried out in pain desperate to stop the invasion. It scoured her memories, quickly discarding the very few she held dear and leaving only those filled with heartache, loss, tragedy, and suffering.

It found her revenge. The black seed of hate cultivating at the very depths of her soul and twisted it into an obsession, a desire, a desperate yearning that would not be sated. An unyielding need encapsulated her very being as anguish spread like a virus through her. She was consumed by this evil. The darkness fed off her hate, draining the energy from her body and leaving only the darkest, most tragic, and broken parts behind—a shell of utter despair.

As her mind undulated with a murky haze and the stench of rot and decay overwhelmed the last of her senses, she knew she was lost forever. The last thing she heard as she slipped from this world back to her own was a chilling laughter and three little words echoing in her mind.

You are mine.

CHAPTER 24

S HE STOOD AT THE BASE of the tree, hidden in the shadows cast by its girth, careful not to be caught by the glare from the streetlight across the way. The park was empty this time of night, the downtown quiet as the temperatures had dipped below freezing. She tugged at the collar of her jacket as the wind whipped by, more from habit than need as the cold did not bother her.

She was immune to human frailties.

Her eyes scanned the street, stopping at the front door of the law firm where Elyse worked. Lights blazed in the windows. Not that she was surprised. Elyse worked longer hours since Cal had gone overseas. It helped ease the loneliness.

She checked her watch.

Five more minutes.

Her fingers drummed the cold bark as she leaned against the trunk. She was impatient and did not like to wait. She was unaccustomed to the lack of precision in this world. It seemed to thrive on the obscure and a chaotic pace. Everyone ran around mindlessly, never seeming to know what or where they were going in life.

Purpose seemed to lack among humans. She thought as another gust of wind blustered through the park. She did not understand why beings with an extremely short lifespan would not focus on accomplishing something every single day they existed. They wasted so much time on frivolous pursuits.

Her thoughts were interrupted by the opening of a door. She watched as both Elyse and Marlee exited the building, laughing as they huddled against the cold wind. She waited until they rounded the corner before emerging from the shadows. Her pace quickened as she crossed the street after them. They were heading to dinner, and she wanted to catch them before they entered the restaurant.

Careful to remain hidden in the shadow of the buildings, she followed. Ducking into a side alley, she ran, crisscrossing behind buildings until she found the exit she wanted. Before stepping into the sidewalk, she glanced cautiously around the corner. The street was empty. She stepped from the alley and began walking back in the direction of the law firm. As she saw them coming toward her, she turned the corner. Their heads were down, hunched against the strong wind coursing along the street.

Gabby pulled her shoulders back and plastered a smile on her face ready to greet them.

"Elyse, Marlee," she said as she met them. "What a nice surprise."

"Gabby, what are you doing in Brighton Hill? I thought you were heading out of town with Stevie and Dane."

"I had a few things to take care of at the store," she lied. She had not been to *Aether* for weeks. After she reverted Stevie and Dane thought it best if Gabby's long-time store manager ran the business for a while.

"Well, it's good to see you. We haven't seen much of you, Stevie, or Dane since our girl's weekend," Elyse said.

Gabby nodded, shaping her face into a look she hoped would pass as regret. "I know, everyone is so busy."

"We were just heading to The Brew House for a burger. Why don't you join us?"

Gabby smiled, "I would love to, but I am meeting someone. Rain check?"

"Of course," Marlee said, hugging her friend. "Soon."

Gabby nodded, waving as they walked away.

"Soon," she whispered, knowing it would never come. She headed back to the park, keeping her head down trying to look like she was bothered by the weather. When she reached the tree, she huddled into its shadow, her brow furrowing as the intense tingling in her blood diminished.

Marlee's scent clung to her skin. The light subtle fragrance wafted around her. The scent of the *fae*.

Dane had been right. Marlee and Elyse were the other two Arcanists.

It had not taken Gabby very long to detect their blood. Fairy scents are fragrant and light but extremely overt, elves even more so. The essence of elven blood made the blood of the celestial tingle. An elemental imbalance in elven magic coupled with their ability to control a person's sight affected the ether embedded in celestial blood. The tingle was an adverse reaction to their proximity. Gabby hated elvenkind; besides their stoic and haughty attitudes, they were the only race from her world that made her feel uneasy.

Their magic was powerful, rooted in an archaic belief that the element air was superior to all the others. It had caused much friction over the centuries between their clans and the other races, many of which ended in bloodshed. It was not until after the war between the elves and the fae that the elven brethren realized their existence depended on a peaceful coexistence with all the other magical beings. They became bearable after that, but Gabby still found them to be the least appealing of the races. Shaking off the remaining tendrils of elven energy, she concentrated on what this discovery meant. They had found all the Arcanists and by daybreak, all but the air realm would be awakened by the Druidstones infusing the ancient worlds with potent magic.

She stood at the base of the tree for a long time. Hidden by the shadows she watched the few people who dared venture out of their warm homes and businesses on this cold winter evening, scurry by. Although she could vividly remember her life as a human, she could no longer connect with the sentiments she had experienced as one. Since reverting, all sense of human emotion had been lost, and she had become entirely detached from her mortal existence. What she had not lost was the understanding of how significantly different her two selves were. She saw it in the eyes of Dane and Stevie.

She also saw disappointment.

It did not trouble her for she was not like them. She was an ancient immortal from another time not a descendant of her race. They did not understand. How could they? They would only ever accept the human she no longer was.

Gabby sighed as she turned and walked deeper into the park, sinking further into the shadows where she found comfort. She was an immortal lost in a world she no longer understood. A supernatural being who longed for the life she once knew—a long forgotten past that lay buried under the ashes of evil.

CHAPTER 25

"YOU WERE RIGHT," GABBY SAID as Dane and Rafe walked through the door.

"About what?"

"The others. Elyse and Marlee."

Sebastian and Kai sat at the kitchen counter the Book of Realms open in front of them.

Dane sighed, "You confirmed, they are the other Arcanists then?"

"The scent of the fae on Marlee is unmistakable, and the other is definitely elvenkind."

"You mean Elyse." Kai snapped.

"Yes."

Dane touched Kai's hand, giving her a look. "It's how she is now. You have to accept it."

"Fine, but I don't have to like it."

Gabby shrugged, unfolding her wings and ruffling her feathers. "Mermaids may be enigmatic but certainly not sympathetic. It is a weakness your kind would not accept. It would serve you well to be less like your mother and more like your ancient ancestral bloodline."

Kai's rage erupted as she leaped across the counter, grabbing Gabby by the neck just as the others walked through the door. A light blue light sizzled in the surrounding air and frost formed on the inside of the windows as the temperature in the room plummeted.

"Kai, NO!" Stevie yelled as she ran toward her.

Gabby raised a hand, stopping Stevie in her tracks. Her venomous eyes locked on Kai as her skin began to shimmer with the iridescent light of the celestials. Kai's eyes widened. Her rage turned to confusion as the hands gripping Gabby's throat began to glow with the same iridescent light.

Sebastian edged closer. "Gabby, you must not."

"She needs to learn a lesson," she hissed.

"You will hurt her."

"Not if I do not intend to."

"Gabby, you will. You are too strong, and we do not know yet how our powers manifest in this world. We need to understand them in this space and time before we actively use them."

Kai's eyes widened as the color drained from her face. In a panicked voice, she said. "My hands are tingling like an electrical current is running through them, but I can't remove my hands from her neck."

"Gabby stop!" Dane yelled, moving toward her friends. "Please."

"Gabby, please," Kai choked.

The iridescent glow ceased, and Gabby pushed Kai backward.

"Next time I will not stop," she said as she turned on her heel and left the room.

"Are you OK?" Dane asked, rubbing Kai's back.

"Yes." Kai shook her hands trying to dispel the remaining numbness.

Stevie grabbed them, checking for any damage.

"What was that?" she asked Sebastian.

"Celestials have the power to use the magic of the ether as a force field. They push magic outward, creating an invisible bubble around them. It is both defensive and offensive as you saw. The larger the force field the more volatile the energy is, creating an electrically charged environment capable of hurting anyone caught within it. You may have noticed how erratic and unstable the Etheriem environment is when you were there."

"Yes, there was lightning in a very angry purple sky," Dane said.

"The ether is powerful. It balances the other elements by consuming all that is unstable. It is why only those born from the ether can exist within its energy for extended periods of time."

"It had calmed before we left."

"Yes, it needs its own magic to be able to balance the others, but it remains a volatile environment that does erupt on occasion."

"I shouldn't have provoked her," Kai said, her eyes brimming with tears. "The kind, caring, sensitive Gabby we knew is not who she is now. I have to accept that."

Stevie hugged her. "I know our Gabby is still in there somewhere. She too is grappling with a new existence, and we will figure it all out, *together.*"

Rafe put his arm around Dane, her hands were visibly shaking.

"Gabriella is a sentinel, a warrior. She has only known one

life. Although we have our differences, she is not a bad person." He hesitated momentarily his green eyes softening. "I am not making excuses for her behavior but in our world, there is an extreme divide between the celestials and the rest of the races. Gabriella has suffered that divide more than others. It is difficult for her to have her destiny tied to others especially those not of her kind. She is very self-sufficient."

"It is difficult for us as well. We have known Gabby for the past thirteen years. She is very different from the woman we called our friend."

"She may not be the same person you knew, but you can trust she will be there for us."

Dane nodded, comforted by the fact they had people around her that knew Gabriella, the celestial, well.

"I recommend no one attack her again," he smirked.

"I don't think that will be a problem."

Gabby walked into the room followed by Sebastian who had quietly left in search of her. She walked directly to Kai.

"My kind is not good at this."

"At what?" Kai asked.

Gabby's mouth tensed. "Apologizing."

Kai glanced at Stevie who squeezed her hand and walked away, joining Drow and Killenn at the far end of the kitchen.

"I am sorry as well. I shouldn't have attacked you."

"It is understandable. I am not yet used to the exceedingly sensitive nature of mortals. Even though I remember my life, I can no longer connect with my humanity." She paused for a moment her eyes darting to Sebastian. "Sebastian has reminded me that I need to try."

Kai jumped up and wrapped her arms around Gabby who tensed under the unfamiliar and unwanted embrace. "I still

love you Gabby, even though you're a pain in the ass."
Releasing her she smiled. "Are we good?"

"I believe we are."

"OK then, so what do we do now?" She asked, looking at
everyone in the room. "Now we must tell Elyse and Marlee,"
Dane said. "All the Druidstones must be reactivated, and each
birthright received before the Second Coming is upon us. We
will need the combined power of our ancestors."

"Convincing them of all this is not going to be easy,"
Stevie acknowledged.

"No, it's not."

"Why would it be any more difficult for them to believe,
than all of you?" Rafe inquired.

Gabby ruffled her feathers. "Of all the Arcanists, those
two are deeply rooted in a fabled institution of faith created by
humans. Marlee more so than Elyse but, nonetheless. In
telling them who they truly are we will shatter a belief system
that has guided them their entire lives."

"I am afraid I do not understand," Drow said looking at
Dane for clarification.

Dane furrowed her brow. "They believe in a divinity
known as God. One singular power who created the universe
and mankind. Unfortunately, the god they believe in is not the
Guardian of Deities. Their god is part of the creation myth of
a worldwide faith-based religion known as Christianity. For
them to find out God is not real, their perception of heaven
and hell is incorrect, and everything they thought about life
and the afterlife is false, well, let's just say it's going to take a
lot for us to convince them."

"Then we may have to show them," Sebastian said.

Dane agreed. "Yes, we may."

CHAPTER 26

S TEVIE THOUGHT TELLING MARLEE AND Elyse in a public place would be a good idea, but she was currently having misgivings.

Peleto's Deli was busy, students grabbing a quick bite in between classes at Brighton Hill University, others using the popular café as a study hall. She found a corner booth big enough to fit the five of them and sat, her hands shaking as she watched for the others to arrive. While she waited she observed the young, eager faces filling the deli, laughing and drinking coffee. Their only worries were passing the midterms and which frat party to attend this weekend, oblivious to the horror buried beneath them. A horror Dane had shared with her last night.

As part of her birthright and a trait of the Dragon Gypsies, her intuition was heightened. She was now more aware of the energy of others and sensitive to the essence of the other dimensions. As a Timestopper, Dane had tapped into that intuition, entering her mind and showing her the past, the one Sebastian had shown her. It had been an unsettling experience, but an informative one. Dane had shown Stevie the devastation thrust upon their ancestor's worlds. The death, destruction, the pain, she experienced it all as if she were reliving her own past. Stevie felt the demise of the supernaturals, the ending of that time. It was, to say the least, unnerving and exhausting, but if need be Dane planned on showing Elyse and Marlee too.

She scanned the students, huddled up with their books and laptops. Nothing was going to be the same for any of them. The only difference between her and the students— they had no idea what was coming, and she was all too aware.

The entry bell rang, and Dane walked into the deli hurrying over to the table with Kai directly behind her.

"Marlee called," she said, tapping her phone as she sat in the booth. "They are running late but will be here in five."

The waiter came over and collected their drink orders. "Would you like menus?" She inquired.

"I can't eat," Kai whispered. "My stomach is in knots."

"Just the drinks, for now, thanks," Stevie said.

"Do you think doing this here is a good idea?" Kai asked when the waitress walked away.

"I admit I'm second thoughts, but it's too late now." She waved as Elyse and Marlee walked through the door.

Kai groaned, laying her head on the table.

"Kai are you not well?" Marlee asked as she reached the table.

"I'm fine," Kai said, her voice muffled.

"Then why is your head on the table."

Kai lifted it up and smiled. "Just waiting for you two."

Elyse shook her head and frowned. "It's so good to see all of you. I feel like it's been forever. Where's Gabby?"

"She's not herself," Dane said, thinking about the exploding anger in her kitchen last night.

"That's an understatement," Kai said under her breath.

"Well, I think she gave it to Kai," Marlee said, scowling at her friend who now had her elbows on the table and her head propped on her hands.

Dane kicked her just as the waitress arrived with their drinks.

"Ouch!" She yelped. "What the hell was that for?"

"Pay attention, this is important."

Kai sulked. Thanking the waitress, she turned her attention back to the conversation.

"So, what is this important news?" Elyse asked sipping her lemon water.

Dane glanced at Stevie before answering. "There is something we need to tell you, about the three of us."

"Four if you count Gabby," Kai interrupted.

Dane shook her head. "Fine, the four of us, but also about you two."

"I'm not sure I follow."

"There is a reason the four of us have been scarce lately. We haven't been out of town for work or too busy to spend time with you, something happened. Something unbelievable to say the least."

Concern etched Elyse's face, and she adjusted her glasses.

Marlee leaned forward. "Is everything alright?" she asked.

"Yes and no."

"Dane just tell us," Elyse said.

"It's not that easy, Elyse. She hesitated. The decreased background noise giving her pause and her eyes searched the surrounding tables to make sure no one was listening.

"Tell them," Kai urged.

"You know how Stevie believes in destiny and is constantly reminding us how we were meant to meet, sure we were brought together for a reason."

"Yes," she said glancing at Stevie, who smiled and shrugged.

"Well, she was right. It wasn't a coincidence. We share a similar destiny. Our paths were meant to cross for a very specific reason."

"And what reason could that possibly be," Marlee asked, her voice breathy.

"To save mankind."

There was an uncomfortable silence as those three words hovered in the air. None of the girls spoke until finally Elyse smiled and broke into an uncontrollable laughter. Tears streamed down her face as she gasped for air. When she finally caught her breath, she looked at the others.

"What are you guys up too?"

"There is no easy way to say this, but what I'm about to tell you is true. You must believe me. The six of us carry the blood of ancient, supernatural beings from another world, in another time. We are descendants of magic and are destined to use the power and knowledge of our ancestors to defeat an ancient evil who has been buried under the Earth for billions of centuries. A prophecy foretold of our ascension and a day of reckoning only we can stop."

Elyse frowned, looking at Marlee whose face was ashen. "This isn't funny Dane."

"It's not meant to be. It's the truth. Kai, Stevie, and I have already received our birthrights. It is why we haven't been around and now it's your turn."

Marlee burst into tears. Her hands shook. "I don't understand. I thought we were friends. Why are you making up such awful things?"

Stevie reached over to take her hand, but she pulled away. "We are not lying to you, Marlee."

Elyse stood up. The volume in the deli had increased as more students flooded through the door, but the noise was irritating, and she was not in the mood to sit here and listen to this nonsense anymore. "Come on Marlee, we're leaving."

Dane stood as well, grasping Elyse's hand. "Please, Elyse you have to listen."

"When you want to explain to us what is really going on, I will. Until then, I have work to attend to."

Behind the glasses, her eyes brimmed with anger and Dane could see the hurt simmering underneath. Shaking off Dane's hand she stalked toward the door pushing past students who were in her path.

"STOP!"

The word rippled through the air, echoing off the silence that erupted simultaneously as everyone in the deli ceased moving. Elyse turned, eyes wide taking in the frozen students. Marlee, frozen in fear, not magic, stood by her side, eyes darting around the interior of the café. Elyse reached out toward the gentlemen beside her, poking him delicately and jerking her finger back when he didn't react.

Nothing moved in the deli, not one single person.

Elyse glanced outside. The same was true out there. Cars were stopped in the street, their drivers unaware behind the wheel. A dog was frozen in mid-jump, chasing a butterfly who was also frozen in flight. All the ambient noise had ceased, and the silence was deafening. Gone were the clatter of dishes, the drip of the coffee maker, and the laughter bouncing off the walls. All that remained was silence, an eerie overwhelming quiet.

Dane looked at Kai. "What did you do?"

"I think we just found out how my powers work in our world."

"Shit. How far does it go?" Stevie asked, running to the deli window to look down the street. It was all frozen as far as she could see. Not a single person or living entity moved, everything trapped in the motion of that very second.

Pulling her shoulders back, Elyse walked to where Dane stood. "I'm listening."

"Are you sure you want to hear everything?"

"Kai just froze the entire town. I think you have some explaining to do."

Dane nodded. "Yes, I do."

After Kai released everyone they quickly paid the bill and left, opting to continue the discussion and any further demonstrations in the privacy of Stevie's home. They drove quickly out of town.

"That is an interesting power," Stevie said from the backseat.

"I wasn't really trying to freeze the entire town. Maybe my subconscious thought it was the best option given the circumstance."

"It seems all our powers become instinctive quickly," Dane said. "You should see what Stevie can conjure."

Kai turned in her seat. "Conjure, like raise the dead or something."

"Not the dead."

"Well, it's kind of dead," Dane retorted.

"Oh, come on, you have to tell me now. What is it?" Kai's eyes widened in interest.

"A smoke dragon," Stevie said.

Kai's frowned. "What the hell is a smoke dragon?"

Dane laughed. "It's a dragon made of smoke."

"Thanks. I figured that much."

Stevie shook her head and rolled her eyes in mock disgust. "My ancestors were Dragon Gypsies, capable of controlling the spirits of the four origin dragons. I am only able to summon the smoke dragon currently as it is the one my blood-line is born from. The others may come."

"What are the others?"

The spirits of the dragons from which the race of Dragon Gypsies was born: fire, smoke, ash, and ember.

Kai was silent for a moment. "I can't wait to see that, it sounds better than my power."

Dane and Stevie laughed. There was much they needed to discover about one another, their ancestors, their powers, and the past. How immortality had changed them, what magic they possessed, and how each fit into the larger scope of their combined destiny. But for the moment they were just three friends, joking around, trying to forget the enormity of the strange direction their lives had taken. Trying, if only briefly, to live in a past that never again would exist.

Dane glanced uneasily at the girls as she drove.

Trepidation hovered around them, its essence weaving in and out of their energy. Acceptance of their new identities and the magic they possessed was only the beginning. There would be times when they would be tested. Their friendship had always been an unbreakable bond, but she sensed that too was about to change. Her hands gripped the steering wheel.

The ancient magic tingled in her blood; a warning. Their future was as uncertain as the one they were destined to save and only time would reveal what was to become of them.

She turned into Stevie's driveway, just as dusk swallowed the sky. The lights of Marlee's car made the turn after her.

The others were waiting—the immortals.

Elyse and Marlee were about to be introduced to a past they didn't know existed and a future they may not want.

CHAPTER 27

LILITH WOKE CURLED IN A fetal position in a dark corner of the mill. Her muscles ached, and her joints were stiff. The chill in the wooden planks of the floor had seeped under her skin, and she rubbed her legs vigorously to get the circulation moving. Gingerly, she staggered to an upright position. Leaning against the wall for support she stretched her limbs until the tingling in her nerves subsided, and she was confident her legs would support her weight.

The pods stretched out in front of her, glowing with a sickly yellow light. The long eerie shadows they cast across the ceiling mimicked dark shadowy fingers reaching out toward the town. Her eyes filled with tears as she surveyed the scene.

There are so many!

Many more than before.

The pods began to hum. A deafening noise filled the mill's large space, and she placed her hands over her ears to lessen the incessant sound. The noise found its way into the recesses of her mind, pounding through her consciousness. Needing to get away from the sickening feeling the pods induced in her, she ran from the noise. As she weaved through them, the stairs her only destination, they ballooned. The pod's outer membrane stretched tautly, and she thought it would split, allowing whatever was entombed inside to escape. An erratic heartbeat swelled from inside each pod as she passed, a disjointed and inhuman sound, and the life breath of something not of this world.

The thumping jarred the floorboards as she ran. The humming grew louder. Perspiration drenched her skin and desperate eyes darted back and forth as she tried to escape the maze of pods entrapping her. They kept swelling as she moved, the bloated sheaths blocking her path. They expanded up and down, the rhythm falling in sync with the horrific sound pulsating from within. With a frantic lunge, she broke free, fleeing upstairs to the rooms where she lived.

The maddening hum went on for hours, dousing the mill with a discordant sound until abruptly it ceased. The mill's interior was dead silent broken only by the creak of the framework that buckled and groaned under the ferocity of the wind outside.

Grabbing the box of matches from the table she lit one. The shaking of her hands made it difficult to light the large pillar candle, but the wick ignited. Its flickering flame chased away the dark shadows as the scent of sandalwood drifted through the air. She stared into the flame's depths, the slow seductive dance soothing the darkness and her frayed nerves. The old mill was quiet now. A comfortable stillness wrapped around the exterior. She didn't dare go back downstairs as she was too apprehensive about what filled the pods. Their energy somehow connected to her and the closer she was to their existence, the more vulnerable she felt to the darkness within.

She began to pace the floor, her heels digging into the brittle wood planks. The rhythmic pattern of her walk achieved a calmness. Her breath steadied, and she gained clarity, her mind again her own.

She was having blackouts more frequent lately. Time disappeared for reasons unknown—hours or days at a time gone. In these moments of lucidity, she tried to make sense of what was happening before it occurred again. Unfortunately, she was unable to recover the time that evaded her. Often the headaches accompanying the clarity were marred by an incoherent murmuring, a whispering just out of reach of her conscious mind.

Was she going mad?

There was no other explanation. She'd been in control only a few short weeks ago and now she felt somebody else was.

Walking to the mill's window she gazed outside. The brightness of the moon still lit up the night sky even though it had begun waning from the second full moon of the year. *That was the last day she remembered! How many days had she lost?* Reaching into her pocket she removed her phone. The battery was dead. She checked her watch. It was almost midnight. The glowing date box noted it was Friday, February 26th.

She rubbed her brow, frowning. The full moon had been on the 22nd—*four days, gone, just disappearing from her memory.* Her gaze shifted to the mill's yard. Shadows elongated by the moon's glow stretched across the wintry landscape. The snow sparkled under the silvery light and a hazy blue essence swathed the land in its ethereal glow.

She hated the moon, preferring instead the comfort of the darkness broken only by the light of a solitary candle. Over the years, the darkness had become her friend, her savior, the one place she could hide from everything wrong and bad. How many times had she escaped her pain by wrapping herself in the shadows that lived in the dark? A pain arising from a broken past propagated by the blood of her families' enemies.

She thought about the Callan witch. She hadn't seen her in weeks, not since her return to the mill to retrieve her dog. Even that encounter was hazy. She remembered fragments interrupted by the empty void that fractured her memory into jumbled puzzle pieces.

She tried to recall the interaction but there were only remnants. The witch had carried a scent in her blood, an essence that hadn't been present the previous times they'd met. The aura revealing her bloodline was stronger. It had been unnerving and triggered an irrepressible darkness hidden deep inside. The loss of control in front of the witch frustrated her but the darkness consuming her very soul terrified her.

As she stood in the window her eyes lost to the night beyond, she recalled the fury that bubbled inside every time she thought of the Callan witch. It had become more intense lately. The rage harder to control. At first, she thought the witch had cast a spell on her, an incantation, a rite, something upsetting the balance of her powers. She knew the witch's bloodline was commanding in the art of spellcasting, and she could not overlook the possibility a spell to bind or disrupt her powers could be conjured. Unfortunately, as days passed she realized the darkness building inside her was coming from something else, something not of this world, and something no mere magic had created. The darkness existed because it was part of her. A suffocating rage seeped through the very fibers of her being and unbeknownst to her, she'd let it fester and take over. Her futile resistance and her own anger toward the Callan witch fed its very soul.

She walked to the mirror hanging crooked on the wall. The glass was cracked and tarnished but reflected an unrecognizable image back to her. Dark circles surrounded sunken bloodshot eyes. Long red hair, matted in knots, and streaked with wiry hair follicles of dank lifeless gray hung from her head. There was a peculiar pallor to her skin and dark blue veins crisscrossing haphazardly were visible just below the surface. She rubbed her face with her hands—bony, knobby fingers topped with dirty, broken nails. Lifting her dry cracked lip, she ran her swollen tongue across her teeth. Some were missing, others had chipped or cracked, but all were yellowed and stained. She studied the reflection in the mirror. She didn't recognize the haggard, unsightly woman staring back at her.

A tear slipped down her cheek as a hopelessness welled up inside of her.

Turning away from the horrid reflection she moved back to the window. The moon had disappeared behind a cloud bank and the mill was cast in shadows.

The dark vestiges of the night enhanced her fears. Every time she became aware of a blackout she felt different, looked different. She was losing herself—*her life energy dissipating slowly*. Whatever was stealing her memory, was also robbing her of time. She was not aging per se, not in the normal sense. It was more a decomposition. Her body betraying her before its time. She caught her reflection in the darkened glass of the window and cringed as the stark image wavered in its panes.

There was a darkness growing inside her. Something she couldn't control. An evil was upon them, a darkness from another time and place. Revenge against the witch was no longer her focus for her hate would not be sated by a Callan death. She needed more. Somewhere inside her festered a dark, unyielding need to destroy, to devour, to watch the world burn. A need so undeniable that it consumed her very soul. Her hatred for the witch weakened her, and now a vengeance not belonging to her and far superior to her own had taken seed.

The pods beneath her began to hum again, and the sickly yellow glow seeped out the mill's windows and onto the snow-covered ground below, interrupting the gloom.

Her eyes flicked to the lane leading to the old mill road.

She sensed a presence beyond the edge of darkness where the ambient glow from the pods ceased to exist. Something was there hidden in the shadows beyond the fringe. Her skin prickled as she felt eyes upon her. There was someone out there, an energy she did not recognize—*watching her.*

The mill seemed quiet. Its massive bulk marred the beauty of the starry night sky. Gabby watched from the shadows, hidden by the pitch black surrounding the building. A cloud bank drifted in front of the moon, and a cold winter wind whipped up cyclones of misty snow, swirling the frigid air around her. The large tree she leaned against groaned. The branches above her head cracked as they bashed violently into one another as the wind gusts intensified.

Her focus never wavered, her attention did not stray as she carefully assessed the quiet escaping from the mill's interior. The abandoned building appeared to exhale in the darkness, its energy expanding and contracting as it watched her as well. Before she left for Dywen, Dane told her of the imprints surrounding this old place. The multitude of stagnant energies caught in the veil claiming the old mill as its own. Surrounded by the dark, she sensed the movement. The ebb and flow of the trapped energies—their anguish, and pain.

Closing her eyes, she inhaled the crisp night air and listened. Her ears found the sounds hidden behind the ones present on this plane. A chorus of whispers greeted her as she focused her senses on the layer of existence just beyond the fabric of this world. The veil, every world had one. The space between one reality and the next. A dimension of nothingness and a brutal unyielding space of desolation. Hollow space where lost and tortured souls felt pain and suffering or nothing at all while enduring an infinite and meaningless existence.

The veil encompassing the Thanissia Universe was not much different, but unlike the veil here, it also provided protection. A magical barrier that hid and shielded them from the millions of other worlds existing in the far-reaching corners of the ether, who existed to harm, impede, or destroy.

Her mind drifted to her past and to the ancient dark who easily breached that magical barrier, entering Thanissia without much resistance. The veil failed them only once, but once was all it took to end the time of the supernaturals.

She opened her eyes, focusing once again on the old mill as she felt a shudder ripple through the air. The whispering ended, and the imprints scattered. Primordial fear tinged their energy in response to the change in the mill—to its secular energy. The interior of the mill began to glow. A sickening yellow light consumed the entire first floor. The light pene-trated the windows and flooded outward over the snow-covered lawn. She could feel the heaviness of the dark magic pulsating within the light. The fractured shifting stilted the night air as it collided with the energy in this world. The magical essence seeping from the mill's interior was not unknown to her.

Her eyes were drawn upward to a window on the second floor. The barely visible glow of candlelight framing the dark silhouette standing in the window, watching.

The dark witch, Gabby thought, her eyes piercing the darkness between them.

She sensed the witch knew she was here, hidden by the shadows. Her eyes drifted down as the glow from the mill's interior intensified. It carried the smell of decay as it crept across the ground toward her. A rotten, earthy scent assaulted her nostrils. It was an odor she was familiar with for it was her past. The ancient and putrid stench lingered in her world even now. A smell she would never forget as it was the very essence of evil. The malodorous odor had stained her world and transformed their existence. It was the mark of the very thing she despised the most.

Her wings spread out behind her and curved slightly forward, so they surrounded her on both sides—a defense mechanism. She must warn the others.

The ancient dark was here.

CHAPTER 28

I T WAS ALMOST MIDNIGHT.

Gabby had returned from the abandoned flour mill a few hours ago and filled them in on her suspicions. As expected, Marlee and Elyse gaped at the real Gabriella. Thankfully, Gabby refrained from insulting either of their ancient races. Maybe she'd learned her lesson from the altercation with Kai.

Sebastian stroked his goatee. "Take Stevie with you. She comes from a long line of proficient alchemists. Maybe she can determine what the dark witch has conjured within those pods and determine if they are similar daemons to the ones you encountered on Dywen."

"If Gabby sensed the ancient dark does that mean it has infiltrated this world? Has the Second Coming already begun?" Stevie asked.

"Its scent was detectable, but I do not believe its powers are as strong here as they apparently were on Dywen," Gabby said. "The dark magic seems to exist only within another. It is not yet its own essence."

Sebastian's head tilted in thought, his green eyes flashed.

"Is it possible the dark witch has unwittingly opened a link to this world the ancient dark is manipulating?"

"It may explain the runes Dane saw drawn around the mill."

Drow stepped forward. "Then may I further suggest Rafe and Killenn accompany you. While I do not diminish your ability to safeguard yourselves, their weapons may be useful especially since the attack on Dywen was so unexpected and vast." His cabernet eyes never wavered from Stevie's face.

"Fine," Dane agreed, a frown creasing her forehead.

"Then I shall go as well," Tauria stated. "My bow will be needed if anything emerges from those pods."

Rafe gave his sister a stern look dampening her enthusiasm somewhat. "You will stay here and engage with Brannon to gain as much insight from the Book of Realms as possible. We have just passed the second full moon of this world's year. If Dane's calculation is correct, we will not have much time before the Second Coming is upon us."

Brannon squeezed Tauria's hand, quieting her.

"We will be here if you need us, old friend."

Rafe nodded. Grabbing his sword, he followed Killenn and Stevie from the room.

"Will you be alright for a bit, we won't be long," Dane asked Elyse and Marlee.

Elyse took a deep breath, her mind still whirling. "Yes, we'll be fine. Go."

She glanced at Marlee, whose huge blue eyes wavered before she too nodded in agreement.

Dane squeezed her hand. "I'm sorry," she whispered.

Silence saturated the night air as they exited the vehicle. An abnormal hollowness engulfed the mill making Dane shudder. She searched for the imprints that normally flowed through the veil but found only emptiness.

"What do you feel Stevie?"

Her shoulders lifted. "Nothing."

"Exactly. The air is absent of its normal energies. Listen, there are no night sounds or ambient noise. We are standing in the middle of a void."

"What do you think it means?"

"Nothing good I suspect."

The mill's darkness reached toward them. No light seeped from its windows. It looked the same as it had for decades, completely abandoned. They walked to the side door. It stood open. The broken lock dangled from the hook. A loud creak broke the silence as Dane pushed it open, the musty scent of abandonment escaping into the damp night air. She turned on the camp lantern as Stevie flicked on her flashlight. The light glinted off the metal equipment. Two more beams ignited and Killenn and Rafe swept their flashlights across the mill's large interior.

They crept forward moving deeper into the belly of the mill's dark, silent interior. Dane could make out the hulking, dark forms of the pods. Hundreds lay quiet on the building's floor. Stevie reached the first pod, placing her hand on its sheath and closing her eyes. Dane watched as a red glow seeped from her fingertips—her magic explored the strange object.

After a few minutes, she released the pod.

"Well?" Dane asked, placing the lantern on the grinder to their left.

"There is nothing normal about the chemistry of the

pods. I can detect traces of magnesium and carbon, but there doesn't seem to be any visible traces of transmutation. The base elements are unknown, but all seem to be in their purest forms." Stevie hesitated, her face clouding.

Noticing the look Dane asked. "What's wrong?

"I just can't believe the shit I know now."

Dane laughed, understanding exactly how she felt. The innate knowledge acquired from their ancestors was immense and it was often unsettling how easily she knew things now that weeks before she was oblivious too.

The beams of Killenn and Rafe's torches swept across the back of the mill searching for any indication the ancient dark had found a way into this world.

"What do you think it looks like?" Stevie asked.

"What?"

"This ancient dark."

Dane envisioned the dark, smoky predator she'd seen sweeping across the universe in her vision. "I am not sure it looks like anything."

Before Stevie could respond pounding feet on wooden floorboards echoed out of the darkness, and the shadowy figure of Lilith lurched forward. She jumped on Dane's back, nails digging into her neck as they fell to the floor.

Stevie yelled.

More feet pounded the floorboards and quickly the onslaught was over.

Lilith screamed as she was dragged off by Killenn and Rafe.

Stevie helped Dane to her feet. "You OK?"

She nodded, rubbing the bloody scratches on her neck where Lilith's fingernails had raked her skin. "I'll be fine."

Rafe and Killenn had Lilith pinned to the floor, Rafe's

hands around her neck. Dane could feel the rage surge through Rafe as his grip on the dark witch tightened. An uncontrollable urge for revenge overtaking his senses. Lilith flailed and shrieked as she struggled to free herself from his grip.

"Rafe," she said, moving in beside him. "Let go."

Her voice was firm, but he did not respond. He squeezed tighter; his mind numb to his actions. Killenn, realizing what was happening, tried to pry his grip open but Rafe's strength was formidable. Lilith gasped for air. Her eyes rolled back as the oxygen she so desperately desired escaped her.

Dane gripped Rafe's shoulder allowing his fury to crash into her. She experienced the overwhelming grief and hatred saturating it. The burden of his tortured past had long ago rooted inside him, growing over time into an uncontrolled hatred for those who killed his family. Lilith, while not the one who wielded the sword, was just as guilty, for she carried the blood of his enemy.

As their binding intermingled their emotions, Rafe began to relax, calmed by her presence and her empathy for the dark witch's plight. Killenn pulled his grip from her neck, and with Stevie's help, dragged a dazed and semi-conscious Lilith away.

"Look at me," she said softly, pulling Rafe's face gently toward her.

His eyes were full of fear. His anxious energy sputtered around them. He was afraid, not of Lilith but himself, of how easily he had lost control and succumbed to his own inner demons.

"I almost killed her," he gasped, placing his head in his shaking hands.

"But you didn't."

His eyes locked on hers, the rage sparked in them once again. "I wanted to," he hissed, turning on his heel.

As she watched him walk into the shadows, Dane felt a sense of relief as the ghosts, lost in an ancient past, retreated with him.

༺༺

Lilith, her wrists restrained by an old electrical cord, leaned wearily against a pillar. Her wide eyes were full of fear as she sat crumpled on the floor bound and gagged.

Dane crouched down beside her, removing the filthy, stained rag from her mouth. Her appearance had changed dramatically since Dane last saw her. She was haggard and aged, her skin no longer flawless, and her hair matted and tangled. Clumps were missing from her scalp. She looked ill. Tears began to flow down her face and her hands trembled as Dane reached for her forearms.

"Please don't," she whimpered.

Dane ignored her plea as the familiar twinge surfaced just below her skin, recognizing her intent. She closed her eyes and grasped Lilith's forearms. Her mind moved forward drifting through time and space until she felt it connect with another. She sensed Lilith's feeble attempt at resistance, but it abated quickly. Dane was only in her memories for a few moments, but it was long enough to gain the information she required.

Releasing her arms, she stood.

"I'm sorry," Lilith said, her eyes wide.

"Let her up," Dane ordered.

"Dane, are you sure?" Stevie asked, her concern evident in her tone.

"Yes."

Killenn removed the restraints, helping Lilith to her feet.

Tears streamed down her face. "I don't know what is happening to me."

Her voice was small and weak, her body frail, yet when she flew into rages her strength was remarkable.

"I think I do," Dane responded.

A chill swept through the interior of the mill. An icy draft slithering around the pods and encapsulating everything in its path. A merciless whisper slid by on its wisps.

Lilith's pale face hardened as blood began to drip from her nose. Lifting a shaking hand, she dabbed at the blood. Her eyes filled with horror at the sight of her stained fingertips. A guttural growl escaped her lips, and she wrenched her arm free of Killenn's grasp, bolting into the safety of the darkness.

Their flashlight beams searched the shadowy mill for her whereabouts, but she had disappeared.

"Now what?" asked Stevie.

"Let the darkness have her," Rafe said stepping from the shadows.

Dane's energy reached out, delicately testing his emotional state. He looked at her with hooded eyes as he grasped her hand and squeezed. No words were needed. He had regained control of the one thing he feared—*himself.*

The cold draft hovered around them and the whispering intensified. The mill's energy was changing. Stevie glanced at the pods. They were still dark, but no longer still. She placed her palm on the outer membrane, the vibration subtle but perceptible. She listened, blocking out the vibration buzzing through the initial layers as her intuition went deeper. There was a sound, something within the pod's center, undetectable before. She concentrated, allowing her mind to infiltrate the pod. Down she went, through the many layers until she reached the center. The sound had an unmistakable rhythm that of an erratic heartbeat.

Stevie yanked her hand from the pod, her own heart thumping in her chest. The pod's structure, its composition made sense. It was a birth chamber and there was something alive inside.

Abruptly, she was pushed to the side as Lilith sprang from the darkness and attacked Killenn. Punching at his middle, she knocked the wind from him. He staggered backward, and she kicked out connecting with his jaw. Blood flew from his mouth. The viciousness of the kick sent him tumbling backward and his head hit a wooden support beam as he fell.

Rafe drew his sword.

"Don't hurt her!" Dane yelled although she wasn't sure they could. Lilith's strength amplified the further into madness she went.

Lilith lunged at Rafe, her eyes crazed. Knocking his sword to the ground her hands clawed at this face. He managed to grab her wrists twisting them away, but she lashed out at him with her teeth. Killenn pulled himself from the ground. Wiping blood from his eye and mouth he staggered forward picking up Rafe's sword from the ground where it fell. Flipping it in the air so that he was holding the blade, he drew back the butt of the hilt and swung it toward Lilith's head. She dropped immediately to the floor as the impact on the back of her skull rendered her unconscious.

"Thanks," Rafe said.

Killenn smiled and handed him his sword.

"Your head," Stevie said, noting the large gash near Killenn's hairline.

"I've had worse."

She lifted an eyebrow, handing him a cloth from her bag. "Put pressure on it. The bleeding will stop soon."

He nodded taking the cloth from her and motioning toward Lilith's body sprawled on the floor. "So, what are we to do with this one?"

CHAPTER 29

THEY TIED LILITH TO THE flour grinder with the electrical cord and an old rope Rafe found hanging from the rafters. With her restrained and still unconscious, they were free to roam the interior of the mill without further incident.

Killenn led them up the stairs to the second level.

The mill's vacant rooms were cold and dusty, years of abandonment visible in the aging, sagging, filthy interior. Most of the rooms were empty and littered with debris left behind by past inhabitants or blown in through broken windows.

Dane closed her eyes, feeling the night's silent penetration. The upper portion of the mill did not vibrate the way the lower section did. The dark energy had yet to taint the second story. She followed Killenn into the largest room. Her eyes drifted around the vacant space stopping on the corner where the thick chain, that once held Tyson captive, lay on the floor beside the broken padlock. She inhaled deeply pushing the image of his sad face from her mind. The others searched the room, picking up clothes, blankets, and garbage, looking for anything indicating Lilith's connection to the ancient dark.

Paraphernalia covered the table in the middle of the room. Dane recognized much of it. There was a black stone scrying bowl, a pestle, mortar, and multiple glass jars filled with herbs, spices, and oils. Small bone fragments filled a wooden bowl, and a human skull sat at the center with a thick pillar candle on top. The dripping wax had congealed, the top of the skull no longer visible under the waxy buildup. Incense smoke hung in the area; a strange scent she couldn't identify. Surrounding the human skull was a circle of powder. She dipped her fingers into it, bringing them to her nose.

Sulfur and black salt.

"Find anything," Rafe asked moving in beside her.

"She's definitely been practicing some rituals, probably on the darker side," she said indicating the bones. "But I don't see anything on this table that's suspicious."

"What about that?"

Dane inspected the athame Rafe pointed to. The tip of its blade was embedded in the wood of the table at the center of a unicursal hexagram.

"In our time the hexagram is used as a portal to the spirit world."

"Yes, it is still used for that now, but it takes a very powerful witch to open a portal to another dimension. Even if Lilith had the power, the ancient dark is not confined to a spirit dimension. According to what Sebastian told me he resides deep in the layers of this world."

"That is true, but portal magic has a way of being," he hesitated, searching for the right word. "Unreliable."

Dane squeezed his hand. Portal magic seemed to be a touchy subject with Rafe. She understood this is how, during the time of Thanissia, they traveled to neighboring realms, but it obviously had a deeper meaning for him.

"I suppose it could have been manipulated to activate a link in the fabric of this world, but it would take precision and extreme concentration." She thought about Lilith's unpredictable behavior, the crazed look in her eye. "Do you really think Lilith has that type of capacity?"

"I don't assume anything when it comes to dark magic. One thing I have learned is its unpredictability tends to lend to its success."

"There is nothing here," Stevie said from across the room. "Just this book." She held up the old tome—Lilith's family grimoire. Dane motioned for Stevie to bring it over.

The old leather tome was in poor condition. Its binding had faded, and a crack ran down one side of the spine. The metal clasp locking it was rusted and broken. As she opened the cover a moldy odor wafted from its pages and the edges of the parchment crumbled under her touch, the fragments scattering on the table. A chill had embedded itself into the paper, the magic weakening. She could feel the energy palpitating from the book as she turned each page. The book was dimming, the magic pulling inward as the secrets contained in the tome faded. Dane shivered as she felt the life force of centuries of witches disappear into nothingness. She had only felt a grimoire go cold once before, and regardless of the family bloodline or the reason for the tome's demise, it is a sorrowful experience. Once familial magic is lost, it can never be returned, and in some small way, the essence of that magic vanishing from the universe affects all witches.

Was the energy bound to this book disappearing because Lilith was dying? Was she the last of her bloodline? Or did the magic sense something was awry and was protecting itself?

She closed the tome. "This will show us nothing."

Rafe too could sense the chill surrounding the tome. "Let's check below where the dark energy is more palpable."

Lilith was still unconscious. They hurried past where she lay, treading carefully through the pods toward the back of the mill. When they reached the small staircase at the back of the mill, Rafe pointed his torchlight into the depths of the basement. The beam sent a family of scared mice scattering into the shadows. A rancid odor infiltrated their senses as they descended the staircase into the mill's basement. Stevie coughed. Rafe's eyes began to water and Dane placed her hand over her mouth and nose. The stench in the air was insufferable.

"What is that smell?" Stevie asked holding her hand over her mouth and nose.

"It is the scent of ancient death," Rafe responded. "Of a dark soul tainted by evil and blackened by hate."

"Well ancient death smells like rat excrement and rotten cabbage."

Even by the dull light of the lantern Dane could see Rafe was not impressed with Stevie's attempt at sarcasm.

"The smell is coming from over there," Stevie said shivering, lifting the light higher, and indicating the unused packing crates tucked into the back corner. A small door hid behind them.

The damp chill permeating the basement sprang from the dirt floor. Ice crystals formed on the surface and Dane could feel the cold seep through the soles of her boots as she walked toward the crates. The cold was not from a typical Brighton Hill winter. This had a layer of evil hidden in its depths, a dark, cold, and unfeeling energy saturating the winter night with stagnated oxygen. It became increasingly difficult to breathe the air trapped in the depths of the mill's basement. The bitter cold rendered deep breaths impossible, and short quick breaths were filled with the decaying stench that pilfered the fresh air.

Dane's ears buzzed as her blood pumped faster trying to compensate for the lack of oxygen. She shook her head, closed her eyes, and stilled her breath, trying to relax. She sensed the others fighting against the same panic as their breathing too became problematic.

Moving behind the crates she grasped the door handle and pulled the small wooden door outward. A creak broke the silence as the hinges protested. She pulled harder. The aged corrosion cracked sending rust particles floating to the ground. A hinge split as the weight of the door pulled the rusted, deteriorated metal from the door jamb. The door shifted downward, the outer corner lodging into the dirt floor, stuck. Luckily there was enough space for them to squeeze through.

Rafe peered over Dane's shoulder into the darkness. No window provided light. The room was pitch black. He looked back at the others, their faces curious.

A puff of air escaped through the open door sending a chill slithering over their skin, sighing as it went. They shivered. The layer beneath the bitter chill was malevolent. Dane could feel a dark energy drift from the room's confines flooding the basement with a vile and unseen substance. It clung to the dark, breathed in the shadows, and dripped from the rotting wood, *waiting*. It sensed them, their magic and their energy and knew who and what they were. She could feel its curiosity as it probed, but it remained at a distance. She lifted the lantern. The warmth of the light flooded into the small space, its soft glow penetrating the small room's dim interior.

They followed Dane through the gap finding themselves in

a storage room filled with burlap flour bags, pulley wheels, and machinery belts. A dusty old ledger sat on a small table beside the door. Dane wiped off the cobwebs, her finger running down the entries.

"It looks like an inventory log," she said. "This must be an old storeroom that housed excess supplies."

"Why here?" Stevie asked, pushing cobwebs from her face.

Dane crouched down, placing her hand flat on the cold dirt floor. She could feel the current that ran under the foundation. The vibration of magic that simmered below the surface. "This is where the veil is most vulnerable."

"The veil?"

She glanced at Stevie. "The earth is surrounded by a dark space. A place between life and death that traps spectral energy, known as imprints, forever. It is an unforgiving, endless void and a place where dark magic could easily fester. It is unrecognizable to humans, but I have always had the ability to detect it, to interact with it and the imprints who reside there. The veil here is thin, the most vulnerable, making it the perfect place for the ancient dark to enter this world.

"Can we repair the veil?"

"The veil is not broken, Stevie. It is an ethereal object. It remains the same as it did from its conception. The only differences are the imprints that exist within its energy and the way that energy manifests."

"Has it changed recently?" Rafe asked feeling an anxiousness deep within Dane's being.

She nodded. "Something has been disrupting the flow of the veil for weeks. The imprints have been chaotic, traces of malice attached to their energies where there was none before. They fade in and out. Sometimes I can feel their fear, their confusion, other times the veil seems vacant like the imprints have disappeared."

"And what does the veil feel like now?" he asked, already knowing the answer as he could sense the concern flooding from Dane.

"Hollow."

She stood and followed the vibration in the dirt floor, detecting its flow by the chill emanating upward. Shipping crates were stacked purposely at the back corner creating a barrier only accessible through a small opening between the crates and the wall. Dane squeezed through first followed by the others. The space behind the crates contained only one thing—a rune carved into the packed dirt floor.

"A hexagram," Rafe whispered.

Without warning a surge of energy exploded from the rune. The invisible pulse throwing them into the crates. The boxes tumbled under their weight. Wood splintered underneath them as they landed on the ground.

"Shit," Stevie said, picking herself up from the wreckage of the wooden crates. "What was that?"

The rune on the floor began to glow a deep orange. The floor shook under their feet. Loose dirt quivered across the floor as the rune's luminosity increased. Rafe pulled Dane back as the light from the rune's edges ascended upward, igniting other runes carved into the dirt walls of the room. Soon, they were surrounded by fiery symbols.

Rafe's tension drifted through Dane as recent memories surfaced in her mind.

The caverns!

Once again Rafe found himself surrounded by the dark magic that penetrated his world and ultimately killed his family.

A sound exploded in her head, a visceral squeal pierced her mind. Her hands flew to her head in a weak attempt to block the sound, but it wasn't penetrating from the outside. It was coming from the rune and was only in her head. As quickly as it had erupted the squeal weakened. The rune on the floor beckoned her. The light glowing at its edges enthralled her with its hypnotic throb. Her body moved forward, the throbbing light pulsing with each step pulling her toward it. She could hear the others yelling. Their voices panicked. They were telling each other they were immobile, unable to move, but she was oblivious to their pleas, content to walk into the center of the glowing rune.

As she stood at its center, her mind warped. The familiar tug accompanying her Timestopper ability surfaced. It reached out, exploring the magic pulsing from the rune and allowing her to see the memories embedded in the energy. Bits and pieces soared through her mind, a past of multiple memories converging into one. As her magic found its way deeper, the squeal amplified.

It sensed her intrusion.

The primeval squeal undulating through her consciousness wasn't a sound at all, but a story, a memory of an existence commencing long before the beginning. This memory manifested before anything existed in the hollow space of time— before her ancestors came to be or magic was born. It was from the period of nothingness when the only extant life in the ether was the ancient dark.

CHAPTER 30

"**S**HE IS POSSESSED."

Drow and Sebastian exchanged confused glances as Dane and the others walked through the door.

Rafe intervened. "What Dane means is that the dark witch has neither opened a portal to the dark sphere nor is actively engaging the ancient dark. It seems it controls her."

Dane nodded. "I don't believe she understands what is happening."

"How is this possible?"

"My abilities as a Timestopper are morphing. They are more intuitive, personal. No longer am I looking through a window. The memories consume me, become a part of me as if they were my own. I have a distinct understanding of their memories and all the layers in each."

"Interesting," Drow said.

"I saw inside her mind, felt the confusion, and the fear. There are also parts missing from her memory, spaces of time where there is only blackness—no thoughts, feelings, or memories, just an empty void."

"And therefore, you think the ancient dark has control of her, because of the missing memories?" Brannon asked.

Dane shook her head. "It is much more than that. This connection I have with the ancient dark, the way I can integrate myself into its consciousness and it into mine. I felt its presence there, inside her mind. The suffocating darkness that surrounds its very existence was dripping from her memories. The voids in her mind are where that darkness is most prevalent."

"So, we have a dark witch who is a vessel for the ancient dark, but how? Brannon inquired.

"I'm not sure yet, but what I do know is that it's more complex than we initially thought."

"In what way?" Drow asked.

"There is a storage room in the basement of the mill. A small room hidden in its recesses. Among the inventory and equipment, we found runes scratched into the surfaces, the floor, and walls. When we entered, they ignited. Dark energy saturates that room and the veil surrounding the mill is at its thinnest there. The room is acting as a gateway for the ancient dark to access the energy of this world. Lilith may have carved those symbols into the surfaces of that room, but the ancient dark is definitely in control."

"If the dark witch is doing its bidding, then she must be killed," Brannon said.

Dane shook her head. "It's not that easy."

"Why? Her death would sever the ancient dark's connection to this world."

"Yes, but it will find another way, another vessel."

Sebastian eyed Dane with interest. "Something else happened in that room."

The others went silent, and all eyes turned toward her.

Rafe shifted uncomfortably, glancing at Killenn whose stoic face stared straight ahead.

Stevie sighed. "Tell them, Dane."

"When we entered the room, the dark magic tried to expel us, and it unwittingly triggered my abilities to enter the minds and memories of others. Only this time I entered the memories of those connected through the dark magic. I accessed the memories of the Tierney clan, all of whose individual memories are now tied to the ancient dark."

"All of them?"

"Back to Vertigan, yes. That is where the darkness began. It has infested this line for generations, causing turmoil and anguish, ensuring the descendants of every generation remain broken. Pain and suffering have continued to feed it for centuries. Hate is what will set it free."

"Lilith is right. Their family is cursed just not by a Callathian," Sebastian said.

"Yes."

"So, she must be killed," Brannon repeated.

Dane shook her head. "Lilith is a victim. This entity is extremely knowledgeable and intelligent, but not in the same capacity as humans nor I suspect the supernaturals of your time. The scope of its existence is narrow. It's using her anguish as a weapon for its own interests. It has a simple purpose. It exists only to survive and will stop at nothing to ensure that survival for it's the last of its kind."

Drow frowned. "This is about the extinction of its species?"

"Yes. It does not possess the same emotions as we do. Nor does it have the capacity to express remorse. Everything it does is instinctual. Its actions are strictly primal, a predisposition to survive not actions born from a malevolent nature. This is not about revenge."

"It destroyed our entire world," Gabby said, her face a mask of anger. "It killed thousands without hesitation or forethought. There was no mercy. It destroyed realms for no other reason than it could, and you now stand here and defend it."

Rafe turned on Gabby. "Dane is doing nothing of the sort. She is trying to understand our enemy's motives so that we can gain perspective and better know how to destroy it."

Gabby flexed her wings, frustration evident in her posture. "How can we be sure it is not driven by pure evil and its innate need to destroy?"

Dane sighed, knowing her understanding of the ancient dark was difficult to accept especially for those who lived through its violent rampage.

"Because we, those with emotions and the capacity to understand right from wrong, look at the ancient dark's actions through a singular lens. Our perceived ideals and experiences shape our views and conclusions. The ancient dark is an extremely old entity born in a time before anything else existed. It has none of the faculties we rely on to guide us nor has it developed emotionally or mentally as we have. Until the time it found your universe, it had been a solitary entity alone in the vast expanse of the ether. It did not destroy your world out of malice but from a primal instinct to survive. You were a perceived threat to its very existence just as this world is now."

"It knows nothing else but survival," Sebastian said.

Dane nodded. "Yes, its actions are driven only by self-preservation. Even though violence is the result, it is not motivated by it."

"How do we stop it?"

"Regrettably, the entity does not have the capacity for reason either. It has engaged in a battle for survival since the day it came to our world. This won't change. If there is another life-form in its midst, it will destroy it. It knows no other way." Rafe said, glancing at Dane for confirmation.

"And the ancient magic?" Drow asked. "We need the power of our worlds to strengthen our powers if we hope to defeat it, but the ancient dark feeds off our magic, consuming it for strength."

"I believe this may be because of the ether. The chaotic nature of the essence that binds all your magic. The ancient dark existed in a time before magic. It is possible that as magic came to be it also became a part of the entity. I sensed from its energy that the power it derives from magic comes from the rawest form of it. Chaos is at its core and it feeds off the uncontrolled essence of the ether."

"How are we to defeat something like that?" Kai asked.

"I don't know," Dane said. Her interaction with the ancient dark at the old mill was nothing like the other times. Her magic had instigated it this time almost as if it needed her to understand the ancient dark's motives. Unfortunately, the reality hadn't changed.

It was a destroyer of worlds and Earth was next.

ॐ

The clock ticked lazily through the night. Dane yawned. It was late, and she required sleep. Marlee and Elyse, subjected to an onslaught of unbelievable information, had gone home shortly after Dane left for the mill. Stevie and Kai had gone to bed about an hour ago. As the remaining immortals left the kitchen, Dane pulled Rafe and Sebastian aside.

"There is something else I believe you should know."

"What is it Callathian?" Sebastian asked.

"Two things actually. Something was missing from the Tierney bloodline. The memories I encountered were fluid through generations until I got to Lilith. Here a black blur mars the bloodline as if someone's memories are hidden. Whoever it is they are somehow connected to both the Tierney bloodline and Lilith, but I'm not sure how. I can't see past the black blur, but I sense it's been there since Lilith's birth, watching." She looked at Sebastian. "Do you have any idea what it could be?"

"I am sorry, I do not. Lilith's mind is obviously not her own, maybe the ancient dark is the blur."

"I didn't sense the blur in her memories. Whoever this is, I don't believe Lilith knows them."

Dane was sure the blur wasn't an imprint of the ancient dark. Although dark magic taints the Tierney family, the blur itself doesn't seem to be affected by it. It didn't foster the pain and chaotic energy apparent in the rest of the families' memories. An ease surrounded the blur. It appeared in control. She shivered at the memory. It had made her feel vulnerable.

"This is another curiosity, then," Sebastian said.

Dane nodded. "I suppose it is."

"You said there were two things. What was the other?"

"Yes." She hesitated, before saying what she knew would cause an emotional reaction. "Vertigan did not intentionally betray either of you."

Instantly, fury washed through Rafe at the name of the man responsible for taking away his family.

"What do you mean?" Sebastian too was stilted.

"The ancient dark controlled him as well. He was the first of his family. It easily manipulated something inside Vertigan and by the end, the darkness completely consumed him. The ancient dark infected him with all the things derived from its survival instincts—pain, suffering, hate, violence. But a small piece of the Vertigan you knew, remained, unable to be destroyed by the ancient dark—*hope*. He died, clutching onto a glimmer of regret for the pain he had caused you both. Remorse for what he had done. It stained his memories as it was the last shred of his humanity."

"How do you know this?" Rafe asked, the fury simmering just below the controlled demeanor.

"The rune in the basement of the mill showed me every memory of the Tierney bloodline. They were dark and painful, Vertigan's worst of all and I almost missed the small glimmer of hope that existed in his core. It flashed by, but it remained in my consciousness. I believe Vertigan needed it to be found.

Rafe's shoulders slumped, and she softened her voice.

"Your friend and the proud Warlician warrior, that small piece of Vertigan not consumed by the darkness was tortured by his betrayal of the brotherhood, and of you.

She squeezed Sebastian's forearm, her eyes filling with tears for Rafe who stood broken in the corner. "I thought you needed to know."

"Thank you," Sebastian said as she exited the room.

CHAPTER 31

"I T IS TIME." SEBASTIAN WALKED into the kitchen where the girls were having a late breakfast and discussing the prophecy.

Elyse and Marlee had arrived about ten minutes ago and Dane was making them a pot of coffee. "Time?"

"To prepare those with magic in your world. We will require all the magic of both worlds to defeat the ancient dark. Your family has magic does it not?"

Dane looked at the others, her friends whom she had kept secrets from for years. "Yes, both sides."

"Your mother is a healer?"

She nodded, "But she has limits."

"Healing magic is infinite. Limitations only exist if created by those who wield this type of magic. Your mother's powers are limited because of the bias present in this world. If she had existed within ours, her powers would be unrestricted and therefore immeasurable."

"Your entire family are witches?" Marlee asked, her face not hiding her surprise.

Dane nodded. "For generations."

"I knew it," Stevie said. "The day I touched your hand in the quad during our freshman year, I felt something in you. I could just never figure out what it was."

"You were the hardest to hide my powers from, Stevie. Your intuition always made me guarded. Now I know why."

Stevie laughed. "I guess you can all stop rolling your eyes when I mention the word *destiny* now."

"I certainly have a deeper appreciation for its meaning," Elyse agreed.

"Sorry," Dane said noticing Sebastian's frown. "You were saying.

"Your parents must be entrusted with the secrets we now hold. They are the link between the two worlds. Magic must be used in unity to protect those without it."

"My father is out of town at a medical conference, but I can certainly have a conversation with my mother. I am sure she can speak with both sides of the family."

"Will it take a lot of convincing?" Gabby asked, her voice short. Her suspicions of mortals, even those with magic, was evident.

"They will join us. My family has engaged in decades of persecution, wars, and magical in-fighting. They will not need convincing, they will be prepared."

To break the tension between Dane and Gabby, Kai intervened.

"How is the existence of magic going to stay hidden from mortals if a fight breaks out and magic is used?"

"It will not," Sebastian said. "Humans will know soon enough magic is real. That the world is not as it seems, and darkness exists outside of this realm."

Gabby agreed. "For those of us who wield magic, acceptance by mortals is not our concern. We have only one—to defeat the ancient dark at all cost. If we cannot, the fact that our powers and magic are known to humans will be inconsequential."

"We also need to understand how our powers will react to the energy of this world. Once all the Druidstones are activated and the ancient magic of all the realms funnel into this world, it is imperative that our magic manifest as it would in Thanissia."

"We should practice tomorrow," Dane said. "Four of the five Druidstones are active so it should give us some idea of the strength of our powers."

Sebastian agreed. Leaving the kitchen, he went in search of Drow and Killenn. He found them in the basement. Their swords clashed together as they jousted. He waited until they noticed his presence before speaking.

"How are you finding this world?"

Drow's cabernet eyes glinted with amusement. "It is familiar to you I suspect."

"In what way?"

"This realm seems very much like Dywen although it is cold and white like Viccinius."

Sebastian nodded. "There is much more to this world than what you see in the immediate surroundings. The Guardian used all the magic of our universe to create this world and each realm is represented within it. You will find much of your world exists here as well. The fires of Kaizi burn deep within its core.

"I almost envy your time here," Drow said.

"It was difficult watching our world disappear and another grow in its shadow but curious as well. I guess I am blessed to have my destiny tied to its existence.

"Will we leave for Athir soon?"

"Yes, day after tomorrow."

Drow nodded glancing at Killenn. "We will escort the Athirians to the Druidstone but from there we must return to Kaizi. I believe the armory will be useful to us. We will bring the weapons we have, here."

"Yes, anything from our worlds that will offer aid must be retrieved."

"The poppy fields are in full bloom," Killenn said, his eyes locking on Sebastian.

"Did she attempt alchemy during her stay with you?"

Killenn nodded.

"And?"

"The talent is there. Her knowledge of the dark art is inborn. We believe she can produce the potions and elixirs just as her ancestors did."

"That would be most helpful."

"We shall bring back the required elements."

"Thank you."

※

Tauria was pacing furiously in the upstairs loft. Brannon leaned against the wall smirking, which only enraged her further.

"You and my brother are not keeping me out of this fight," she fumed. "I am not a little girl anymore."

"That is not what I am saying, Tauria. Will you please calm down? You may not be a child anymore, but you are acting like one at this moment."

She whirled on him, her eyes flashing, her skin flush. "You take that back Brannon Draagorn."

He laughed at her use of his full name. "Now you are just being a brat," he teased. Taking her by the shoulders, he pulled her toward him until she was only inches away. His eyes looked deeply into hers. "You will fight, just as you did on Dywen. Your brother does not intend to keep you from harm's way, he just wants to ensure you understand the danger, as do I."

She gazed at him. Her anger diminished under the strength he exuded. Pouting, she said. "He is always trying to protect me."

"That is what brothers are for."

"And you, what are you for?" she teased.

Brannon stared into her green eyes, his body reacting to her closeness. Tauria was his best friend's little sister. He thought about pushing her away, but he could not. His willpower weakened when it came to her. She had enthralled him from the moment she had awakened, and he could no longer ignore the way she made him feel.

She was no longer a little girl.

He bent his head. His lips hovered over hers, waiting to see if she pulled away. Instead, she moved in closer. Her arms encircled his neck.

"Are you done being angry?" he whispered.

"For now," she said as her lips touched his.

He kissed her, inhaling her scent. She was intoxicating and at that moment he knew he could never want another.

"I see Dane was right."

The sound of Rafe's voice startled them.

Brannon pulled away abruptly. He locked eyes with his best friend who stood stoically at the top of the staircase. The three immortals stared awkwardly at one another until Rafe finally broke the silence.

"She said you two were attracted to one another. She first noticed it on Dywen."

"I am sorry, friend," Brannon said preparing himself for Rafe's anger.

Rafe moved forward, his indifference unsettling.

His eyes met Tauria's who returned his gaze defiantly. "You will need to test your bow skills tomorrow and ensure your shot is as accurate here as it is on Dywen. There may also be a need for healing potions to be mixed."

Her eyes squinted in response, her head tilting to the right. She stayed quiet waiting for her brother to continue.

He turned to Brannon. "Drow and Killenn are returning to Kaizi after we escort the last of the Arcanists to the Druidstone in Athir. They intend to retrieve weapons and supplies and bring them back here. I suggest we do the same."

Brannon nodded uneasily. "Of course."

Rafe turned and walked back toward the stairs. "I am happy for you both. Love should never be ignored."

Without a backward glance, he disappeared down the stairs.

"Did we just receive your brother's approval?"

Tauria stood silently staring at the empty staircase. She shook her head in disbelief, her hand finding Brannon's chest.

"I believe we did."

CHAPTER 32

THE CADENCED TICKTOCK OF THE clock in the hallway shattered the quiet of the dark house as Rafe opened the door.

Brannon and Tauria said goodnight as Dane showed them to the spare room.

"Do you mind sleeping on the sofa Sebastian?" Dane asked over her shoulder.

"That will be fine."

Upon her return, she got a blanket and pillow from the hall closet and handed them to Sebastian. Kissing him gently on his cheek, she smiled.

"Goodnight, then."

"Goodnight," he responded affectionately.

Turning out the light she followed Rafe into the bedroom.

He closed the door gently. His energy shifted as the barrier went up between them and the others occupying the house. It became softer, intimate. He crossed the room and wrapped his strong arms around her, pulling her close. His eyes shone with affection and he kissed her tenderly. Dane could feel the familiar pull of the binding as their magic responded to one other. He placed his forehead on hers, looking deep into her eyes.

"I don't know what I would do without you," he whispered.

She cradled his face in her hands. "You won't have to find out."

His eyes darkened. "Fate is never that simple."

They stood in the middle of the room, wrapped in each other's arms for a few more minutes. He picked her up and carried her to the bed, climbing in beside her.

"You were right about Brannon and Tauria."

"How do you feel about it?" She knew how protective of Tauria he'd become since their parents' death.

"I want her to be happy and Brannon is a good man."

"That doesn't answer my question. How do *you* feel about it?

Pulling the blankets tightly around them, he kissed her forehead and wrapped himself around her. "I hate it," he chuckled.

The town was burning. People screamed as they ran helplessly through the streets. The daemons had birthed from the pods at the mill and now thousands of them spilled into the streets from all directions. The chaos was immeasurable and the violence endless. People lay in the gutters, dead or dying, some disemboweled as daemons fed on their innards.

These daemons were different from the ones they encountered on Dywen. They weren't rotting from centuries buried far beneath the ground. Their skin was ashen, the membrane thin and fragile yet completely intact. Rot and stench did not secrete from their skin only the dirty yellow glow that once throbbed from their pods illuminated their hollow, black eyes. Their talons were long and sharp. Blades of bone extended far past the end of their deformed fingers and easily severed the flesh of those they attacked.

Dead eyes turned toward her as she gasped alerting them to her presence. Thin lips curled into wicked sneers, displaying jagged teeth, dingy and broken. Black blood seeped from the corners of their eyes; a dark tear stain marring their ghastly gray face. One threw the body it was dragging to the ground, gutting it in front of her. As it shrieked with pleasure, it pulled entrails from its victim's stomach. Blood pooled on the ground, gliding slick and fresh across the asphalt and into the sewer grate. The daemon laughed, taunting her before returning its attention to the chaos.

Dane looked at the town, the streets littered with the bodies of its residents. Dead eyes stared up at her accusingly. The daemons had killed specific individuals—the old, the sick, the weak.

It was a culling.

Those healthy enough to run from the massacre did so without purpose, blindly running in every direction. Some were captured by the daemons, chained together, and dragged off into the dark, while others hid, hoping their lives would be spared. Rivers of blood ran down the streets. The stench of death burned Dane's nostrils as her bloodshot eyes searched for the others. The burning buildings sent ash and embers floating across the town. They fell slowly in the night sky, lazily drifting in the breeze until they settled and ignited something else. She stood at the end of the street, watching helplessly as the town burned. The screams of people she knew echoed in the night.

She needed to find the others, the Arcanists. Spurred by the fear rearing up inside she ran toward Gabby's shop.

That's where they will be, she told herself, momentarily quieting the roar of uncertainty throbbing in her head.

Smoke billowed around her. The flaming buildings illuminated her way as a strange orange glow lit up the sky. Pools of blood lined the street, her boots were slick with it, but she pushed on determined to find her friends.

Rounding the corner, Gabby's shop came into view. Her heart sank as she saw the store engulfed in flames. The sense of loss and failure overwhelmed her as she ran to the storefront. Tears fell hot and sticky, blurring her vision and tracking a path down her sooty cheeks. Wiping them away she looked frantically for any sign of life inside, but only the roaring fire greeted her. The storefront window exploded. Shards flew in all directions. She covered her face, turning away from the projectiles in a feeble attempt to avoid their path. Shards bit at her skin, small tiny pricks of searing heat. The flames roared higher and as she shook glass from her clothes and hair something above the door caught her eye. Flames licked upward from the fiery interior igniting something on the storefront.

It was a symbol burning in fire.

From deep inside she felt the ancient magic erupt, pushing through her veins like a torrent of water. Her palms exploded with green energy, spitting and flaring in her palms. A sense of knowing encapsulated her mind in an unshakable serenity as the ancient magic took hold. Standing in the center of the street, she lifted her hands in the air. The magic of her ancestors streamed from her skin surrounding her in a whirling vortex of green energy. The ancient power pushed outward, expanding around her and penetrating everything in its path. As she stood, eyes closed, unleashing her power on the unsuspecting town, the ground beneath her began to quake. Cracks fractured the pavement under her feet. As they rippled outward, the town began to crumble, collapsing into the fractured earth. The earthquake rumbled around her as she became the epicenter.

She woke with a jolt, the dream still fresh in her mind. The ancient magic pulsed through her blood, its energy reacting to the vision. Rafe slept undisturbed beside her, his face awash with moonlight. He didn't stir as she grabbed her robe and padded across the room, closing the door noiselessly behind her.

She sat at the office desk and pulled the Book of Realms toward her. The fragile pages crackled as she turned them, looking for the information the old tome wished to reveal. Stopping on a blank page near the middle of the book, she waited. Seconds ticked by before the paper's surface began to morph. A thick black ink rose from the parchment and began to bead, moving across the paper in every direction. The beads slowed and began to spin. Each rotated in place in a counterclockwise motion, then as a group in a circular pattern. The ink beads melded together forming a symbol that stained the parchment as it sank back into the page. She stared at the tome dumbfounded. Its magic had created the same symbol she had seen burning in her dream.

Her finger traced the dark ink, the tip following the sharp curves and endless lines. A tingle spread through her finger as she continued to trace the symbols outline, over and over. Her mind relaxed under the methodical movement, the book's magic melding with her own.

As the tome's magic surged through her, she fell into a dream-like state. A voice, long gone, whispered in her mind. At first, the whisper echoed without providence, an inaudible sound lulling her further into the trance. As her mind's eye opened, the whisper reached out from the depths of the ethereal plane wrapping itself around her awareness. The more she succumbed to its presence, the more focused her mind's eye became on the voice. Discernible words formed as the whisper repeated its warning.

Use the darkness, do not become it.

The unfamiliar voice had a distinct Celtic dialect. It was not from this period or any existing in this world, but she knew instinctively to whom it belonged.

It was the last Druid—*Adaridge.*

The connection severed, and the mist of the trance faded from her consciousness. The words still buzzed in her ears as she looked down at the Book of Realms. Warmth sprung from the page and seeped into the tip of her finger. The symbol glowed as additional black ink appeared on the page, the ancient magic revealing a message hidden in the tome.

Her breath hitched as she read the words multiple times. The tome's magic hadn't just connected her with the last Druid it also revealed the meaning behind the shadow of separation clouding their true destinies.

The Arcanists were not just saviors.

CHAPTER 33

AFTER A RESTLESS NIGHT, DANE rose. A feeling of dread penetrated her skin, but she ignored it as she prepared breakfast and packed supplies to take back to Stevie's house. The others were already in the backyard when they arrived.

"You can feel the ancient magic. It surrounds us." Stevie said.

"The magic has always been here, it just required the power of the Druidstones to release it," Sebastian replied. "Now it is fusing with the natural environment and amplifying our powers."

It was a crisp, sunny winters day, and they spent the remainder of the morning outside practicing how to manipulate the magic of their individual realms. The solitude of Stevie's property was perfect to keep prying eyes at a minimum. The four Warlicians took turns throwing energy balls at targets Rafe and Brannon constructed from plywood and two-by-fours. Tauria turned it into a competition by shooting arrows at the targets, trying to beat the energy balls. Showing off, Kai swept snow and ice together, constructing a ten-foot wall; then just as quickly, she brought it crashing down into a pile of slushy rubble. Not to be undone, Stevie conjured a smoke dragon sending it soaring through the air below the tree line.

"I can't wait to see that smoke dragon in action!" Kai said, turning to Dane her face a mask of disappointment. "I wish I had been with you in Dywen when you fought the daemons."

"The dragon was impressive, but I am glad you weren't there Kai. There will be a time when your life will be at risk, I'm just thankful it hasn't happened yet."

Kai shrugged, turning back to the others. "What powers do you think you two will gain?"

Elyse glanced at Marlee, her mouth set in a grim line. "I guess we will find out soon enough."

Marlee smiled, her bright blue eyes crinkling at the corner. "I just hope whatever they are I can wield them as well as you three do."

"That won't be a problem," said Stevie. "You will instinctively know what to do. The magic becomes a part of you, like something you have possessed forever. Immortality gives you a sense of freedom. It is indescribable, but you will understand soon enough."

Marlee's face clouded.

Dane could sense the anxious energy begin to swirl around her when Stevie mentioned immortality. She walked over to where her friend sat.

"Nothing will change Marlee. You will still be the same person you are today, just more powerful, physically and mentally. The knowledge your ancestors provide is invaluable, but it doesn't change the person you are. You will always be you."

"Gabby changed."

"That is different. Gabby became who she used to be. The prophecy did not change her, nor did immortality. Her journey is much different from ours."

Marlee absently pulled on her blond hair, twirling a strand around her finger. "Thanks, Dane."

"Of course," she said squeezing her friend's hand. "Speaking of Gabby, I'm going to check on that cranky celestial."

Marlee laughed. "OK." As she watched Dane walk toward the house the laugh faded, and she wrung her hands. Stevie and Kai appeared to accept their fates willingly, a casual ease that mimicked their mortal lives. Even Elyse did not seem dissuaded by the magnitude of immortality. *Why then was she so terrified?*

Sebastian stopped Dane as she crossed the yard.

"Kai's abilities are vastly different here than on Viccinius."

"In what way?"

"Mermaids have the power to manipulate water, but it must be fluid. Ice and snow are not. Kai's mastery of engaging with the kinetic energy of water even in its stagnant forms is far superior to her ancestor's impressive abilities."

"Stevie's powers as well," she said, watching as the smoke dragon circled overhead.

"The Arcanist's powers are manifesting quickly. The ancient magic does not seem to be weakened in this world, in fact, it appears quite in balance with Earth's energy." He hesitated, his voice lowering. "This is encouraging as you will need all the knowledge and magic you can conjure to defeat the ancient dark."

"Every trick in the book."

Sebastian frowned, his lack of understanding apparent.

Dane smirked. "Never mind. There is something else I wanted to discuss with you."

She felt Rafe's eyes on her, but she ignored him. He had been badgering her all morning about the change in her energy and it made her uncomfortable. She wasn't ready to discuss the implications of the dream to him yet, not until she spoke to Sebastian. "Something strange happened last night. I had a dream," she whispered. "Well, a nightmare."

"Prophetic?"

"In a way, I suppose. I am not sure."

"Dreams are never as they seem," Sebastian noted, concern evident as his voice lowered.

"It felt real. Like I was immersed in a reality that hadn't yet happened."

"Did you feel the ancient dark?"

Dane shook her head.

Sebastian clasped her shoulder. "If the vision has meaning, it will be revealed to you in time. Do not fret."

"There is something else."

Sebastian's eyebrow raised. "Another dream?"

"No more like a trance. It was after the dream. I felt lured by the Book of Realms; its magic called to me. When I touched it, I was engulfed by a strange haze. I heard a voice."

"A voice?"

"It was Adaridge."

"How can you be certain?"

"I can't explain it. I just know."

Sebastian thought for a moment. "A Timestopper's mind is powerful and connects to the ether and energy in ways we have never really understood. It is a strength but also a weakness. Adaridge would have the ability to exploit that if he deemed necessary. If anyone has the power to communicate through time and space, it is he. The same way the ancient dark entered your mind so would the Druid."

"So, you believe me."

"It is not a matter of belief Callathian. It is fate. If Adaridge has something he must tell you, the message will eventually become clear."

"There is more."

"Should I sit?" he said sarcastically as a smirk played at the edges of his stoic expression.

Dane ignored his attempt at humor. "The book revealed something to me. A symbol. The same one I'd also seen in the dream."

"What kind of symbol."

"The mark of death."

"It cannot be," Sebastian said, his hand rubbing his forehead.

"What do you know about this mark?"

A shadow darkened Sebastian's features as he lowered his voice. "The mark of death is part of an ancient superstition. It is a symbol of the end times."

"When was the mark last seen?"

"It has never been seen. It is a myth. A fallacy propagated by an ancient belief system revered by the Druid priests who first inhabited the Thanissia Universe. Where within your dream did it appear?"

"Burning in the front of a building. Gabby's store to be exact."

Sebastian's eyes widened at the revelation.

"This means something," Dane said, her eyes squinting.

"The legend says the mark of death will be carried by those who are harbingers of the end times and used as a warning of impending resurrection, destruction, and death. It is said the mark will appear first in fire, then in blood, and finally in flesh."

"Flesh?"

"Those who rise from the ashes of the past to execute the end times will be marked by the symbol."

Dane squeezed his arm. "Thank you. I think I understand now what the Book of Realms was trying to tell me. We need to gather the others. Can you meet me inside?"

"Of course."

The kitchen smelled of sage as she entered.

"You lit a candle."

"I like the smell," Gabby answered tersely. She was her usual surly self, refusing to partake in the 'antics' going on outside. Instead, she retreated to Stevie's kitchen to mull over the Book of Realms.

"You miss it," Dane said watching as the smoke dragon touched down in the backyard. A silent roar coming from its open jaws.

"What."

"Etheriem. Home."

Gabby's iridescent eyes sparkled. Her face contoured slightly with her frown.

"I do not belong here."

"Maybe not Gabby, but you were sent here for a reason. The importance of your destiny is undeniable. We are lucky to have you."

Gabby stared at Dane. Her eyes flickered with the light of the ether. "I suppose you are."

Dane smiled clasping her hand. "Anyway, I'm getting used to having the new you around."

"I assumed you no longer liked me."

"Why would you think that?"

"It is obvious. I am not the Gabby you became friends with long ago. That human was not me. I am unsure if you can accept who I truly am."

Dane hesitated before answering. "We are all very different now Gabby. Maybe you are more so but it does not make you any less of a friend. We will always love you no matter what."

A small smile appeared on her lips. Her wings fluttered slightly, but before she could respond the others came in from the backyard.

CHAPTER 34

THEY SAT AROUND THE KITCHEN island, her best friends. Linked by friendship, magic, and destiny, and hunted by evil. They had not asked for this burden, but each had accepted it willingly.

Dane searched their curious faces. She no longer needed to hide her powers from them or her past, but instead of feeling a sense of relief she felt only sadness. They too were now burdened with the power of magic and a destiny that would change each of them forever.

The others stood behind them, immortals caught in the web of time. Pulled into a future that fate had irrevocably linked to their forgotten past. Their world, like hers, was in danger. If they failed, neither would survive.

"The prophecy reveals that only by combining our powers can we hope to defeat the ancient dark, but what it does not disclose is, the same is true if we fail."

"What are you saying?" Elyse asked, pushing her glasses up.

The other girls had the same look on their face, confusion shadowed with fear.

Dane flipped through the Book of Realms until she found the page she was looking for.

"Our destiny is not yet written because we are marked by the shadow of separation, right? According to the book, this means at some point we will be faced with a choice, one that will determine the direction of our fates and reveal our true destiny. Unfortunately, it does not expand on what that choice may be or any consequences that may arise because of our actions." She hesitated, looking apologetically at her friends. "I believe I know what that choice will be and its ramifications.

The room went deathly silent. All eyes were focused on her.

"If we are unable to defeat the ancient dark and save mankind; then we must destroy it."

Rafe frowned at Dane from the corner, his face distorted by the shadows cast by the candles. She could feel his energy wrap itself around her, the beat of his heart increasing as he tried desperately to understand the meaning of her words.

Dane shook her head. "I'm sorry." She glanced at her friends. The sacrifices they would have to make, faced with such a daunting task, an unknown future, and an unthinkable decision.

"Do not be sorry Callathian, explain," Sebastian demanded.

She nodded, fidgeting as she spoke.

"We've been given the ancient magic of our ancestors, their knowledge, and powers, but we have also received a unique power only the Arcanists possess. I believe it is the reason Stevie can cause volcanos to erupt. How Kai can push the ocean into tidal waves and why I, with one hand placed on the ground, can cause it to crack open and splinter into a cavernous void." Hesitating, her eyes sought out Marlee and Elyse. "I suspect once you gain your birthright that you both, in some way, will be able to command air."

Elyse's face was somber.

Marlee looked away, tears welling in her eyes. Dane knew this was the most difficult for her. Even though she'd accepted her fate, she hadn't embraced it as the others had.

"Unlike our ancestors, we can control the elements, and bend them to our will. We can summon the most destructive and devastating aspects of it; volcanic eruptions, earthquakes, tsunamis, a smoke dragon." Dane caught Stevie's eye. "We have been given the power to destroy the world and everything in it."

"Yes, to use against the ancient dark so that it does not exterminate us," Stevie said.

Dane shook her head, reaching for the Book of Realms. Carefully, she turned the delicate parchment until the marked page was visible, pushing it across the table toward them.

"The ancient dark does not plan to eliminate the race of man like he did with the inhabitants of the Thanissia Universe. He means to enslave it, to cultivate an extension of his extinct race." Her hand shook slightly as she pointed to the ancient symbol on the page. This is the mark of death, an ancient symbol meaning—*the end of days.*

Gabby leaned in. "But how do you know the ancient dark wishes to enslave us or that the mark foretells of the Arcanists and not the ancient dark?"

"Because of the words appearing below it."

Rafe scowled moving in closer. He read the words aloud.

"When the mark of death appears, first in fire, then blood,

and finally in flesh, the earth will succumb to evil and be judged by darkness. The darkness will call upon the elements to cleanse the earth of its suffering, ending its captivity, the evil, and all that is good."

The room was fraught with tension as an anxious energy burned in the air.

Dane's finger tapped the page. "The darkness is us. Those who can manipulate the elements."

She hesitated. "We are the end of days."

All the eyes in the room widened, but no one dared utter a word.

"I have already seen the mark in fire and I suspect the others will reveal themselves in time. It is an omen, a warning, and a directive. If the Arcanists can't defeat the ancient dark, then we must use our inherited powers to harness the vast power of the elements. We must end the suffering that will come from the ancient dark's rule. We will have no choice but to *end the world*."

CHAPTER 35

THE RAYS OF THE BRIGHT morning sun were just breaking the tree line. The rustle of pines wafted through the early morning air as Dane stood on the back deck, her hands warmed by a mug of hot tea.

"We will meet you in Athir," Sebastian said closing the door behind him and joining her at the railing. "From the Temple of Air, the journey is half a day northeast to the Galenvale Grove. Inside its depths is the door to the Druid sanctuary. Follow the white blooms, they will lead the way."

He handed her a crude map.

"If we are to gain an understanding of why Adaridge's spirit is communicating through time and space, it will make itself known there," Sebastian continued. "Take this portal ring. It will allow you to access Athir from anywhere."

She accepted the ring a smirk on her face. "Rafe doesn't like these."

Sebastian nodded, understanding her meaning. "He has a unique relationship with portal rings."

"Did something happen?" she asked, sensing Sebastian knew why Rafe disliked using them.

"It is not my story to tell."

She took a sip of tea, dropping the subject. She knew the Warlician code made it impossible to breach trust, but the special bond between Sebastian and Rafe made it even more so.

"We won't be far behind," she assured Sebastian.

"We will make ready the Druidstone and meet you at the sanctuary."

The concern on Sebastian's face betrayed his calm voice.

"What is it, Sebastian?"

He moved closer and lowered his voice. "The Temple of Air is the final Druidstone and the most powerful. Two races exist in the realm of Athir and their combined magic is extraordinary. My fear may be premature, but once the ancient magic of Thanissia is at full power, the ancient dark may come forth sooner than the predicted full moon."

"We will be ready," Dane assured him. "Elyse and Marlee are the last of the Arcanists, once they receive their birthrights we will be at full strength."

She sighed, thinking of the vagueness of the prophecy and the limited information contained within the Book of Realms. "I realize how much is at stake Sebastian, for all of us. We won't fail. We can't."

Sebastian's eyes flashed as he clasped her shoulder. "Your interpretation of the mark of death and the cryptic message found in the Book of Realms is a dire one. The Arcanists possess immense power, but a power prophesied to defeat the ancient dark not to be used against mankind. I hope this is not how the end times will come about."

"Me either."

Rafe came outside, his gaze softening when he looked at her. "May I have some time?" he asked Sebastian.

"Of course," Sebastian replied, going back inside to join the others.

Dane could feel his heart. The beat fell into rhythm with her own. It had become commonplace over the past weeks as their bodies, their energies, and their emotions synced. When he was near, her body involuntarily reacted. There was no hiding from the immortal warrior who stood gazing down at her.

He lifted his hand, caressing her cheek. "Are you sure you do not want me to come?"

"No, Stevie and I will be fine. It's a quick trip to my parents' house. We won't be too long. We will meet you in Athir."

"Be careful."

"Of course."

A shadow crossed his face. "What is it?"

She shrugged. "It's nothing."

"Dane, I know something is going on. What has happened that you are not telling me?" He tilted her chin up, so he was looking directly into her eyes. "Secrets are no longer your burden to carry alone."

She inhaled deeply, her mind whirling. If she told him of her trance, the message from Adaridge, he would worry. If she didn't he would probably still worry but not let her go to Salem without him. Her brow furrowed.

"Is it the ancient dark? Did he find his way into your mind again?"

"No, nothing like that."

"Secrets bare no power, only weakness." His eyes turned

dark, and she could feel the frustration seeping through his energy.

"It's Adaridge."

Rafe straightened at the Druid's name. "The last Druid?"

She shifted uncomfortably. "He spoke to me."

Rafe's brow furrowed as his energy shifted, frustration mixing with curiosity and concern. His protective energy reached toward her. "When?"

"Last night. You were sleeping. I had a nightmare. Brighton Hill was burning. Daemons ran through the streets. Everyone was dead." She took a breath. "That's the condensed version. The dream is where I saw the mark of death in fire." Tears welled in her eyes as the feelings evoked by last night's dream overwhelmed her. "When I woke, I could feel the Book of Realms' energy beckoning to me. I went to it and it revealed a page, one which hadn't been there before."

"What was written on it?"

"Nothing at first, just a blank parchment. Then the mark of death appeared and as I traced its outline, a feeling of euphoria and drowsiness came over me pulling me down into a trance. Whispering surrounded me, then clarity. I recognized the voice even though I had never heard it before. I knew instinctively it was Adaridge and his words, they felt like a warning."

"What did he say?"

"Use the darkness, do not become it."

She felt Rafe stiffen.

"Do you know what it means?"

He looked over his shoulder as he ran his hand running through his hair. "No one knows this, not even Sebastian, but I spent a lot of time with Adaridge, long before the Great War. The Druids were fading into Thanissia's past and although he could not pass on his power to another, he could ensure their ancient knowledge did not disappear. I never understood why he chose me as the vessel for their knowledge, only that one day my destiny would require it."

"So, what is Adaridge trying to tell me?"

"The Druids believed there was darkness in all of us. Something uncontrollable that if unleashed would be all-consuming."

"What is this darkness?"

"That I do not know. He said it was different for everyone."

Dane thought about Adaridge's words. "Do you think he was warning me about my own darkness?"

Rafe shrugged. "Druids are often cryptic. Even the knowledge he granted me was vague and when I asked for more information he would only say 'the seeds of knowledge would grow when enough time had passed'."

She sighed as he pulled her in close. Her cheek rested on his chest, and she breathed in his familiar scent. Closing her eyes, she listened to his heartbeat, the metrical rhythm connecting his life to her own. "I love you," he whispered.

Her stomach clenched at his words as a chill slid over her skin—a predictive sensation of dread that she may never hear those words again.

After going over the plans again and ensuring Sebastian, they would meet him in the Druid sanctuary in Galenvale Grove, Stevie finished packing the Jeep for the drive to Salem. Dane had spoken to her father at his conference, but her mother hadn't answered when she'd called. Stevie knew she would try again from the road.

Snow had just begun to fall, and the temperature dropped as the morning waned.

"Are you sure you don't want me to go with you?" Kai opened the Wrangler's door for Diego, who awkwardly jumped his bulk into the cramped back seat.

"We will be fine. It's a quick trip to speak with Mrs. Watts; then we will use the portal ring from there to Athir. We'll be back with you in no time."

Kai groaned. "You are leaving me alone with Gabriella, the cranky celestial," she huffed, pointing her thumb toward where Gabby stood with Drow.

"You are hardly alone," Stevie responded, looking at the group of seven immortals who would accompany Kai, Marlee, and Elyse, to Athir.

"You know what I mean."

Stevie smirked. Her eyes narrowed as they skimmed over Kai's outfit. The ski pants and boots were normal, but she wore only a fleece vest over a long sleeve Henley. "Aren't you cold?"

Kai laughed, pulling at the long braid over her shoulder. "You would think, but not anymore. Mermaids are cold-blooded, and apparently, we thrive in cooler temperatures. I have a suspicion it might be the hot summer months I hate now."

Stevie's eyes raised at this revelation. "How ironic."

"Isn't it?"

"What's ironic?" Dane asked, joining them at the Jeep.

"Kai was just telling me she is a big fan of winter now, *loves* the cold and ice."

"Mermaid blood. Yes, Sebastian told me. It is rather ironic," Dane agreed.

"Yes, well, I think *love* may be a strong word, but I certainly have fewer complaints about it."

The three friends laughed, their world so different from the way it was a few weeks ago.

"I'll see you soon," Kai said as she walked away.

"Soon," Dane responded, getting into the Jeep next to Stevie.

She glanced in the rearview mirror as they pulled away, her eyes connecting with Rafe one last time. As she turned onto the road and lost sight of him she felt the familiar sensation as his voice echoed in her mind.

"You will come back to me."

CHAPTER 36

MARLEE HELD THE PORTAL STONE in her hand, the smooth surface cold and unresponsive. "What's it supposed to do?" she asked, glancing at the others.

"It should respond to the blood of its realm," Rafe answered.

Gabby walked up to her and sniffed.

"What are you doing?" Marlee said, pulling away.

"Fae blood is scented. It is sickly sweet, reminiscent of the strange flora that grows on your lands," Gabby responded. "She is definitely fae, maybe the elf should try."

"Oh, *the elf*. Is that me?" Elyse said as she walked to the tree. Cynicism dripped from the words as she scoffed at Gabby and rolled her eyes. Retrieving the portal stone from Marlee's outstretched hand she placed it in her own palm. The stone sat cold in hers as well.

Sebastian, perplexed by this hindrance, began to pace, his muttering intensifying the faster he moved. His cloak swept the forest floor scattering bright colored leaves into the night breeze as he mused.

"Both the fae and the elves resided on Athir and the portal stone should react to both their kind. Why is this stone different from the others? What was the Guardian of Deities plan?"

Gabby glanced at Rafe and shrugged.

"Maybe it requires both their blood," Drow said.

Sebastian stopped pacing. The corners of his green eyes crinkled as he pondered Drow's suggestion. "Only the blood of two shall once again open one world to the other."

"What does that mean?" asked Elyse.

Sebastian strode to where they stood. He placed the portal stone face-up in Elyse's hand. "It is part of the peace doctrine signed by the elven and fae races after the war." Grasping Marlee's hand he placed her palm face down on Elyse's, so the portal stone was wedged between them.

No one spoke as they waited.

The wind stirred the leaves of the Elder Oak, the rustle of its crisp, dead leaves the only sound to break the tension. It groaned as its branches swayed back and forth.

"The tree recognizes a portal stone," Rafe said, pointing at the yellow glow escaping from Elyse and Marlee's hands.

"Come," Sebastian said, placing his hand on the Elder Oak and revealing the hidden panel. The other stones still lay in their respective niches, each one glowing with coordinating colors: green for Dywen, red for Kaizi, purple for Etheriem, and blue for Viccinius. On Sebastian's urging Elyse and Marlee placed the glowing portal stone into the remaining spot. The yellow glow intensified as a mist sprang from the rune's center, quickly spreading through the clearing. The air warmed slightly as the mist floated upward and circled lazily overhead. As it collected at the center of the clearing, it began to shimmer. Tiny sparkles of light flecked the mist as it funneled downward to form a swirling tornado.

"To Athir," Sebastian said as he disappeared into the swirling funnel of mist beckoning the others to follow.

·﹀﹀·

A shimmering mist hovered over the lands as they emerged from the portal.

"This is Athir?" Kai said, whistling her appreciation.

"Remarkable is it not," Sebastian said, his eyes scanning the vast lush lands laying before them.

"That would be an understatement."

They stood on a grassy hill. Small yellow flowers dotted its silky, green surface. Acres of lush flatland lay to their right, to the left a thick forest; its trees in perfect alignment stretched for miles toward a serene mountain in the distance. Rows of white flowers edged a dirt path as it meandered through the acreage. The sun's rays combined with the shimmering haze creating a sparkling golden-hued atmosphere that swirled lazily above them. Sweeping gold-tinged cloud banks embraced the mountain range in the distance. It was breathtaking. Everything on Athir moved slowly, swaying softly in the apple-scented breeze. An imperturbable ambiance enveloped Athir.

On the horizon, Kai could see something glinting. "What is over there?" she asked pointing toward the light.

"Tariedrelle, home of the fae." Sebastian pointed toward the perfectly symmetrical forest. "Deep within the dark forest, you will find Niramyst, land of the elves."

"It's amazing," Elyse said.

He nodded. "If I dare say, Athir is the most beautiful of all the realms in the Thanissia Universe. The dual magic of both the fae and elves is extraordinary and visually appealing."

"The mist is unusual," she said looking skyward.

"It is elemental magic."

"Magic?"

"Athir's magic is ruled by the air element. It is a magic born from above. When the Druidstone has been reactivated and the full power of your ancestor's power is reborn, the mist will infuse every part of this world."

"Is the magic of every realm as obvious as this?" she asked.

"Elemental magic is noticeable in each of the realms, but not as apparent as here. The fae and the elves pride themselves on beauty and cohesion. The elegance of their magic is constantly on display."

"I guess we have much to learn," Marlee said.

"Once you receive your birthright, you will gain all the knowledge of your ancestors."

"Does it hurt?" she asked, her blue eyes wide.

"What?" Sebastian asked, his brow furrowing.

"Becoming immortal," she whispered.

"This is unfortunately not something I am familiar with. I was born an immortal. Kai is the one you should be asking."

Marlee glanced at Kai who was laughing with Tauria and Brannon. "Maybe later."

They walked in silence, ten strangers in a forgotten realm, a fragmented world existing only in memory. Each of them represented a singular destiny, connected through time and space—the past and present converging into a shared fate.

Rafe glanced over his shoulder. "Come, we must continue

to the Temple of Air if we hope to be there before nightfall. The sun is passing through its second phase and the triple moon will replace it shortly."

"Triple moon?" Marlee asked.

Rafe smiled. "It is something one needs to see to experience but the races who resided in Athir worshiped the triple moon for its magical energy. Moon magic enhanced many of their powers."

He lifted his pack and signaled for Brannon and Tauria to lead the way down the hill toward the lake. Killenn and Drow dropped back to bring up the rear. Sebastian moved in step with Rafe.

"Do you think Dane and Stevie will accurately traverse this world without guidance?"

"They have good instincts, they will find us."

"Even when the mist descends?" Sebastian asked.

"I am confident the last of the Callathian line can find her way through the home of the elves. Claaven was an exceptional tracker; let us trust she too has the ability."

"And what if they go west instead of north? The Oberon Fen does not react well to those who do not carry the blood of the fae."

"The portal ring you provided them with will open directly behind the Temple of Air. You instructed them to go northeast from that point. The Fen is to the far west. We must not concern ourselves with something unlikely to happen."

Sebastian's eyes flicked to the west. An ominous gray sky hung heavy over a portion of fae territory. Its darkness malevolent as lightning flashed behind its roiling clouds.

Rafe clasped his shoulder. "It will be fine, old friend."

Sebastian nodded as his eyes strayed back to the part of

Athir where the Oberon Fen waited. It was a dark scar on this otherwise perfect realm. A land stained by hate and the only part of Athir left unhealed after the war between its races. He watched as the dark sky churned in anger above the tainted land. Even now it continued to fester, haunted by the arrogance that destroyed it.

CHAPTER 37

THE HOUSE WAS DARK AND STILL.

It was after midnight when Dane pulled up to her parents' house.

"She's probably sleeping," Stevie whispered.

Dane stared at the house. Erratic energy swirled around her as she noticed the street was also dark. The streetlights were extinguished plunging the entire neighborhood into darkness.

"Something is wrong."

Stevie glanced at Dane. "What?"

"I don't know," she said getting out of the car. Her mother always left lights on when her father was out of town. The complete darkness of the house was disconcerting.

Stevie exited the passenger side letting Diego out of the back. She stood beside Dane and waited. The house *was* too quiet, the entire street shrouded in an eerie silence.

She shivered. "Are you sure you want to go in? We may frighten your mom. Maybe we should call first."

Dane ignored her and walked toward the house. Stevie could see her hands clenching as she disappeared into the shadows at the side of the house.

Stevie hurried after her. Thankfully the moon hadn't waned considerably, and strands of moonlight still glowed, lighting her way through the Callan's heavily treed yard. As she rounded the corner, she saw Dane standing at the back door, eyes closed, hands shaking.

"Dane, are you OK?"

Diego growled. His thick fur bristled as the moon went behind a cloud and plunged the large backyard into a shadowy darkness. As she moved closer, Stevie could sense what Dane focused on. Beneath the pressing quiet lingered a scent of decay; like food left to rot in the sun or the carcass of a small dead animal was nearby. Stevie allowed her intuition to follow the odor. Her eyes scanned the dark windows of the house.

Whatever was emitting the smell came from inside the house.

Dane moved quickly to the back door using the extra key her mother hid underneath the flower pot on the back porch. As the door swung open, a strong smell of decay wafted by them.

"Oh my god," Stevie said, putting her hand over her mouth and nose. Diego growled again, sniffing the air precariously.

Dane flipped the light switch to her left. Nothing. She walked to the kitchen island and flipped the switch located on its side. Still, nothing.

"Power must be out," Stevie said, trying to convince herself nothing was amiss.

"Maybe," Dane said producing an energy ball in her

palm. Its glow lit their way as they moved cautiously through the kitchen. The tick of a clock echoed through the midnight darkness, the only noise interrupting the eerie stillness.

Stevie reached for Diego's collar giving it a quick tug. "Close," she commanded as they walked cautiously toward the staircase. She knew this house well. She'd spent a lot of time here during their college years and after. The Callan's were like family, always treating her and the other girls like one of their own. A chill ran over Stevie's skin as they reached the bottom of the staircase. The air was ripe with the foul odor that clung to the interior of the house, but there was another scent mixing with it as if floated down from the second floor. Diego whined as he sniffed the air. His fur bristled on his back, and he moved in protectively beside her.

The stairs creaked as they made their way up. The dank smell intensified the closer they came to the second-floor landing, the other odor also grew more obvious—a pungent, tinny smell. Stevie's senses tingled in warning. She could feel the darkness now, not the one that comes with the midnight hour, but the evil seeping ominously from the walls. She knew this is what Dane sensed from outside, and the reason she knew something was wrong.

Dane turned left at the second-floor landing, and headed directly into the large master bedroom, disappearing into the shadows. Stevie hurried after her but as she reached the doorway, a guttural howl erupted in the darkness of the bedroom. A wail of despair so unnerving it stopped Stevie in her tracks —frozen with shock and fear. Diego, baring his teeth, lunged into the master bedroom, snarling at whatever emitted the anguished scream.

Stevie's blood ran cold as her mind slowly recognized the noise.

DANE!

She ran into the bedroom, her heart pounding in her chest, as terror gripped her mind. The moon had found its way from behind the clouds. The ethereal glow washed the bedroom in its silvery light as it poured through the large bay window. Dread gripped her in its cold vice and her stomach lurched at the horror she saw waiting for them in the shadows of the dark, silent house.

Ella Watts was naked, splayed open, cut from sternum to pelvis, and hung from the bedposts. Thick, barbed wire secured her hands to the posts; its razor-sharp barbs severing one wrist to the bone. Her intestines had been pulled from her body and wound around her like a rope. The pungent metallic smell filled the air. Blood stained the walls. It flowed from her wounds saturating the sheets and pooling on the floor.

It was a slaughterhouse.

Stevie's stomach churned, and bile rose in her mouth. She closed her eyes. The room spun, and she desperately tried to calm herself. The stench of blood and death overwhelmed her as the staccato sound of dripping blood echoed through the quiet. She wanted to run. To get away from the horror, but she was rendered immobile, her body unable to react to what her brain demanded. Fear and shock paralyzed her.

Opening her eyes, she tried to rationalize the abhorrent surroundings. Her heart clenched as she looked at Ella Watts, her lifeless body desecrated. A pentacle had been crudely carved into her chest, another into her forehead. Her head lolled to one side, her broken neck angling it backward. Her dead eyes stared up, unseeing.

Stevie followed her gaze.

Scrawled on the ceiling in blood was the mark of death

and one word—*WRATH*. Tears filled her eyes as a hollow retching sound erupted from her throat.

"Who would do this," she choked, her mind still grappling with the violence on display in the room.

Dane stood at the foot of the bed, anger rising as her despair consumed her. Without acknowledging Stevie, she turned and ran from the room, magic exploding all around her. Pictures flew from the walls, tables toppled, carpets buckled under her feet as she exited the house in a blind fury.

Stevie ran through the house after her, ducking objects as they flew in all directions. Exiting through back door she halted when she saw Dane on the back lawn, kneeling at the center of her mother's flower garden. The black withered stalks of dead vegetation a stark contrast to the white snow covering the frozen earth. Dane's shoulders slumped as her body heaved. Grief poured from her energy as her aura darkened, defeated.

Tears flowed down Stevie's face as she reached out to touch her friend. Her hand gently caressed her shoulder.

Dane stiffened under her touch. Shaking off Stevie's hand she stood and turned to face her, bright green eyes burning with fury. Her face, an unrecognizable mask of grief-filled hate, contorted as the ancient Warlician magic flickered erratically under her skin. Flashes of green energy erupted from her palms as her controlled demeanor slipped. A coldness simmered in her eyes, her face dead and emotionless.

Stunned, Stevie moved a few steps back. There was something in her friend's cold eyes that frightened her. Dane had changed.

Diego whined as he sensed the change shifting in the surrounding air. Suddenly, the energy in Dane erupted. The magic of the Warlicians flowed under her skin, bursting outward and enshrouding her in a vortex of green warrior magic. Stevie could sense the volatility of the ancient magic as it churned around her. Through the magic Stevie heard her friend's voice, a tormented whisper its tone saturated with grief.

"I will be the Wrath."

As those words hovered around them, Dane's magic calmed and disappeared. Without a word she moved past Stevie and vanished into the shadows leaving her alone with Diego in the backyard. The chilly night air pressed down on her as she stood staring after Dane. The sound of the Jeep leaving echoed through the night. Attempting to stop the violent shaking in her hands she clasped them together, but it intensified as a cold dread crept over her skin. She thought about Dane and her volatile reaction, the fear she felt when that volatility changed to an unnerving calm as an emotionless void embraced her.

Killenn had warned her about this. How the ancient dark didn't just feed off a person's magic but also their hate. Making it grow until they were consumed by it. She thought about the prophecy. Perhaps the ancient dark did have a plan, maybe it too had evolved. Like Sebastian, perhaps it had watched and learned from this world. Was killing Dane's mother an attempt to weaken her? To control her and thus the Arcanists?

Pulling her phone from her jacket pocket she scrolled through the contacts until she found the one she was looking for. As Stevie listened to the hollow ringing at the other end she trembled, remembering the look in Dane's eyes and the unambiguous power she felt swirling around her. It hadn't broken her, it had transformed her and now she was out there somewhere alone, swallowed up by grief and rage. Maybe the ancient dark had unwittingly unleashed something even the powers of the Arcanists couldn't control.

"Hello," said the groggy voice on the other end.

Stevie began to cry. "Something's happened."

End of Book 2

ACKNOWLEDGMENTS

To my amazing beta readers Ashley, Effie, and Kristen. Thanks for your hard work, honesty, insight, and friendship. Sometimes fate puts people in your path for a reason. To the MMI crew, thanks for supporting me and reading my books, and for pushing me to get this one written in time for boating season.

And to the characters of The Scrying Trilogy who have been an integral part of my existence for the past seven years. Bringing you to life and telling your stories has been a challenge and a joy, sometimes a pain, but always an adventure.

ABOUT THE AUTHOR

Jaci Miller is a dark fantasy author originally from Ontario, Canada. She graduated from University of Phoenix with a BA in English and has worked in both the legal and real estate mortgage businesses. Jaci enjoys paddle boarding, yoga, and her Peloton. She currently resides in Vermont, with her husband, Dale and their Parson Russell Terrier, Ike.

ALSO BY JACI MILLER

The Scrying Trilogy

The Scrying

The Hallowed

The Arcana

The Dark Kingdom Trilogy

coming 2020/21

Short Stories

Neverland: The Iron Fortress

The Dark Season (republishing 2020)